I, Claudia

Marilyn Todd was born in Harrow, Middlesex, but now lives in West Sussex with her husband, one hare-brained dog and two cats. For the last ten years she has run her own secretarial business from home.

I, Claudia is the first in a series of Roman mysteries featuring Claudia Seferius. The second novel, *Virgin Territory*, is published in hardcover by Macmillan. Marilyn is currently at work on the latest Claudia mystery, *Man Eater*.

Marilyn Todd

I, Claudia

A Mystery, 13 BC

PAN BOOKS

First published 1995 by Macmillan

This edition published 1996 by Pan Books
an imprint of Macmillan Publishers Ltd
25 Eccleston Place, London SW1W 9NF
and Basingstoke

Associated companies throughout the world

ISBN 0 330 34414 5

1 3 5 7 9 8 6 4 2

A CIP catalogue record for this book is available from
the British Library

Phototypeset by Intype London Ltd
Printed by Mackays of Chatham PLC, Chatham, Kent

For Kevin

Acknowledgements

To Marjorie Rogers, who may only have slipped into the next room, but who has somehow managed to keep the door wedged open a fraction, I have just one thing to say: Thanks, Mum! For everything.

I

(Rome, 13 BC)

Even for July, the streets seemed hotter and busier than ever as Claudia pushed her way across the Forum, grateful that she didn't have to walk very often. She'd got the litter to drop her at the arch of Augustus, but there was no escaping the last few hundred paces she'd have to cover on foot. One of the senators – she thought it might be that odious little Ascanius – was waving his arms and ranting on about food subsidies to a gathering crowd, so to avoid recognition she pulled her palla low over her eyes and pointed her face to the ground. Turning into the Via Sacra, she collided with a small boy in porridge-stained rags, his filthy hands clutching a pig's head which he'd undoubtedly stolen.

'Out of my way, you poxy little oik!'

Claudia elbowed him aside and thought she caught the words 'Up yours, missus', but when she spun round he'd disappeared into the crush of lawyers, vendors, fortune-tellers and dancers. Dodging a porter's pole, she turned left into a narrow sidestreet, then, glancing over her shoulder, ducked down a deserted alleyway, from which point her sense of smell led her forward.

Jupiter, Juno and Mars, how could anyone live in such squalor! Claudia covered her nose and carefully negotiated her way past broken pots, fleabitten cats and the contents of slop pails emptied from upstairs windows. What a din! Babies bawling, dogs howling, women scolding, children squabbling, and, in the midst of this racket, water-carriers touting their wares at full tilt. And the stink! Rotting food, over-subscribed toilets, unwashed bodies, all exacerbated by the stifling heat. Grimacing, she picked her way up the stone staircase. If there was any justice, Quintus would have grown tired of waiting and she wouldn't have to hang about in this cesspit any longer than was necessary. For heaven's sake, was it her fault she'd got delayed by the old linen merchant's funeral procession? Since she was in her own litter at the time, with its distinctive orange canopy, she could hardly pretend to ignore it, could she? Especially since that awful Marcia woman had caught sight of her and pretended to mourn, the hypocritical cow. As if she hadn't spent half the old sod's fortune already!

Claudia paused at the top of the steps, where large lumps of plaster had cracked and flaked away. The landlords must positively rake in money from these tenements, cramming in, what, two, three families to a room? You'd think they'd learn, wouldn't you, but no, every now and again fire would sweep through and roast the tenants alive, or else these flimsy structures would simply crumble and fall. And who really gave a damn about the mangled bodies inside?

Now what directions had Quintus given her? Two flights up, third on the left, wasn't it? She turned and walked slowly up the second staircase. Good life in Illyria, suppose she'd made a mistake? Suppose it was three flights up, second on the left? The prospect of barging into the wrong apartment was too dire to consider so she shook the dust and plaster off her hem and smoothed her stola. Oh well, she could always try to convince Gaius she was here for humanitarian purposes, she supposed. She tapped on the door.

'Quintus?'

Silence. She screwed up her eyes and prayed again that his patience had run out. Why he wanted to meet in this sordid place was beyond her. Perhaps the sleaze added a bit of spice – more excitement, greater risk, heavier gamble . . . qualities Claudia was only too familiar with.

'Quintus.' She raised her voice slightly. 'Are you in there?'

It was unlikely she'd been heard above the din and clamour from the surrounding rooms. She could slip away, say she'd got lost, that Gaius had come home, that she'd been forced to tag along with the funeral procession – oh, she'd think of something. But then again, Quintus was prepared to pay handsomely for his fun and games in this abominable room, and when she owed that bloodsucker, Lucan, the best part of a legionary's salary, she couldn't afford to be too particular.

Juno, that door looks less than clean! Claudia felt a distinct reluctance to put her ear to the wood.

'Quintus,' she hissed, glancing up and down the deserted corridor.

For all its squalor, it was still better to slip that little scumbag Lucan a few denarii to keep him sweet than risk him calling at the house and making insinuations. Kicking aside a cabbage stalk, Claudia eased open the rickety door, offering silent prayers to whatever lowlife gods inhabited this stinking threshold that it was the right bloody one. And if I catch anything from this damned sewer, Quintus

Aurelius Crassus, you can bloody well stump up for the doctor's bill, too.

The senator lay face down on the bed, stark naked, his feet bound with a leather strap, his hands held behind his back in handcuffs, the sort they use to restrain slaves. Unlike the long, low, comfy couch at home, this was nothing more than a straw-stuffed, lice-infested mattress which Quintus, quite sensibly in Claudia's opinion, had covered with his toga. Three filthy cushions supported his stomach, pushing his podgy, white buttocks up in the air. Claudia smiled. Fat chance of him leaving – he'd trussed himself up like a chicken and there was no way he'd get out of this without help! She pulled out the rawhide whip, hidden under her palla, and cracked it.

'Right, you despicable little man!'

The professional had taken over.

'Let's see what you're made of!'

Claudia let her palla slip to the floor and slid out of her stola. She cracked the whip again, this time a finger's width from Quintus's balding head. He didn't flinch, but she wasn't surprised. They either jumped like a scalded cat or else they lay perfectly still like something on a butcher's slab. Given a choice, she thought she preferred the latter, but a job was a job and she didn't care to dwell too long on the matter. He'd jump soon enough, when the whip burned his buttocks.

'What do you say, Mr Senator?'

Off came the tunic, and she tossed her breast band on to the bed where he could see it.

'Will you plead for mercy?'

His poor manhood hung limp. Perhaps it needed the pain to jolt it into life?

'No?'

Of course, at his age, it might not ever come to life!

'We'll have to see about that!'

Her thong landed on top of the breast band. If he wasn't excited by now, there was something wrong with him no matter what his age.

'Take that, you smug, arrogant bastard!'

The whip should have left a raw, red wheal across his white flesh. His buttocks should have clenched. In fact, his short, fat body should have jarred with the pain. Instead, his body remained as flaccid as his manhood.

'Oh, shit!'

Claudia ran over to the bed. Don't tell me the silly sod's had a seizure, that's all I need! She touched his flesh. It wasn't entirely cold, but you didn't need to be a doctor to know this man was going to need the same hired mourners as the old linen merchant. She looked around to see where he kept his money. There was an obsidian brooch tucked into one of his high patrician boots, a soft leather pouch inside the other, containing nothing more than a few copper quadrans.

'Bastard!'

He hadn't intended to pay her, the scheming little cheapskate! Unless – yes, unless he hadn't trusted her and had hid his silver under the toga? Claudia's fingers glided over the wool, ignoring whatever livestock might be inhabiting the filthy straw below them. No coins. She slid her hand underneath his lifeless body.

'Damn!'

This was her own fault, of course, arranging to meet an old buffer like Quintus without knowing the first bloody thing about him. She wondered who it was who put him on to the exclusive services she offered, because usually she approached punters direct. She straightened up and moved round to explore the other side of the toga.

'Sweet Jupiter in heaven!'

Quintus Aurelius Crassus, respected senator, loving husband of Livilla, father of five sons and two daughters, grandfather of a dozen lively grandchildren, had most certainly not died of natural causes.

Quintus Aurelius Crassus had had his eyes gouged out.

II

In the four and a half years since Claudia had married Gaius Seferius for his money, a day hadn't passed when she'd been neither cooled nor soothed nor refreshed from walking in off the hot, bustling street to the quiet serenity of the atrium. Burning braziers gave off sweet-smelling scents, fountains rippled and tinkled, marble statues smiled in welcome, while cranes and doves and a hundred exotic animals pranced and danced on the walls. Except today.

'Melissa!'

She snapped her fingers and marched straight upstairs to her bedroom.

'Melissa!'

By the time the young slave girl came running up, Claudia had already divested herself of every item of clothing.

'Burn these!'

'Madam?'

'Don't gawp, girl. You heard me, burn them. And, Melissa – see to it personally, or I'll slit your nose right up the middle.'

Obediently the slave girl gathered up the garments. She was used to odd requests from her mistress, but this was the strangest yet. She would burn them herself, she didn't trust the other slaves, but oh, what a tragic waste of beautiful apple-green cotton.

'Oh, for heaven's sake, what's that terrible wailing? Isn't there anyone in the house man enough to put a stop to it?'

Melissa stuck the sandals under her arm. 'That's your daughter, madam.'

'Flavia? Dear Diana, how many times do I have to tell you, she's Gaius's daughter, not mine. My own poor, dear family – well, you know full well what happened. I don't need to go over it again. Besides,' she scowled at the dark-haired girl standing complacently in the doorway, 'I'm nowhere near old enough to have a daughter of fifteen. Now give me a hand with this breast band.'

She waited until the fit was comfortable before asking, 'What's the matter with the silly bitch this time?'

'The bridegroom, I gather.'

Claudia puffed out her cheeks. 'That awful child's never been happy about one damned thing in her life. Tunic! I hope her aunt's here with her.'

Flavia was the youngest of Gaius's brood and when her mother died in childbirth, she had been fostered out to Gaius's only surviving sister. Many times Claudia had pondered the conundrum: was Julia frigid because she was childless, or was she childless because she was frigid?

'I thought you disliked Miss Julia, madam.'

'Frightful woman. Can't stand her. Stola, please, Melissa!'

But even a sister-in-law has her uses from time to time.

Sweeping into the courtyard in fresh, ice-blue linen, she threw wide her arms. 'Julia, darling! I had no idea you were here.'

Her sister-in-law, bony, birdlike and a decade older, shot her a sideways glance. 'I thought you were out,' she said sharply.

'Oh, you know what slaves are like these days!' Claudia waved an arm dismissively. 'I was lying down.' She tapped her temple. 'Headache, you know.'

Julia's eyes became even more hawklike, but Flavia saved the day by bursting into another fit of tears. 'I don't want to marry him,' she howled.

'Want doesn't come into it,' her aunt snapped. 'It's arranged and wed him you will. Your father's fixed a good match with Antonius. He's a leading figure in the Treasury, isn't he? Draws a top-grade salary and is an old friend of your father's as well. What more can you ask for?'

'He's old . . .'

Julia and her sister-in-law exchanged glances. 'Mature,' Claudia corrected. Antonius was the same age as Gaius.

'It's not fair.' Flavia began to chew nails which were already down to the quick. 'First he was engaged to Calpurnia and when she died he was foisted on to me like some old hand-me-down.'

'Exactly my point.' Julia slapped the girl's hand away from her mouth. 'Your father thought him good enough for his eldest daughter, didn't he? Give thanks Antonius is still interested in the family alliance.'

Flavia pouted. 'He wants babies straight away and I don't. I'm too young.'

'Nonsense,' Claudia said briskly. 'I'd already had one daughter by the time I was your age and was heavy with my second.'

It wasn't true, of course, but if she stuck to the story

well enough, in another year or three – who knows? – she might even come to believe it herself.

Julia moved closer to her sister-in-law. 'I think it might be the, er, physical side that's putting her off,' she whispered.

'Fennel.'

'Oh?' Julia's eyebrows raised in surprise. 'Does that make you . . . more . . . or less . . . you-know-what?'

'I meant for her nerves,' Claudia snapped.

'Oh!' The older woman inched further towards her. 'Actually, I was rather hoping you'd have a word with her about the wedding. Or to be more precise, about what happens *after* the festivities.'

'Certainly not.'

'But you and Gaius . . . the age difference . . . I mean, you're Flavia's stepmother, it would reassure her—'

'No. And for goodness' sake, do get the child to shut up!'

Deaf to her stepdaughter's tearful protests, Claudia clapped her hands and called for wine. Flavia's wedding arrangements were part of her duty. Regrettable, but there you are. She resigned herself to lengthy discussions and prayed Jupiter would send a thunderbolt to break up the proceedings quickly. Instead Julia's thin claw held out her latest pendant.

'I wanted to canvas your opinion on this,' she said. 'I'm not sure the silversmith has got it right, the balance seems somewhat uneven. What do you think?'

Claudia stood up, vowing to make a really good sacrifice to Jupiter first thing in the morning. Maybe a nice white calf?

'What I think is that my head's thumping. I'm going to lie down.'

She'd established her presence, there was no need to prolong the ghastly encounter with this constipated old cabbage.

'Oh?' Julia hopped forward and peered closely. 'Hmm. I suppose you don't look too well. Very pale.' The hooded lids finally conceded defeat and Julia gathered up her belongings. 'And rather waxen, too,' she admitted. 'You're not coming down with anything, are you?'

Claudia shrugged noncommittally. 'Who knows?' she said feebly. 'Who knows?'

The veiled threat was sufficient to send Julia and her snivelling stepdaughter packing with all speed, and Claudia sincerely hoped it might be sufficient to keep the tiresome pair at bay for at least another week. Snatching up a goblet and a jug of honeyed wine, she marched back up to her bedroom and threw herself down on the couch. A small Egyptian cat with a wedge-shaped face and blue, crossed eyes bounded up beside her, rattling with pleasure.

Melissa poked her head round the doorway. 'Would you like—'

'Get out!' Three fat cushions hurtled towards her. 'And stay out!'

The cat poured itself into the hollow of her shoulder, butting Claudia's chin with its head. Stroking it thoughtfully, Claudia sipped at her wine.

'Well, Drusilla,' she said at last. 'Have we pulled it off?'

Sooner or later someone would walk in and discover the dead senator, mother-naked and trussed like wildfowl, and the search would be on for his killer. A noblewoman dressed in the very finest cotton would stick out like a snake among sweetmeats in that tenement, and you simply couldn't count the number of people who'd seen her go in and come out. That stola was the trouble.

'Still, it would've engendered a damned sight more gossip had I discarded that fine and distinguished symbol of Roman womanhood, don't you think? Anyway, the point is – would anyone there be likely to recognize us?'

Drusilla began to knead gently, the tips of her claws snagging at the fine linen.

The cat and Claudia had been together for seven years, long before Claudia took up as a dancer in Genua, and having found each other, both of them lonely and starving and living off their wits, there wasn't a single secret they hadn't shared since.

'Prrrrrr.'

'Me neither.'

Melissa had burned the evidence, Julia and Flavia had provided the perfect alibi. All the same . . .

She drained the goblet in one swallow. She'd seen some sights in her time, but many moons would wax and wane before Claudia, inured as she was, would forget the corpse of Quintus Aurelius Crassus, a stab wound to the heart and two bloody, raw holes where his eyes should have been. This made the fourth such murder in the past six months and each of the victims had been a respectable, high-ranking official. The authorities, under that foul-mouthed midget Callisunus, were no doubt sweating their sandals off in the search for a common link. So far they hadn't found it, but Claudia knew what – or rather, who – that link was.

Her.

'We've got a problem here, poppet.'

The cat snuggled up under her ear and drew a long, deep, contented breath.

'It can only be a matter of time before they latch on to us, then dear old Gaius will know what we've been up to. Now we can't have that, can we?'

'Mrrow.'

Gaius Seferius was old and he was fat and his breath smelled, but he was frightfully rich and, praise be to Hymen, he didn't pester her for sex. His family was grown up, and he didn't want another, although his position as one of the most successful wine merchants in the city had dictated that he ought to remarry – so why not take pity on the young and lovely widow of a judge from the Northern Provinces, grieving for an entire family wiped out in the plague? Providing she didn't interfere in any of his activities, commercial or personal, Claudia had everything at her disposal. She bridged her fingers in concentration.

'Shame patricians were out of the question, eh, Drusilla?'

Too bloody canny, that's why. Never dream of taking anyone on face value, no matter how tragic the circumstances. Pity, really, because Claudia was hellbent on having aristocratic children. She might not make the grade herself, but by Jupiter she'd get at least one son in the Senate if it was the last thing she did. One million sesterces, that's what it needed. One measly million. Still. She had settled for a leading light in the equestrian order, the next best thing, and although the marriage hadn't been consummated, compensation came in the knowledge that Gaius's chest pains occurred with increasing regularity. It could only be a matter of time before tragedy struck and she was widowed 'again' – and *then* she could think about bearing sons for promotion to the Senate.

Yes, indeed. It was merely a question of waiting . . .

Unfortunately, after less than a year of mixing with empty-headed matrons with whom she had nothing whatsoever in common, Claudia realized, somewhat to her disquiet, that wealth, social standing and a life of luxury were nowhere near enough. It wasn't that she regretted the wheeling and dealing that had been necessary to hook Gaius, far from it, it was simply that she'd been living on the edge for too long to suddenly give up the thrills. In short, she needed stimulation. Thus to feed the giant cuckoo she had hatched, Claudia had resorted to her old business activities.

'What do you think we should do?'

Drusilla's rough tongue was abrasive on her cheek, but she made no effort to draw away.

'So do I, poppet. Because if we don't find out who's knocking off our clients, someone else will and that'll really put the fox among our comfy little chickens.'

She kissed the cat between its ears and swallowed a whole goblet of warm, honeyed wine. Drusilla lifted her face, twitched her ears in the direction of the door and let out a short, guttural growl. Claudia tapped the side of her mouth thoughtfully.

'Yes, that had crossed my mind, too.'

The cat's eyes had become mere slits. 'Rrrrow.'

'I know, Drusilla. Irrespective of who he is, we're going to have to kill him, aren't we?'

III

'There's a very handsome gentleman to see you, madam. Gives his name as Marcus Cornelius Orbilio.'

Claudia glanced at Melissa in the mirror. 'To see me? Not my husband?'

'You, madam.'

She was in a good mood. They had just returned from the Field of Mars, where, victorious from his campaign against the Alpine tribes in Gaul, Augustus unveiled his testament to success, the magnificent Altar of Peace. Watching the Tiber roll gently past as the Emperor expounded on a glorious age of sunshine and gold, where civil war was a thing of the past and expansion of the empire the only way forward, there wasn't a Roman left standing who wasn't bursting his tunic with patriotic pride. Mighty restorations had already begun – roads, bridges, temples, the lot. Why, in Rome alone eighty-two major renovation works were in progress. Day and night hammers reverberated round the city, turning brick into marble, clay into stone.

'Then don't just stand there, girl. Show him into the garden!'

She dabbed scent delicately behind her earlobes, prodded a wayward curl back into place and slid another gold ring on her long, slim finger. As an afterthought, she clipped a black onyx brooch to her tunic.

He was sitting on a white marble bench in the shade of a sour apple tree. High patrician nose. Firm square jaw. And a mop of dark, curly hair which showed no signs of thinning. Claudia doubted whether there was an ounce of fat on his body and conceded he'd make a formidable adversary, although at the moment he seemed to have met his match.

Back arched and hackles raised, Drusilla advanced sideways, growling menacingly in the back of her throat.

'Pretty kitty.'

Claudia thought his voice lacked a certain conviction.

'Mrrrrow.'

'There you are, poppet.' She scooped the glowering cat into her arms and turned to her visitor. 'I see you've met Drusilla.'

Marcus Cornelius Orbilio stood up. 'Claudia Seferius?'

'Do I look like one of the slaves? What do you want?'

Orbilio glanced at Drusilla, who was scowling at his face as though she'd like to shred it to pieces, and squared his shoulders.

'I'm empowered by the Security Police to investigate the murders of four high-ranking officials—' He paused, and Claudia's quick wits sent her bending to park an indignant Drusilla on the ground, knowing it would pass off the flood of colour to her face.

'And?'

'And I wondered whether you could spare me a little of your valuable time.'

Valuable time! Claudia clapped her hands and called for wine and figs and some pecorino cheese, which was her favourite. Then she forced herself to stare him out.

Drusilla jumped up on to the sundial and copied her mistress.

'Yes, well . . . Perhaps I can begin with asking you how well you knew Crassus.'

'Who?'

'Quintus Aurelius Crassus, the senator whose body was found in, shall we say, *unusual* circumstances last Saturday.'

'Oh, him. Hardly at all. Why?'

'Didn't he dine here a week or two back?'

That was a shot in the dark, she thought. If he knew for certain, he'd name the date. 'Everybody dines here at some stage,' she said. 'Was he the one who'd just come back from some dire little outpost?'

She turned to the dark-skinned slave girl hovering with the tray who was obviously hanging on every word.

'Clear off, you. I'll see to this.'

A smile twitched at the side of Orbilio's mouth. 'Something like that, yes. Did you know where his body was found?'

'I heard a rumour.' She thrust a glass of wine in his hand. 'I heard it was in some ghastly slum.'

'Then you heard right. It was one of the buildings owned by Ventidius Balbus. You know him, I presume?'

'Everyone knows him,' Claudia said, making a great show of helping herself to raisins. 'What's this got to do with my husband and myself?'

Orbilio leaned back to rest his spine against the bark of the tree. 'Now who said this has anything to do with Gaius?'

Had the sun gone in? It seemed rather chilly all of a sudden.

'Come to the point, Orbilio.'

He fished in his pouch and came out with a torn scrap of apple-green cotton. 'This is the point,' he said quietly. 'It was found on the door of the room where poor old Crassus was killed. Looks like you caught it in your hurry to leave.'

Claudia took the proffered scrap. 'It's not mine,' she said, tossing it over her shoulder, where it landed to adorn a rosemary bush.

'Oh, but it is.'

'Rubbish. I wouldn't be seen dead in that colour.'

'I rather thought it would suit you,' Orbilio replied, smoothly retrieving his evidence. 'It would complement the tints in your hair.'

Claudia narrowed her eyes. 'Then perhaps I should order some,' she said sharply.

Orbilio smiled. 'But you already have, remember? I know, because I spent all yesterday traipsing round mercer after mercer to see who sold this particular cotton in this particular colour, and Gratidius, now – Gratidius remembers quite clearly it was the wife of Gaius Seferius who was so taken by the subtlety of the shade.'

'Gratidius is old and he's a fool with it. I'll have you know, I'm not in the habit of visiting malodorous slums, Marcus Orbilio—'

'Then you won't mind if I have a look around, will you?'

Claudia jumped to her feet. 'Yes, I bloody well would! How dare you come in here, you jumped-up little mongrel, and presume to search my house!'

Orbilio studied his thumbnail. 'Would you prefer someone with higher status?' he asked indifferently. 'Someone, say, like Callisunus, who would bring his soldiers with him?'

'That sounds suspiciously like blackmail, Orbilio, and I don't like blackmailers.'

Orbilio sighed. 'Sit down, Claudia, and try to remember I'm investigating the brutal murders of four of our most prominent citizens. Just to refresh your memory, that's one prefect, one aedile, one retired senator and a jurist.'

'Which you assume gives you the right to trample over decent folk in the process.'

'For pity's sake, woman! I'm busting my baldrics in the hope of reaching this lunatic before another unfortunate sod has his eyes gouged out and if that offends your sweet sensibilities, I couldn't give a stuff!'

Realizing one of the slaves might be watching, Claudia seated herself with a show of indifference and nibbled an olive. He was whistling in the dark, she decided. He couldn't prove she'd bought the fabric, and besides, if push came to shove, she could always slip Gratidius's assistant a spot of silver – between them, they could manage to persuade the old mercer his memory was at fault here and she'd done nothing more than simply admire the colour.

No. What really irritated her was the fact that she'd slipped up. By heaven, she'd chop that wretched Melissa into pieces for not checking the stola was intact!

'I'll be discreet,' he added, reaching up and plucking a sour apple.

'Young man,' she said. It sounded so pompous when he was the same age as herself. 'There's no way in the world I'm having your greasy little fingers poking around in my underwear *and that's final*.'

'Would you mind, then, if I requested your husband's permission?'

He was up to something, the bastard. She could smell it. He knew damn well she didn't want Gaius involved.

'Not at all,' she said. 'Junius!'

A muscular young slave appeared as if by magic.

'Junius, fetch my husband, will you?'

'I'm sorry, madam, but the master's already left for the baths.'

She shot Orbilio a glance. 'How long ago?'

'About an hour,' the boy replied.

Curiously enough, it was shortly after that when Marcus Cornelius Orbilio came to call. Well, well! What a coincidence. She dismissed Junius with a curt nod. When she first thought this man would make a formidable adversary, she hadn't expected him to be hers. No matter, she could be as sharp as a wagonload of monkeys when she chose. Four and a half years of easy living might have softened her physically, but Claudia Seferius had never once afforded herself the luxury of letting her guard drop. She picked a pink, sniffed deeply, then gave Orbilio her sunniest smile.

'Why don't we compromise?'

That seemed to shake him.

'MELISSA!' As did the pitch of her voice. 'Ah, Melissa. See this,' she pointed to the snippet of green cotton, 'do I have anything in this colour?'

'No, madam.'

The investigator frowned and pressed the fragment into the girl's palm. 'Look carefully,' he said, his eyes darting from slave to mistress for signs of hidden communications. 'It's very important.'

Claudia studied her onyx brooch, careful that her eyes never once met Melissa's.

'Madam has nothing in this colour,' the girl said, looking him coolly in the face before turning back to the house.

Claudia let her breath out slowly. 'Anything else, Orbilio? I mean, you don't want to turn the house upside down to see whether we're concealing a chest full of eyes as well, do you?'

Orbilio pursed his lips sullenly. 'No. That's all for the moment, thank you.'

'Good!' Claudia swept to her feet and flounced along the shaded colonnade. 'Then you can see yourself out,' she called over her shoulder.

IV

Orbilio heaved himself off the naked, glistening body of the girl beneath him and rolled on to his back. Mother of Tarquin, he had difficulty remembering who was who these days! Was this Vera, the Sardinian fish-trader's daughter, or Petronella from the locksmith's place? He wiped his brow with the back of his hand and wondered whether the locksmith either knew or cared who his woman slept with. He reached for the flagon, but it was empty.

'Damn.'

He slumped back on to the bed, his hair falling across his eyes. He couldn't go on like this much longer, he was burning himself out. Eighteen hours a day, seven days a week for the past six months he'd searched for clues that would bring him closer to trapping a demented killer, seeking solace at night in wine and women – and finding it in neither.

If only he could get a break, and, Juno's skirts, it wasn't for the want of trying. There had to be a connection between the four men. There *had* to be. That foul-mouthed, sour-faced boss of his didn't think there was, but then again, Callisunus hadn't exactly risen through the ranks because of his brains, had he, the oily bastard? A propensity to take full credit for his officers' findings if they were successful and to swiftly disown them if they fell short had secured his position as Head of the Security Police. That his men might despise him mattered not a jot to Callisunus. Small and squat with pug-like features, he sat like a spider in his web of complacency knowing that even if Orbilio's theory happened to prove sound, he could still come up smelling of lavender. Except in this instance, Callisunus was convinced the killings were random, leaving Orbilio to follow his nose . . . providing it was during his own free time. No matter. There was a link, he was sure of it – but what?

His mind ranged back over the information to date, but so far he hadn't found one single shred of evidence to link any of the men with the others, particularly Crassus who, having retired from the Senate, had recently completed a long stint in Isauria. He'd driven himself into the ground, delving into every business transaction they'd ever entered into, and so far he'd found bugger all.

Of course, there were plenty more leads to follow, but assuming there was no professional connection what other motives were there? Someone with a grievance? Crassus had been a miserable old curmudgeon with a reputation for cheeseparing, but Tigellinus, the man responsible for the metropolitan water supply? Horatius, organizer of the Megalesian Games? Such occupations attracted laurels rather than grudges. Fabianus the jurist might have been a possibility, had he not been widely respected for his sense of balance and perspective. Nevertheless, he might have offended someone – a man with a twisted sense of justice . . . Orbilio groaned and rubbed his eyes at the thought of the enormous number of trails still left to follow. And why were there no witnesses to any of these crimes?

'Mother of Tarquin, is the man invisible?'

How much simpler if he could have unearthed (as he'd hoped) a conspiracy to assassinate the Emperor. Now that would have sent him winging up his ladder of ambition faster than a bolting steed – and the kudos, oh, the kudos! Unfortunately, the conspiracy theory held as much water as a leaky sieve and he was left without a single suspect and the barest minimum of clues.

Regardless of the amount of effort he'd put in, hadn't Callisunus remarked that very morning, in his inimical silver-tongued fashion, that if Orbilio didn't stop farting around with dead-end theories he'd put Metellus on the case instead? The worst part was he'd follow through, dammit, because if Callisunus suspected this dissent was halfway contagious he'd ditch him at the earliest opportunity.

'I want evidence!' he'd stormed at the briefing. 'Concrete fucking evidence, not pansified piffle. The Emperor would kick my butt from here to Hades if I trotted out your far-fetched farrago, so I suggest you get your arse back to work before I lose patience completely.'

'Well screw you, Callisunus,' Orbilio said aloud. 'You'll see I'm right, you just wait.'

'Huh?' Petronella – or was it Vera? – lifted her head. 'Did you say something?'

'No. Go back to sleep.'

Cupid's darts, what was he doing here, night after night? It was like when he was young. No matter how many of those saffron yellow honey cakes you ate, they never filled you up. Well, this is pretty much the same thing, isn't it? He turned his face to the window and stared at the silver semicircle of the moon. I ought to marry again, he thought. Start a family. Work is work, but at the end of it a man needs something good to go home to. I want to be surrounded by laughter and squabbling. I want to be getting involved in my boys' schooling, my wife's family and my own duties as a senator. Because I *will* make the Senate, make no mistake, I'll be there! Being born into the nobility helps, but it's by no means a foregone conclusion; you still need to apply yourself – and Marcus Orbilio had certainly done that. Two years' legal duties, two years as a tribune and eighteen months working in criminal justice. Six more months and I'll be eligible to put myself up for a quaestorship, with automatic admission to the Senate – just the right amount of time to ensure people wouldn't forget.

'Orbilio? Fine fellow. Solved those gruesome murders, you know.'

'Oh, yes. First-class work.'

'In a matter of months, too, and he had virtually nothing to go on.'

Orbilio tugged on his lower lip. That would remain the stuff of dreams unless he could get to the bottom of this nasty business. Motive! If he could only find a motive! Having exhausted the obvious possibilities, his mind had turned to the less obvious. Tigellinus's murder suggested a lunatic, literally, since he was killed two days before the moon was full, but Horatius was murdered when it was in the first quarter, Fabianus when it was waxing and Crassus halfway. Cross that off.

Then he realized Tigellinus was killed on the Festival of Juturna, Horatius at the start of the Megalesian Games.

Could that be a connection? Both had been heavily involved in their respective ceremonies – Tigellinus because the festival was celebrated by men whose business was connected with sacred water and since the pool of Juturna was the source for all official sacrifices and seeing as how Tigellinus was responsible for the city's water in general and this shrine in particular, how much deeper could you be? The same with Horatius, responsible for organizing the games from start to finish. Unfortunately neither Fabianus nor Crassus fell even remotely close to the ceremonies and this theory had fallen by the wayside. Supposing he checked again? No, no. He'd gone over this, time and again, it was pointless running down the same blind alleys.

The thing that kept nagging at him was: why the eyes? Each man had been killed by an expert, with one savage, upward thrust into the heart. Oh, that makes it easy! He punched his pillow. That narrows it down! Dammit, there should have been witnesses . . .

It was odd, thinking about it, Tigellinus being lured away from so important a date in his calendar. The temple was right in the Forum, too, yet not only had he slipped away, he'd gone home and sent his servants, slaves and family packing. Horatius, too, had been killed at home, having dismissed the entire household and again, despite the density of people at the start of the games, no one had seen or heard anything. Fabianus was a different kettle of fish altogether. Unlike the other two, he was a man of low profile and equestrian, rather than patrician. He lived meagrely, ran a small household, yet he too was killed, some time between going to bed and waking up.

But why, why, why rip out their eyes?

One thing was certain, the murders were becoming

increasingly frequent. Tigellinus was killed two days before the Ides of January, leaving the authorities to follow up what appeared to be a purely domestic affair. Except Orbilio could find no motive. The prefect was a popular man, loved by family and friends alike. Twelve weeks passed before the next victim and what should have been the start of a week of celebrations, of theatrical performances, processions, banquets and races, had culminated in another brutal murder. Orbilio's mind raced on. Suppose Horatius was the intended victim, with Tigellinus killed as a decoy? He didn't think so. April was a time of beginnings. Flowers open, so do the seas. Land travel becomes once again possible, campaigns begin in earnest and he was sure this would turn out to be a campaign of wits. He was right. Seven weeks passed, then Fabianus was killed, six weeks later Crassus . . . who was the most bizarre yet. What in Tartarus was he doing in a backstreet slum tied up like a pudding?

Orbilio had just one tangible piece of evidence: that snippet of green cotton. He folded his hands behind his head. She was there. Without doubt, she was there! She was lying through her lovely teeth – and so, dammit, was the slave girl. He just couldn't prove it. Not yet, anyway. He grimaced at the memory of that evil monster of hers. That bloody cat was enough to frighten the dead away. They were well matched, those two, scowling and spitting and attacking head on if they thought they were being threatened!

The furrows in his brow relaxed as he thought about Claudia Seferius. Venus, she was lovely! Orbilio was no ladies' man, but he could tell that no matter how many pins she stuck into her hair, nothing was going to restrain those luxuriant dark tresses for long. There were terracotta tints in there, and old gold and bronze and amber. He'd seen them when the sunlight caught it. Seferius was a lucky sod – assuming he ever got past that damned cat of hers. Oh yes, Gaius got his money's worth with that one, and he'd like to bet she wasn't such an abrasive bitch in bed. He pitied her, though, having to satisfy a fat old slob like Gaius when half the young men in Rome would give their right arm to have her. But of course, half the young men in Rome put together didn't have one quarter of Gaius's fortune . . .

He hadn't missed the way that strong-backed slave Junius had looked at her, either. She was certainly a woman to love, was Claudia Seferius, rather than a woman to merely make love to. She'd make a man possessive and if she was in Marcus Orbilio's bed he wouldn't want her underneath him. Oh no! He'd want her on top, straddling him, so he could see every luscious curve of her body. It would be daylight, too. He'd watch her arch her back and thrust out her breasts. She'd throw back her head and . . . Realizing the prospect was arousing him, he turned on to his side and cupped his hand over Vera's breast. Claudia's breasts were fuller and rounder.

'Marcus, I'm trying to sleep.'

His hands began to explore.

'Leave off.'

Vera shrugged her shoulder, but he pulled her roughly on to her back. Yes, much fuller and rounder. His mouth closed over her nipple. Underneath that brittle veneer he was sure he could sense a pulsating passion in Claudia Seferius.

'Marcus, stop it!'

'Claudia!'

'Who?' Vera tried to roll over on to her side, but he pinned her down. Claudia had long legs, they would be slender like her arms and neck. She would call out his name.

'Claudia!'

He climbed on top of Vera, who was frantically pushing at his shoulders. 'Get off me, you self-centred, two-timing, double-crossing lizard.'

If he closed his eyes, he could pretend it was Claudia wriggling underneath him in the throes of passion, not Vera fighting him off. Except with Claudia it would be long and slow, not a few quick thrusts like this. It would take from midnight until daybreak just kissing and arousing her, then when dawn finally broke, when sunlight flooded the room, the rhythm would begin. The age-old rhythm that would have them sweating and groaning and panting and screaming . . .

'Oh, Claudia, Claudia!'

The last words Orbilio heard before he climaxed was a woman's voice snapping, 'I'm Petronella, you stinking, slimy bastard.'

V

Sliding into her seat, Claudia felt the same old sensations take over. The racing pulse, the trembling hands, the brightness in her eyes. A ripple of pleasure shuddered her body as she surrendered to the excitement ahead. Good old Apollo! Eight delicious days in his honour! The last games, the Fishermen's Games, were a month back and a decidedly inferior affair, too, lasting one mingy day. High spots of colour rose in her cheeks as the babble around her increased. The raucous chuckles of the men, the high-pitched giggles of the women, the delighted squeals of the children. Well, if any one of them extracted a mere fraction of the pleasure Claudia would get, they could count themselves jolly lucky. She smiled to herself. That Gaius was beside her, unaware of her cravings, added a certain piquancy to the occasion.

'Seferius!'

One of his business associates clapped him on the back.

'Seeing as how you're here early, I don't suppose you could spare me ten minutes?'

Gaius and his colleague settled into an animated discussion about wine – quantities versus price – while Claudia absorbed the atmosphere of the amphitheatre. It was filling up now. Amazing how so many working people still managed to squeeze in the time to attend these lavish spectacles and she wondered whether that ferreting investigator, Orbilio, had found time to indulge himself today. Probably not, he'd be too busy grubbing around in filthy tenement slums to relax with simple pleasures! She wished him joy.

While musicians sought to make themselves heard above the din of the crowd, Claudia adjusted her cushions and drummed her fingers, impatient for the entertainment to begin. Gaius had secured seats near the front, reflecting his privileged status, but not for Claudia the savage thrill of the bloodlust. She began tapping her foot and glanced round for the seventeenth time to catch the eye of her slave, Junius. As usual, the muscular Gaul was watching attentively and signalled acknowledgement with a slight incline of the head. He was a good boy, was Junius. Knew precisely what to do!

The parade began as the lump of lard that was her husband resumed his seat, chortling because he'd talked his colleague into taking another two hundred amphorae without so much as dropping his price by one copper quadran. In a flurry of gold and purple cloaks, the gladiators strutted round the arena, followed by slaves holding aloft their plumed helmets and weaponry. That was typical of Gaius, she thought. So damned shrewd. Through sheer hard work and enterprise he'd amassed a veritable fortune – yet he saw nothing contradictory in spending the same amount of money on a small consignment of Black Sea caviar for his banquets as he did a yoke of oxen for his farm. Both were justifiable expenses in his eyes, and he'd flay her alive if he learned she was squandering his money on fripperies.

Except that her gambling was no idle pastime. It had become an addiction, a monster of Olympian proportions, forever ravenous and totally out of control, and not for nothing did Claudia Seferius spend more time on her knees propitiating Fortune than any other deity.

The gladiators marched out, the musicians upped their tempo and, to a crash of cymbals, an elephant lumbered into the arena to be matched against a bear. Claudia felt her whole body tense. Already her mouth was dry, her heart pounding. Using a secret signal, she indicated to Junius, 'Bet on the elephant', and wiggled five fingers, intimating the bear would be dogfood within the space of five minutes. The way she tilted her head told him to bet two quadrans. She always started low; it was part of the game. Small bets gradually became large bets which in turn became almost impossible bets and, dear Diana, she couldn't help herself, the daring was all part of the exquisite torture. The same way your heart freezes as you wait for the dice to land, or when your charioteer tries a tight manoeuvre at the end of a circuit and you just don't know whether he'll make it.

Unfortunately Fortune seemed deaf to her prayers, or perhaps Minerva had thrown in her might with the money-lenders. Either way, Claudia's debts had spiralled. She'd tried to stop herself, but be it a simple game of knuckle-bones or a full-scale race at the circus, she was there and it wasn't unheard of for Claudia Seferius to be hanging around the training schools, betting on the practice fights. What, initially, was a straightforward case of syphoning off the household expenditure fell at the first hurdle when Gaius had begun to comment, and thus she set out to find another well to dip into. The answer, when it came, was amazingly simple.

To pay for her own vice, others could pay for theirs.

Not that hers was a service she bandied about. On the contrary, these clients had been carefully cultivated for their unusual proclivities and little could she have envisaged the scale on which it would take off. Magistrates, merchants, high-ranking civil servants were suddenly queuing up to be spanked or whipped, tortured or humiliated, and whilst they didn't deserve to die for their perversions Claudia had scant sympathy for them. Except maybe Quintus, for no one deserved the indignity of being found in that frightful flyblown room.

She signalled to Junius. Two quadrans on the panther tearing the lion's throat out within four, no – three minutes. It would be a lie, of course, to say Orbilio's visit on Tuesday afternoon hadn't shaken her. Probably the best thing was to go back to that dreadful dive, in full view of everybody, and confound the boots off possible witnesses. And she'd have to do it pretty smartly, she supposed. Memories, in slums like that, would be relative to their lifespans. Meaning short in the extreme. Tomorrow morning? Why not? Let me see, that would make it the, ah yes, the Nones of the month, she could excuse herself, if necessary, by pleading attendance at one of the ceremonies. Splendid.

Come the interval she was five asses and a quadran ahead and should have been feeling pleased at the strict limits she'd imposed on herself. Instead it rankled that she still was no closer to finding the murderer than before. Gaius, bless him, shuffled off to talk to one of the praetors and his wife, but Claudia remained seated. Who could possibly have discovered what she was up to? She had a nasty suspicion it was one of her clients, but who? In each case, discretion was everything. Only old Quintus approached her direct, and because his request to meet in the tenement was unusual, even by her standards, and she'd exacted such an exorbitant fee she hadn't bothered to enquire further. Until he'd been murdered.

She stood up and stretched. Junius was nowhere to be seen, so she set off in search of refreshment. Rumours were spreading fast of a maniac abroad, gouging out the eyes of the nobility to keep as grisly souvenirs, and locksmiths could charge double (and often were) for the protection the governing classes were seeking with such desperation. Callisunus had scores of men working day and night to catch the demented lunatic, but Claudia's intuition told her that Orbilio was working silently and secretively to find a link.

'There you are, my sweet.' Gaius handed her a quince decorated with thorns to resemble a sea urchin. 'A dainty treat, what?'

Claudia wrinkled her nose and swapped it for a pomegranate. Speed was certainly crucial here, because should Gaius catch wind of her activities, he'd throw her into the street without so much as a backward glance. Hadn't he insisted on both prudence and fidelity as part of the marriage contract? Under no circumstances would this man allow himself to be made a fool of. Oh yes, she'd really have to move fast.

'Gaius, old man! You're looking well!'

'Ventidius Balbus! Well, I never. Claudia, you remember Ventidius?'

Remember him? How could she forget him? The mention of his name had sent shivers down her spine when Orbilio had thrown it into the conversation – but for reasons he could never have imagined. The very last thing she wanted was to see the fellow today!

'Of course. How are you, Ventidius?' Dying of leprosy, I hope.

Six, seven years ago in Genua, when he was an ambitious young magistrate, Ventidius Balbus would hire nubile dance troupes to entertain at his banquets and she honestly couldn't remember whether she'd slept with him or not. Good tippers she'd recall, but otherwise a punter was a punter, you never looked at his face. Especially one as bland as that pasted on Ventidius Balbus! She studied him now. Puny as ever, eyes like boiled gooseberries. When she'd taken on the persona of the other Claudia, the one whose family had been wiped out in the plague, there were precious few people in Rome who might recognize her and Balbus had been one. Luckily for her, she'd been installed as Gaius's wife for nearly a year before their paths crossed and when they did meet at some function or other it was patently obvious he hadn't made the connection. Nevertheless, prudence was one of Claudia's saving graces and it didn't hurt to avoid him wherever and whenever possible.

'Can't complain. But you, my dear, you look more ravishing as time passes.'

Claudia bared her teeth in the semblance of a smile and was about to turn away when she remembered *why* Orbilio had mentioned him. She heard Gaius saying:

'You've been buying property in the south, I hear?'

'Vulturnum, do you know it? Dull town, despite its—'

Claudia wasn't interested in dreary chitchat. 'You're landlord of the apartment block where they found Crassus, aren't you?'

Both men looked startled. 'Why, yes—'

Gaius picked up her hand and patted it. 'Claudia, my sweet, you don't want to concern yourself with that terrible business.'

'Rubbish. If there's a madman on the loose what decent person dares sleep soundly in their bed?'

'One understands the fellow only picks on men,' Balbus said. 'One would assume—'

'One assumes nothing of the sort,' she retorted. 'A madman is a madman. Who knows what's going on inside his lunatic skull? Until he's in chains, I for one won't rest. Has anyone been round asking you questions?'

Balbus blenched. 'What rumours have you been hearing?' he asked. 'One doesn't like to think one might be a suspect.'

'Don't be so silly. I meant do they have any witnesses, things like that. I mean, if it's so terribly overcrowded, you'd think someone would have had their eyes open, if you'll pardon the expression.'

'People keep themselves to themselves in those places,' Balbus said.

'I thought that was the very thing they couldn't do,' she snapped, 'packed together like feathers on a duck. Gaius, you really ought to lobby someone—'

She found her arm being slipped through her husband's and a distinct pressure on her elbow.

'Claudia, my sweet, we should be getting back to our seats. Let's meet, Balbus, say, three o'clock at the baths tomorrow?'

'Excellent. Hope to see you soon, then, Claudia.'

'Ghastly little man,' she said to Gaius, knowing Balbus might well be within earshot still. 'I don't know why you put up with him.'

'If I stopped dealing with ghastly little men, my sweet, I'd be out of business by the end of the month. He's got fingers in all sorts of interesting commercial pies and as I so often tell you, it is frequently the indirect contacts which prove more fruitful than the direct.'

'Well, I hope you never bring him to the house.' She tossed the pomegranate over her shoulder. 'I didn't like the way he was looking at me.'

'Every man in Rome looks at you the same way.' Gaius gave her arm a gentle squeeze. 'But I'll probably invite him to the banquet.'

'What banquet? Gaius, I wish you'd consult me more often.'

'Claudia,' he replied patiently, 'I told you about it weeks ago. The one on the Ides.' An ominous edge crept into his voice. 'I hope you're not telling me you've forgotten, because I've invited some very important people.'

Damn, damn, damn. It was Melissa's fault, of course; she should have reminded her!

'Oh *that* banquet.' She shrugged indifferently. 'I thought maybe you'd slipped in another one.'

Nine days. She'd really have to steam to get the bloody thing organized in time! And how was she going to find the time to track down a killer as well?

More cymbals, more animals, more bets, more losses.

'Our paths cross so rarely these days,' he remarked eventually.

Often enough for my liking.

'You always seem to be out, Claudia.'

'You always seem to be busy, Gaius.'

And not only with work.

'I don't bring it home, though.'

'Even *you* aren't that insensitive!'

Gaius pursed his lips. 'Now, why are you so prickly today, my sweet? You usually enjoy the games.'

'I'm always prickly,' she said, and Gaius's heavy body shook with laughter.

'You're right there.' He leaned conspiratorially towards her and lowered his voice. 'Fancy a small bet? I know it's illegal but once in a while maybe . . . ?'

Claudia shook her head. 'Can't be bothered,' she said, frantically signalling to Junius to put a whole denarius on the leopard. 'Maybe when the gladiators come on.'

The midday executions had been a bit of a disappointment. Either Rome was getting safer or criminals were getting smarter, but whatever the cause, only five men went down on to the sand and none of them lasted long. Watching the pairs slug it out had been pitiful and the survivor, the snivelling coward, had positively hurled himself at the wretched tiger in the end. What did he think? That because he'd beaten the others he was free to go? Claudia had lost several sesterces on him, because until then he'd proved a tough character and she'd bet double that he'd fight like a man and last a good fifteen minutes. However, she couldn't complain. Geta, one of Rome's finest bestiarii, had got himself disembowelled by a rhinoceros before he could fire off a second arrow and her rash bet on the rhino had left her well ahead of the game.

'You're looking pleased with yourself.'

Startled out of her reverie, Claudia spun round to gaze into the bearded face of a tavern-keeper she hadn't seen for over five years.

'Ligarius!'

Quickly composing her features, she signalled Junius to keep an eye out for her husband's return.

'They said you'd done well for yourself.'

'I thought you were in Genua.'

He shrugged. 'Not since last November. You're looking lovelier than ever, Claudie.'

'What do you want?'

'Nothing.' He folded his arms across his broad chest. 'Just came over for a chat, that's all. I thought it might be nice to talk about the old days.'

'I disagree.'

'Oh, come on, Claudie. You can spare an old mate ten minutes, can't you?'

'Go away.'

'I only want to talk.'

'Ah!' She was beginning to understand. 'How much?'

'Pardon?'

'Is this man bothering you, Claudia?'

Julia's husband, a man with the face both the colour and texture of an underripe mulberry, slipped his arm around her shoulder. She could feel a damp patch forming, but resisted the urge to flick his hand away.

'Marcellus, kindly convince this fellow I'm not Livilla Flaccus. He won't take no for an answer.'

Her brother-in-law ostentatiously adjusted his toga.

'This,' he said pompously, 'is the wife of Gaius Seferius, the wine merchant. His sister is my wife. Now clear off and pester someone else.'

Ligarius opened his mouth to speak, then changed his mind. 'Sorry,' he mumbled to Claudia, backing into the crowd.

'You can remove your sticky hand now, Marcellus.'

He ran his palm lingeringly over her shoulderblades and down her backbone.

'*Now*, you bastard, or I'll slap your face in full view of everybody!'

'All right, all right.'

When he smiled, she could see the gap in his teeth. Thank Hymen Gaius had a full set! Even if they weren't that good.

'Keep your hair on, Claudia.'

'I do,' she snapped. 'It's your wife who runs up the wigmaker's bills.'

'She needs the adornments,' Marcellus replied, running the back of his hand down her cheek. 'You don't.'

'Oh look, there's Gaius.'

'No, it's not. Stop teasing.' He inched closer. 'I'm serious. You don't need cosmetic aid, not even round those lovely big eyes of— Ouch!'

Claudia was grinding her heel on his little toe.

'Remus, I love a woman of spirit. Suppose we make sweet music together?'

That he'd been drinking heavily was in little doubt, yet Claudia had the impression he was making genuine overtones.

'Frankly, Marcellus, I'd rather throw myself to the lions.'

Yes, the killer must be a punter, because someone's tongue was definitely loose. No matter; when she found him, she'd loosen it for good!

'Second thoughts, I'd prefer to throw you to the lions.'

There were limits, after all, on what a girl would do, even for money. Small wonder Julia was frigid!

Having despatched the reptile that passed for her brother-in-law, Claudia was laying into Junius for allowing Marcellus to get within ten paces when Flamininus the censor sidled up.

'Tomorrow morning?' he whispered, pretending to look the other way.

'No.' She'd have to give up working for a while. It was the only way to stop the bloodshed.

'But you promised!'

Or was it? The killer might be working through a list. Great heavens, Flamininus himself might be responsible. She decided to meet him as planned and question him. Maybe she wouldn't have to go on to that smelly tenement afterwards.

His voice took on a wheedling tone. 'Please, Claudia. I'll make it worth your while.'

You bet your sweet life you will! 'No.'

Urgency crept in. 'Claudia, you must. I'll double the price.'

'Treble it.' If she was to clamp his testicles and lead him around by a halter while he called her filthy names, the least he could do was pay for the privilege.

'Very well. Treble it is. Goodbye, Claudia.'

When she turned round, he'd melted into the crush. Now, perhaps, she might be able to enjoy a peaceful moment to herself.

'There you are, my sweet. Look who I've found.'

Gaius was standing beside her with a huge grin pasted across his face.

'A long-lost cousin from the north. You might not remember him, of course, you were very young at the time, but he assures me he remembers you very well.'

There was no one from the north who could remember her, that was the point. She had chosen her new identity with extreme care. The other Claudia had no family, her relations by marriage were killed by the plague. Every last one of them.

'Hello, Claudia.'

Her face set like marble, Claudia slowly turned round.

'Remember him now, my sweet? Marcus Cornelius Orbilio?'

VI

'Little Markie! My word, how you've grown!'

The sarcasm flew right over Gaius's head, as of course she knew it would.

'You recognize him, then? Splendid, splendid!'

'I'd know him anywhere,' Claudia replied sweetly, watching Orbilio squirm. 'And to think I believed myself without a relative in the whole wide world.'

Whatever reaction the miserable worm had been expecting, it wasn't being welcomed with open arms. She smiled. And whatever devious game he was playing, she could match it in spades.

'Oh, well – it's a very distant connection . . .'

'Yes, indeed. Remind me again, Markie, my poor mind's gone completely blank.'

'Ah, well . . . Your mother was my mother's, er, second cousin. Yes, that was it. Of course,' he said apologetically to Gaius, 'Claudia and I rarely saw one another.'

'Nonsense, you used to visit an awful lot, Markie, don't you remember? Your mother couldn't wait to get shot of you.' She tilted her head to one side. 'You might not believe it, Gaius, but Marcus here was a perfectly horrible child. Always following me about, forever poking his nose into matters that didn't concern him and asking the most preposterous questions.'

43

Orbilio gave a brittle smile.

'Not much family resemblance,' Gaius said, cheerfully peering from face to face, 'although you're both fine-looking specimens. Must have been a damned handsome family on your mother's side, what?'

'Absolute stunners, the lot of them,' Claudia chipped in before Orbilio opened his mouth. 'Although underneath Marcus's mother was a frightful old boiler. Gave him a terrible childhood.'

She stood on tiptoe and whispered loudly in Gaius's ear.

'No one can say for certain exactly who Markie's real father is.'

It was clear Gaius attributed Orbilio's colour and discomfort to the airing of his family background. Claudia linked her arm firmly through Orbilio's and drew him away.

'So how is the old bat these days?'

'My mother? She's dead.'

'Fancy.' Claudia placed the flat of her hands against his chest and pushed gently until he was sitting on the stone seat. 'Then I'd really appreciate it,' she said quietly, 'if you'd be kind enough to go and join her just as quickly as you can.'

She patted his mop of curly hair and returned to her husband.

'Loathsome fellow,' she said. 'Never want to see him again.'

'I think you're being unfair, my sweet. He's your only living relation and I'm sure he'll have mellowed over the years.'

Claudia followed his glance to where Orbilio was sitting, frantically combing his hair with his fingers.

'Doubt it. See? Still sulking like he used to. Oooh, look, there's Octavia. I'll catch up with you later, Gaius.'

Elbowing her way towards a make-believe friend across the other side of the amphitheatre, Claudia wondered whether she'd been a trifle hasty in disposing of Orbilio so quickly. Maybe she could have wheedled some information out of him? No matter. He was up to something and in her experience a pre-emptive strike always proved the most effective form of attack. She was still congratulating herself as she summoned the rugged young Gaul.

'Junius, I want you to run an errand for me. You know Gratidius, the mercer? Good. Well, I want you to find his assistant . . .'

The slave listened attentively, repeating Claudia's instructions back to her practically verbatim.

'Oh, and Junius.' She was feeling quite sublime about the way she was handling this dodgy business. 'Drop my winnings off at Lucan's counting tables on the way.'

The Gaul's mouth twisted. 'There are no winnings, madam. You bet them all on the Nubian.'

'Bugger!'

Claudia slapped her forehead. This is all that bloody Orbilio's fault, she thought. Odious little snooper.

'Listen, if that investigator chappie comes slinking round asking questions,' she said, 'you just smile and nod and say yes to everything he asks. And I mean everything.'

He'll think the boy's daft or unable to understand the language properly, and either way it suits me right down to the ground.

'There'll be a sesterce in it for you,' she added, because

loyalty was a fine quality in a man but you couldn't always take it for granted. Especially in a slave.

There was a comic turn in progress when Claudia finally resumed her seat. In the arena, two women of truly enormous proportions were pretending to be gladiators, clashing wooden swords and oohing and aahing all over the place. Like real fighters, they too were naked and when one fell in a mock wounding, she cast aside her shield in imitation of the plea for mercy except instead of raising her left hand, she shook her breasts in a most lascivious manner to the deafening roars of the delighted crowd and, thus pardoned, the fight recommenced. The Seferius party didn't seem to have even noticed. Gaius was installed with his arm around Flavia, who – surprise, surprise – was grizzling loudly, while Julia sat on the end, tight-lipped as usual. Thank goodness Mulberrychops was nowhere to be seen.

'Claudia!' The relief on Gaius's face was overwhelming. 'Perhaps you could have a word with my daughter. Seems she's a little concerned about the, er, honeymoon activities.'

'Why, Gaius, I'd be delighted.' She smiled radiantly at her sister-in-law. 'You should have asked, Julia.'

Julia's face darkened with indignation, but she remained silent as Flavia disentangled herself from her father and latched on to Claudia like a leech. Claudia pushed her away, forcing herself to leave what she hoped would be translated as a motherly hand on the girl's shoulder, but refusing to move any closer. Juno, that child could use a bath! If this was a ploy to escape her honeymoon activities, she was certainly going the right way about it.

'Gaius!'

Talk of the devil.

'Antonius! You know my sister, of course, but I don't believe you've met my wife. Claudia, allow me to introduce Flavia's fiancé, Antonius Scaevola.'

The newcomer smiled. 'You're absolutely correct, Seferius. I don't believe I've had the pleasure.'

Liar. Several times, if memory serves me right. And at twenty sesterces a shot, no less.

Antonius settled himself beside Flavia and slipped a proprietorial arm around her shoulder, his hand brushing against Claudia's as though by accident. He wasn't a bad looking fellow on the whole, she thought, and he had more energy than most men half his age. The best advice anyone could give Flavia, now she thought about it, was to get herself fit. After all, Scaevola was no once-a-night man; his bride would need stamina by the bucketload. She glanced at Gaius. He was surprisingly fit, in spite of his bulk. And fast with it. His chins wobbled as he laughed and suddenly Claudia was glad his energies weren't invested in the marital bed.

'What do you make of Crassus, then? Tied up and stark naked, too. Something of a new development.'

Antonius moved away from Flavia, ostensibly so he could see the arena better, but Claudia had caught the wrinkling of his nose.

Gaius turned to look at his friend. 'I hope Callisunus nails the bastard soon, because you never know who's going to be next.'

Julia let out a small whimper, but no one took any notice.

Scaevola's mouth turned down at the edges. 'There's a lot of men hiring bodyguards—'

'Ooh, Julia! Think of all those broad, muscular bodies round the house,' Claudia whispered to her sister-in-law, wondering whether she was supposed to have been chastened by the withering look she received in return.

The fat women waddled off, to wild cheers and whistles, and the serious fighting began.

'—and they say there's another new development. A mysterious noblewoman, according to Callisunus.'

Claudia's ears pricked up. 'Sounds highly unlikely, a woman of our class skulking round backstreet slums,' she said. Oh yes, the sooner she returned to that dump the better. 'Do they seriously think the killer's a woman?'

'Could be,' Antonius replied. 'Callisunus hasn't ruled out the possibility that the Woman in Green is his man, so to speak.'

'Woman in Green, eh? Could be you, Julia. You favour green a lot.'

Another withering glance. She'd have to be careful baiting her sister-in-law in public, she decided. One of these days the old bag would turn. But in the meantime there was a great deal of fun to be extracted from the game.

'Balbus won't pay attention to rumours.' Antonius paused to cheer on the net fighter. 'His opinion is that the scum who rent those places would sell their children into prostitution for a copper quadran, and, heavens, he ought to know, he takes enough of their money.'

Claudia had heard quite enough about Ventidius Balbus for one day, thank you.

'You promised a bet, remember?' She nudged Gaius in the ribs. 'What about us all wagering a little something on the next fight?'

Her enthusiasm was pounced on by the other four, and while Scaevola organized the stakes, she sincerely hoped it wasn't her future son-in-law who was responsible for the murders. He was good fun to have around, by and large. It would be a bloody shame to kill him.

VII

More than ever the tenement resembled an ant's nest as Claudia wove her way across the large, open courtyard. Maybe it was the threat of thunder that hung heavy in the air, or maybe late morning was simply the busiest time of the day, but the bawling and wailing seemed louder than ever, the smell worse than she remembered. This time, resplendent in peacock blue, she arrived by litter, drawing the crowd she'd intended. By the second landing, however, a tongue-lashing had disposed of the curious and Claudia was once again alone.

Dark and comfortless as before, the room had not been touched. Crassus's bloodstained toga sprawled over the mattress, his boots waiting patiently under the window for their owner to collect them. Dust lay thick on the rickety table, a shrivelled onion and a broken pot beneath it. In the far corner, flies hummed round the charcoal brazier. Claudia was on the point of leaving when her eye caught one object which definitely had not been there the last time.

'Forgotten something, Claudia?'

Marcus Cornelius Orbilio slowly unfolded his arms and prised himself off the flaking plaster.

She couldn't speak. For one awful, heart-stopping moment she pictured him propped up against the wall, silently watching her undress, holding his breath while she cracked the whip before witnessing her search for the senator's money. Hysterical nonsense, of course. She'd been utterly alone and, besides, any witness could only have been the murderer. In which case, she'd be dead. She drew a deep breath and cleared her throat.

'Don't tell me – you can only get off by frightening people.'

Orbilio smiled. 'No, but I'm prepared to make an exception in this case.'

'You're just feeling smug because I put one over on you yesterday.'

He flexed his shoulder muscles. 'Don't I have every reason? I knew you'd come back. It was only a question of time.'

'Let's get one thing straight, Orbilio. I haven't come *back*. I'm here solely because my name's been dragged into this mess and I intend to clear it.'

'And you couldn't think of a better way?'

Why he seemed amused was beyond her. 'Certainly not. Ask any one of those people downstairs, I very much doubt whether a single person is able to lay claim it was me they saw.'

'You mean "willing", not "able". How much did you pay them?'

'Orbilio, grow up. Hundreds of people live in this slum; do you honestly believe I've gone round bribing every single one?'

'I meant just now. I watched you throw a handful of coins in the air. Don't tell me that wasn't to – how shall I put it? – sway their judgement?'

'Orbilio, I wouldn't tell you the time. Now get out of my way, you're blocking the door.'

'Since you're so observant, perhaps you can tell me what you saw last time? Apart from the corpse.'

'There was no last time. Get out of my way or so help me I'll scream the place down.'

'Feel free, no one'll come – assuming they even hear you. That's the way it is here. What were you doing in this room last Saturday?'

Claudia folded her arms across her body and stood firm, confident that sooner or later her wall of silence would wear him down.

'Was Crassus your lover?'

No response.

'I suppose you'd have to meet somewhere out of the way, in case Gaius found out, although personally I'd have chosen a rather more salubrious setting.' In bright sunshine, with thyme-scented hills as a backdrop.

Claudia pretended to study her nails.

'It's against the law, too.'

Silence.

'Claudia Seferius,' he said mildly, 'I'm calling you an adulteress.'

'Yes, dear, and you'll soon grow tired of it.'

A smile tweaked at his mouth. 'Was Crassus protecting your reputation? We all know how strongly the Emperor feels about adultery, especially in view of his own daughter's behaviour . . .'

He trailed off. Everyone knew the story about the woman's voracious sexual appetites and how deeply it embarrassed the Princeps, flying in the face of his own moral preachings. It's always the same,

Claudia thought, one law for one sex, another for the other.

'Cousin Markie, if husbands paid the same price for their affairs as women pay for theirs, there'd be a damned sight more lonely men about, I can tell you.'

Cousin Markie! It served him right, he supposed, saddling himself with a label like that. He'd thought he was clever. He'd thought he could wheedle his way into the Seferius household. Claudia would rebuff him instantly, but at least it would get him an introduction to social gatherings where he could pursue his enquiries. Instead the tables were turned so completely it had been humiliating. He congratulated himself that he'd managed to even the score by waiting in this sordid room until she arrived. He smiled. He knew she would. She was always going to point her horns and charge straight in to attack. Mother of Tarquin, she was lovely!

Provoking a reaction by suggesting adultery with that bloated old haddock Crassus failed miserably. Not that he gave the idea serious credibility; he'd thrown it in to create ripples, but the water remained calm. Too calm. Why hadn't she torn his throat out at the mere suggestion?

'How long had he been dead when you found him?'

Claudia watched the slow progress of a cockroach crawling over the peeling plaster.

'I have three grounds for placing you at the scene of the crime.' He had nothing to gain by holding back. 'One.' He ticked them off on his fingers. 'A snip of green cotton.'

'We've been through that.'

Orbilio grinned. 'So we have. First Gratidius says it was you, then he's not sure because his assistant suddenly swears it wasn't. Incidentally, that's the same assistant who's just settled a long-standing doctor's bill. However, you missed something.'

It was no good her pretending indifference.

'You forgot to bribe the porter who delivered it to your house.' Hooray, that brought a spark of life to her eyes. Even though she covered it quickly. 'Two. You returned to the scene of the crime. Perhaps not evidence in itself, but highly suggestive and a trait common to most criminals.'

'Want to arrest me?'

'And, three, I have a witness. You were seen coming in and going out of this room.'

Orbilio opened the door wide. Frowning, Claudia looked up and down the empty passage.

'You don't see him?'

She pulled a face.

'Rufus!'

A bundle of rags in a doorway formed itself into a small boy.

'Rufus, do you recognize this lady?'

The urchin shuffled closer. 'Yep. That's her.'

'Nonsense!' Claudia turned to Orbilio. 'How much did you bung this little guttersnipe? One ass? Two?'

'She called me a poxy little oik.'

Her eyes flashing, Claudia looked the boy up and down several times. 'That's hardly conclusive. I should imagine everybody calls you a poxy little oik.'

'And up yours and all, missus!'

Orbilio watched recognition dawn on Claudia's face, but instead of a feeling of triumph an iron claw gripped his guts.

'I remember this horrid little ragbag now. It was in the

Forum.' She turned to Orbilio. 'He rammed me with a pig's head. The snout, if I recall correctly, caught me right here.' She jabbed her navel.

'You was wearing green.'

'*You* was running from the shopkeeper.'

'You was here.'

'I was not!'

'You was. I'd know that swagger any place.'

'I most certainly do not swagger!' Claudia spun round to Orbilio, who quickly covered his mouth with his hand. 'Are you seriously considering the word of this offensive little street arab against mine?'

The investigator scratched the back of his neck. 'Yes,' he said at last. 'I rather think I am.'

Claudia glowered at the boy. 'Hop it, you. I want to talk.'

Orbilio tossed him a copper and nodded assent. 'Come back inside, Claudia,' he said quietly, sweeping his arm round the room. 'Because I very much want to listen.'

VIII

Under a sky which made promises of rain it had no intention of keeping, Claudia sat in the cool of the peristyle, half-heartedly strumming a lyre. Around her, tiny birds in cages, their plumage brighter than jewels, trilled to drown the melody. By rights I should be enjoying the second day of the games, she thought, weighing strength of elephant against armour of crocodile or cheering dwarfs as they cartwheeled through the legs of giraffes or cavorted with ostriches. Instead I spend half my morning ploughing through riffraff and dross in some sleazy backstreet slum. Drusilla came running up, tail erect, and began rubbing against Claudia's shins until, eliciting no response from this tactic, she jumped on to the seat beside her and yowled at the top of her voice.

'I'm sorry, poppet, I was miles away.' At the foot of the Quirinal, holding my nose to be precise. Claudia clapped her hands. Why do they build tenements, with no water and no sanitation, in the bowls of hills where the smell can't escape? 'Fetch some chicken, bread and cheese, will you,' she commanded the slave who answered the call, 'and root out a sardine or two for Drusilla.'

The girl made no effort to pick up the cat and carry her off to the kitchen. Scars on her wrists had taught her not to tangle with the animal, especially when its mistress was at home. It ate with her, slept with her, followed her around like a shadow. But just you try to stroke it and it would go for you like a wild tiger.

'Fetch some dates, too,' Claudia called out. 'And check whether that idle sod Verres is back yet.'

Bloody cook, never around when you wanted him. Probably come up with some ridiculous excuse that he was out choosing food for tonight's dinner. Why he didn't send some of the slaves was beyond her. What on earth was the point of having them, if you did the job yourself?

'You wanted to see me, madam.'

Bloody cook, always creeping up when you never expected him!

'Yes, Verres. I wanted to talk to you about the banquet Saturday week.'

'What banquet?'

'Come, come, Verres. I told you about it weeks ago. The one on the Ides.'

'No, you didn't.'

'Don't contradict.'

If he wasn't such a good cook, imaginative as well as subtle, she'd sack him on the spot. Who did he think he was, anyway, arguing with her like this? Not that it mattered. By the time she'd finished with him she'd have him believing black was white and that she actually *had* told him about the bloody thing.

'But I—'

'Stop wittering, sit down and concentrate. Now, at our last feast you did something rather clever with a pig's innards, if I recall.'

Verres, as plump as a boiling fowl, beamed with pride.

'The sow's womb I stuffed to look like a fish? You want me to do that again?'

'Great heavens, no!'

Gaius had to believe she'd invested the utmost care and attention in its long-drawn-out planning.

'This has to be exceptional, Verres. I want their eyes popping out on stalks at this . . . this magnificent extravaganza, so think carefully.'

'Ummm. Dormice in honey and sprinkled with poppyseeds?'

'Yes, yes, by all means. Whatever delicacies you can come up with. But I'm talking about a particularly lavish spectacle. Think, man. What can you produce that'll be the talk of the Senate for months afterwards?'

For a while it looked as if Verres had lapsed into a coma, but eventually a broad grin split his face. 'I've got it! A wild boar which, when you carve it, lets loose a score of live thrushes which I'll sew up inside at the last minute!'

You had to hand it to the man, he was a genius. 'Excellent! Well, you go away and work on that—'

'We'll start with oysters and leeks stuffed in a peacock, then move on to tuna disguised—'

'Wonderful, Verres, absolutely splendid. Now go and plan it alone, there's a good chap.'

He looked a mite crestfallen as he stood up, but Claudia had no interest in domestic trifles and shooed him away with the back of her hand. Drusilla, meanwhile, having cleared every last scrap of sardine, was helping herself to chicken off Claudia's plate.

'Melissa!'

A boar filled with thrushes, eh? Oh yes, that'll make 'em spill their wine.

'MELISSA!'

The cat jumped and a lump of chicken fell out of her mouth, which she promptly scooped back up when she realized there was no sign of danger.

'Oh, there you are. Look, there's a list in my husband's room of the people attending the banquet. Don't look so blank, the feast next Saturday, I told you about it weeks back. Now run off and fetch the list – and bring a jug of wine while you're about it.'

It'll be interesting to see who he's inviting. With any luck, Gaius will have forgotten about adding that boring old fart Balbus to the list – but suppose he'd thought to invite Orbilio? No, no, he couldn't. He wouldn't have seen him since yesterday. Which was just as well, really. She didn't fancy another round with Cousin Markie. She nibbled on a date. Well, not yet, anyway.

'Here you are, madam. Is there anything else?'

Claudia spat the stone across the courtyard. She was getting better. One of these days she'd hit that sundial. 'Yes, as a matter of fact there is.'

She picked up the lyre again and began to strum. 'We need entertainers. Singers, dancers, acrobats, that sort of thing. See to it, will you, Melissa?'

'Me? But I can't—'

'Don't talk rubbish. Here.' She unclipped her obsidian brooch. Well, it was Quintus's really, but . . . easy come, easy go. 'This might sugar the pill.'

The girl's eyes widened. 'For me?' She'd been given the odd sweetener from her mistress before, but never anything valuable.

'One problem, though. It might be short notice for some of them, but do what you can, Melissa, and, failing that, bribe the buggers to say they'd double-booked and it was the other party's misfortune, not ours.'

Hopefully at least one of them will put a spoke in the wheel of that Marcia trollop. Claudia closed her eyes and offered up a silent prayer to Minerva to be with her rather than with the linen merchant's widow on this. Anything to outdo her! Twenty-two and inherited a fortune indeed. Well, it's your own fault, she chided herself. You would pick Gaius. More fool you, because the linen merchant was older and had no living children, whereas Gaius had four waiting to inherit, didn't he? Furthermore, she'd actually wished that spotty little gold-digger luck with the linen merchant. He was a grumpy old sod and a real tightwad, but now the boot seemed firmly on Marcia's dainty little foot, the bitch. She sighed. It was too late grumbling. Wheels were in motion, there could be no turning back now.

'What on earth are you babbling about, girl?'

'I was asking about tumblers, madam. Do you want—'

'What I want, Melissa, is for you to go away and organize it without pestering me.' She jerked her head towards the house. 'Go on, off you go.'

The girl's fingers wrapped themselves tight around Quintus's brooch as she ran off, leaving Claudia to scan the list in peace. When Gaius said his guests were important, he meant instrumental in furthering his business activities rather than any reference to the political hierarchy, though there was a healthy smattering of magistrates, prefects and the like. No less than seven, she noted, were punters. There was a heavy night ahead, then, questioning seven men without letting any of them – or Gaius – suspect a damned thing. Still, it was the sort of challenge she could rise to standing on her head and, if the truth was told, even enjoy. She'd track that maniac to his grave, so help her – though she'd be a lot happier if that damned Orbilio wasn't so fly.

'Quick as a coney he was, Drusilla, double-checking with the mercer's porter about that wretched bale of cotton.'

The cat paused in her washing and cocked her head.

'I could have kicked myself for that.' Lack of foresight was not one of Claudia's faults. 'Or Junius. He ought to have thought of the porter, the numbskull. And as for that little arab Orbilio winkled out – well!'

It was difficult to tell how much that obnoxious little snoop had believed her over in that stinking tenement. On balance, hardly at all, she concluded . . . but he couldn't prove a bloody thing.

'Come inside,' he'd said smoothly, thinking he was about to crack this tough little nut at last, 'I very much want to listen.'

Listen to what? Did he honestly expect her to pour out a startling revelation? Oh yes, I was passionately in love with darling old Quintus, but please, please, please don't let my husband know or he'll divorce me on the spot? Hardly. Whatever else he might be, Orbilio wasn't gullible. Maybe he was expecting a different sort of admission? The-swine-was-blackmailing-me type of confession? Well whatever, he was completely hamstrung by the time she'd finished and it served him damned well right.

She'd wasted no time. The instant the door closed behind him, she'd spun round, wagging her finger.

'Listen to me, you filthy little meddler, I've had it up to here with you. I do not own, and have *never* owned, a

61

garment in that vile shade of green, and however much you paid that abject little tramp, it wasn't enough. A bump in the Forum is not proof.'

'Proof enough,' he'd said mildly.

'You aren't listening,' she hissed. 'If I hear so much as one more syllable drop from your lips on this subject, I'll personally cut your tongue out, chop it into pieces and feed it straight back to you, do you understand?'

'Is that a threat?'

'All I need to do is tell my husband how dear old Cousin Markie laid his filthy paws on me and the rest, as they say, is mystery.'

'Ah! A bribe as well.'

Damn you, Orbilio.

'Any foul insinuations you make after that will brand you as a vindictive lecher who was spurned once too often and resents it like hell. You'll be ridiculed from here to Hesperus and you can kiss all your ambitions goodbye.'

If that hasn't disposed of the irritating little tick once and for all, I'll eat my shift for breakfast.

A sparrow landed in the courtyard and Drusilla hunkered down, alert and ready to pounce. Claudia threw the bird a piece of bread, which it snatched up and flew off with. The cat stretched and began washing again, too full, too satisfied to think seriously about hunting. The edge had gone. And suddenly Claudia wondered whether her edge had been blunted, too. Without doubt, the hunt was exciting, but what would happen when it came to the kill?

'Come, Drusilla, we've guests arriving shortly.'

Was she too full, too satisfied, to carry it through when it came to the crunch?

The sparrow landed a second time, twisting its head

on one side as it hopped closer for more bread. Cheeky little beggar. She smiled at its comical gait and its beady eye and broke off another crust. Suddenly there was a blur of cream and brown. Feathers fluttered in the air. Drops of red splashed over the tiles. And Claudia Seferius had her answer.

'I'm sorry, what were you saying, Gaius?'

'I said, I've invited Ventidius Balbus to my little do.'

Bugger. Now she'd really have to watch her step next Saturday. The slightest hint of any spurious extra-marital activities and he might just make the connection with Genua. Especially when there's a nubile young dance troupe breezing around all over the place! Bugger, bugger, bugger.

'Something the matter, my dove? Your face is all screwed up.'

'Oh, Balbus is as dull as boiled asparagus. I was merely wondering where to seat him.'

'Next to Ascanius, I think. I don't see why he shouldn't get a dose of the senator's views on food subsidies, do you?'

Claudia laughed. That was the thing about Gaius, he could at least make a girl laugh. Which is more than you could say for the old linen merchant!

'I'll put them both near the door where they can bore the sandals off each other without troubling the rest of us. Uh-oh, that sounds like Old Sourpuss arriving.'

Gaius patted her shoulder. 'Don't be like that, Claudia. It's not Julia's fault she's turned out so . . . so solemn.' He picked up his clean tunic. 'Help me into this, will you, my dove? We so rarely spend time together, I don't want to spoil the moment by calling a slave.'

Sweet Jupiter, what a sordid amount of blubber! There were several red marks round his neck and over his chest, which she chose to disregard, but Gaius had caught her noticing them.

'Yes – um, I can manage the rest.' Embarrassment darkened his already florid features. 'Why don't you go on down and greet them?'

'Let's go down together.' Let Julia think she'd interrupted a bit of hanky-panky. That would stick in the old trout's craw. 'Marcellus won't notice we're missing, he'll be too busy eyeing up the slave girls. Julia will be inspecting for dust, Flavia will be trying to avoid Antonius and Antonius will be . . . well, he'll just be Antonius.'

If only Flavia could let her hair down, she'd be in for a wonderful time with Scaevola. So what if he was forty years older than her? He was wealthy, generous, virile. Grey rather than bald. Give him the babies he craved and she'd not know she was born. Silly cow.

'How do I look?'

Frightful. 'Wonderful. And me?'

'Claudia, you look as ravishing now as the day I married you.' He clucked her under the chin, then paused. 'Tell me, my dove. There must have been times over the last few years when you've wanted . . . a spot of male company, shall we say?'

'A lover?'

The more direct you are about things, the more it unnerves people. Especially husbands.

'Ah, well, I wouldn't go so far as . . .'

'Gaius. I assure you, sex is not a problem.' Or, in our

case, the distinct lack of it. 'I wonder what your sister will find to carp about tonight?'

Gaius chuckled. 'These interchanges are good fun, what?'

Claudia made a noncommittal sound in the back of her throat.

'Seriously, my little dove.' Gaius picked up an ivory comb and ran it through his hair, covering the front where it receded. 'Sweet, domesticated wives are ten a quadran, whereas Seferius has a treasure beyond price.'

'Oh?'

'A wife with balls. Rarer than teeth on a duck's arse.'

They were both chortling when they emerged from his bedroom, and Claudia was delighted to see that Julia looked as though she'd bitten straight through a lemon. Just in case the frosty old turnip had missed the point, she pinched Gaius's bottom and got a playful slap on her own in return. Her stepdaughter's jaw had dropped open and Claudia wished someone would have the sense to snap it shut for her. Of Gaius's four children, Flavia was the least likeable. Whereas her sister, Calpurnia, was a lively, amusing creature – until her untimely death at the age of fifteen. Poor old Gaius wasn't having much luck with his offspring, really. His youngest son, Secundus, a snide little bastard if ever there was one, had managed to fall under the broad wheels of a wagon. He wasn't much of a loss, though, and Claudia didn't think even his father had mourned him for longer than a week. Still, he'd at least had a sense of fun, that boy.

'New tunic, brother?'

'Pure Campanian wool. Like it?'

Julia wrinkled her nose, but said nothing as she followed them up the other stairs towards the smaller dining room. It was strange to think there were twenty years between brother and sister, Claudia reflected. His zest for life and his passion for the wine business knocked years off Gaius, yet Julia could pass for a decade older. The party paused to admire the new frescoes depicting scenes from Greek literature. In the doorway, Marcellus blocked his hostess's path.

'Good, was it?' he sniggered, nodding towards Gaius, who was now gingerly lowering his bulk on to the couch.

Claudia treated him to a sickly smile and patted his pockmarked cheek. 'Better than you'll ever be, brother-in-law, better than you'll ever be.'

She wriggled in between Flavia and Antonius, certain the arrangement would suit them both, although that wasn't her motive.

'Could any man want for a more beautiful mother-in-law?' Scaevola asked, tilting his glass at Claudia. 'Or a prettier bride?'

Claudia spluttered into her wine. Pretty was stretching the imagination, wasn't it? Flavia had been sulky and sullen even before the prospect of marriage came along, sitting round-shouldered and biting her nails. Of course, a smile would be a great improvement, but that didn't seem to be part of the girl's wardrobe. On the other hand, when you were fifty-three yourself, maybe any fifteen-year-old looks attractive?

The slaves came round with the eggs and salad. She would be a very wealthy woman one of these days, would Flavia, now there was only herself and Lucius to inherit the Seferius fortune. Gaius had made sound provision for his wife, but his children were the chief inheritors.

'There's a lot of talk going round about you, Claudia.'

Julia's birdlike features seemed more pronounced than ever tonight.

'Oh?'

You bastard, Orbilio! I'll nail your balls to a post for this!

Julia sniffed. 'I'm afraid so. Brother, you ought to be more careful, we don't want the name of Seferius sullied.'

Gaius stiffened. 'No, indeed.'

His eyes narrowed as he looked at his wife. She opened hers ingenuously wide and shrugged. Lips pursed, Gaius turned to Julia.

'What have you heard, sister?'

All eyes were on Julia as she laced her fingers together. 'They say that if it's good enough for the Emperor's wife, it's good enough for Claudia Seferius.'

'What, exactly, are you driving at, dear?' This time it was Claudia who spoke, her lips parted in what she hoped would be taken as a smile.

'Spinning, of course! I mean, honestly, Claudia, you don't do any of the weaving and clothmaking expected of a woman of your social standing, it's an absolute disgrace.' Two spots of colour had appeared on her cheeks. 'The Princeps won't consider clothes unless made by Livilla's own hand, just like my Marcellus would never dream of wearing anything other than homespun, would you, Marcellus?'

All eyes turned to Mulberrychops, who reminded Claudia of a beetle wriggling on the end of a pin.

'Flavia won't let you down, Antonius,' Julia said

primly, 'I assure you of that. Oh yes, you'll have a wife to be proud of, because she sews a very fine seam, does Flavia.'

All eyes turned to Flavia.

'I do,' she said smugly. 'I sew a very fine seam.'

Claudia was aware that if she restrained her laughter much longer she'd wet herself, and when she glanced at Gaius it was obvious that the image of his wife happily playing with distaffs and spindles was too preposterous to take in. His whole body was shaking.

'I do not find this amusing, brother. Simple pleasures are always the best.'

Claudia couldn't help herself. 'Did you say "thimble" pleasures, Julia?'

Marcellus laughed so heartily that food fell out of his mouth and down his tunic and Gaius's eyes were watering when Leonides, the lanky Macedonian steward, entered the room.

'I apologize for interrupting dinner, sir, only Rollo, the bailiff, is downstairs. Shall I ask him to wait or do I show him straight up?'

Gaius wiped the tears from his eyes. 'Oh, bring him up, Leonides. He's ridden for two days, poor devil, he won't want to hang around here for too long. Not when there are taverns and whores waiting.'

Seferius had immense respect for his bailiff. Originally a slave set to work on the farm, Rollo had shown such flair for viniculture that Gaius had quickly given him his freedom and promoted him to supervise the vineyards. Within less than five years, Rollo had risen to become bailiff of the entire estate.

He looked as though he'd ridden for two weeks, rather

than two days. His face was drawn, he could pass for forty instead of thirty.

'Master Seferius, it's bad news, I'm afraid. It's your son . . .'

'Lucius?'

'Aye. There's been an accident.' He shuffled his feet and stared at his large, square hands. 'I'm most terribly sorry, sir – he's dead.'

IX

Claudia was engrossed in thought as her entourage wove its way through the maze of temples, arches, halls and rostra that comprised the Forum. Progress through the throng of orators and philosophers, barbers and beggars was slow, and donkeys carrying stone for the restorations were becoming bad-tempered in the stifling heat. To her left rose the twin peaks of the Palatine where the imperial residence and a sumptuous temple to Apollo dominated the skyline, while on her right work was in progress on the Capitol in the form of a temple to Jupiter in praise of Augustus's escape from lightning during his recent Spanish campaign. At times the builders' hammers threatened to drown the clamour in the Forum. Claudia snapped shut the distinctive orange curtains of her litter.

Poor Gaius. The death of his favourite had come as a body blow; he'd crumpled instantly and remained inconsolable. She chewed her lip. Terrible business. From the moment of his birth, Lucius had been groomed to take over the business, to ensure Seferius wine continued to reach the same exacting standard expected of it, and over the years the boy had proved himself a capable organizer, a hard worker in the mould of his father.

Rollo explained he'd died from eating bad fish and round the table heads nodded solemnly in commiseration.

There was hardly a Roman in the empire who didn't know of a friend or relative who'd perished along the same unfortunate route. Yet, glancing round the dining room the instant the news was broken, Claudia noticed that, with the exception of Gaius, none of the family looked particularly distressed. Including herself, it had to be said. Surprised, yes, but no signs of grief – even from the boy's sister. And for Flavia not to snivel was, in itself, rather interesting.

'Alms! Alms!'

A leprous hand, bound with filthy bandages, thrust itself under the curtains of the litter. Claudia hit it as hard as she could with the sole of her sandal and watched its hasty retreat. The oath that accompanied it lacked a certain charity, she thought.

Driven by grief and a desperate need to oversee this season's transformation of fruit to wine, Gaius had left at first light the following day, accompanied by the poor bailiff who had been forced to repeat the arduous journey without so much as a decent night's sleep. Claudia had kept her head down in the fervent hope her husband might have forgotten her until he was well underway – by retiring early and cocking a deaf ear to the clatter of hooves and the shouts of the grooms right under her window – but luck wasn't with her. She was hastily summoned to his room on the point of departure and issued with a long list of instructions, culminating in the inevitable: she must join him and the family at the villa when she'd finished; it was her duty.

'Bugger.'

As the litter lurched, she picked up a fan of ostrich

feathers and frantically began flapping. Bugger, bugger, bugger.

'We can't stay long,' Gaius had said miserably. 'I need to be back in time for the Wine Festival.'

For a wine merchant, this was the second most important event in the calendar, although little consolation that was! Not when there's a whole blessed month in between with nothing to do except stagnate at that wretched farm. Claudia ground her teeth. I'll miss all the fun of the festivals, and I do so enjoy the Lucaria! People would congregate in the groves, singing and dancing and picnicking for two luscious days, followed by ten whole days of the Caesarian Games. Then there'd be all the processions, the parties, the thanksgivings – oh, dammit, Gaius, I'll miss the whole bloody lot! Mind you, I told him straight. This is the Nones, I said, there's no way one poor helpless female could possibly work through that onerous list before the Ides. No way at all. Sceptical even in grief, Gaius compromised on a week and even as she waved him off Claudia congratulated herself on screwing seven days out of him; two were more than adequate. Oodles of time to lap up what's left of Apollo's Games!

Not that she'd forgotten her quest, because Claudia was well aware that for some poor sod time was running out. It didn't take a mathematical genius to work out that the murders were being committed with greater frequency and that, by definition, the killer's confidence would be growing with each one. There had been times, of course, when she'd wondered whether the fact that the four dead men happened to be punters was pure coincidence. Those thoughts, however, were confined to moments when the moon was high and her spirits were low. Of the five clients she'd cornered this week, every last one expressed profound shock at the suggestion they might have revealed the relationship. To them the arrangement was as sacrosanct as it was pleasurable, they said – although she freely acknowledged their sentiments may well have been swayed by the knowledge that, if their family and friends found out, they'd be both ostracized and ridiculed.

Moral austerity was the order of the day, with the Princeps introducing more and more laws to tighten any lapses. If the penalties for adultery were crippling, it was nothing compared to those for the type of activities Claudia's clients were paying for. It was ironic, when you thought about it, such strict decrees from a man who once prostituted himself for three thousand gold pieces and negotiated his inheritance to the Empire by agreeing to become Julius Caesar's catamite.

Using charm and guile, she'd also managed to establish alibis for three of them, including Flamininus the censor, who was away in Lanuvium at the time. Claudia continued to flap the ostrich feathers. Pity, really. He'd have been easy to kill and his wife would probably have been exceptionally grateful. She sighed. Such is life, she thought. Never as straightforward as you'd like.

Oh well, she might find out more at the baths this morning, and if not, then there were plenty of compensations to be gained. The steam room, a hot bath, a spot of gossip, a good rub-down – not to mention the prospect of a wager or two on the men in the exercise yard. How many press-ups they could manage, how many balls they could juggle, even silly bets, like how many sausages they might eat. There was always another like mind eager to swap coins.

'What the . . . ?'

The mood of the crowd had changed suddenly, turning ugly and riotous and her slaves could no longer maintain the litter at shoulder height. It was now joggling from side to side. Claudia edged the curtains apart a fraction. They were halfway between the Forum and the baths, taking a short-cut down one of the side streets, but the chants and jeers were too close for comfort.

'Turn back, Junius!'

All too often the populace turned nasty about their handouts of grain – something to do with not getting them, she supposed. Nevertheless, it wasn't her business.

'Juno!'

Without warning the litter tipped over, tossing her on to the pavement like a sack of turnips. She managed to land safely, suffering only grazes in the process, and looking around decided she could count herself jolly lucky. Tempers were flaring. Fists were beginning to fly.

'Down here!' Claudia beckoned her slaves, but when she glanced over her shoulder she was alone. She paused on the corner. Sweet Jupiter, where on earth were they? 'Melissa? Junius?'

Now she looked carefully, all seven servants seemed to have been swallowed up in the fighting, including the women.

'Damn!'

Sending up a quick prayer to Mars to keep an eye on them, Claudia decided she could waste no further time. She picked up her skirts and ran full pelt down a dark, deserted alleyway between two tenement blocks. As she raced past the coppersmith's, an arm lashed out and pulled her into the workshop. She tried to scream, but a strong hand clamped itself over her mouth.

'Hello, Claudia.'

The voice was soft, low – and very menacing.

Squirming and wriggling, she managed to bite into one of the fingers. 'Let go of me, you bastard.'

'I can no do that, Claudia.' She'd bitten deep, but he'd not so much as winced. 'Not until we have quiet little chat.'

She spat out his blood. 'Let me go!'

Her feet were kicking his shins and her nails were clawing at the arm round her waist, but she was held fast. There was a clatter of metal as they crashed into buckets, bowls and sheets of copper.

'Now, now, Claudia,' He spoke with a thick Thracian accent. 'We got few things to sort out, yes? Like, you know, the money you owe Master Lucan.'

She could place him now. It was Otho. The man who breaks legs for a living.

'Sod off, bonehead.' She reached for a hammer, which he kicked away. Jupiter, he was a big bugger, too. Made of iron, most like. All Thracians were, weren't they?

'Tch, tch, tch. That no very ladylike. Why don't you and me go to the back and talk this thing through? I'm sure we can come to an arrangement to suit everybody, yes? After all,' his voice sounded quite conversational, 'you don't want house calls, no?'

'Go fuck yourself!'

Suddenly she was slammed against the wall and a huge paw gripped her chin. His thumb and forefinger pinched deep into her cheeks.

'Listen to Otho, you foul-mouthed bitch. You no in position to tell *anybody* what to do, understand?'

Her head was hurting badly from where it hit the wall, she'd bitten her tongue and she was also feeling sick. Whether the nausea was from the knock or from fright wasn't really important.

'What do you want?'

'Good girl.' The voice was back to its low, sibilant menace. 'Now let's go out back and talk, yes?'

He jerked his thumb towards the terrified coppersmith cowering in the shadows.

'And you. Start hammering or you won't have no hand to hammer with.'

Claudia found herself bundled into the back of the workshop, the ringing of the metal making her dizzy. To her surprise, there were tears in her eyes. Otho shoved her towards the back wall. Close up, she could see there was a deep red scar running the length of his cheek and she shivered. What befell the man who made it didn't bear thinking about.

'How much does he want?' Dear Diana, was that squeak hers?

Otho placed his hands flat against the wall. She wasn't pinned, but the result was the same. 'How much you owe Master Lucan?'

'T-t-two thousand sesterces.'

'Two thousand four hundred.' Otho bared his teeth. 'You forgotten the interest.'

That much? Bugger. This visit was turning into a right bloody mess, she couldn't let it continue.

'All right. I'll send him a hundred sesterces by . . . by

the middle of next week.' Miracles do happen occasionally, but this at least would buy her time.

Otho leaned forward, his face almost touching her own. 'Three hundred,' he whispered. 'By the weekend.'

She felt whatever colour was left drain out of her face. 'I can't do that!' Even if I throw myself on Gaius's mercy and for some unbelievable reason he said yes, it was still impossible. 'My husband's away. There's been a death in the family.' Good heavens, was this pitiful babble really her? 'I can't raise three hundred in time.'

One finger gently traced a line down her cheek. 'Three hundred, Claudia. Or you and I, we be matching bookends. You have my promise on that.'

Her mind made rapid calculations. Would Gaius divorce her if she was disfigured? Not if she told him it was a vicious street gang. Except . . . except she'd look like a bloody chequerboard by the time Otho had finished and Lucan still wouldn't be any closer to getting his account settled!

'Look. Maybe you and I could do a deal.'

She tried to calm her breathing. 'Instead of spending your money on tavern girls, suppose you and I . . . got together?'

The raddled old whores only charged eight asses, it would take three lifetimes!

'Maybe.' His accent was so thick now, it was almost unrecognizable. 'But first let Otho see what he'll be getting.'

His left hand slid slowly along her shoulder, down her upper arm and across to her breast. She shuddered involuntarily and watched his face split into a grin. Claudia thought she'd never seen anything more closely resembling a death rictus. Her heart was thumping. This man enjoys hurting people. She forced herself to look him in the eye as his hand moved inside her stola and under her tunic.

'Nice tits.' He began to squeeze.

She could bring her knee up, now, and . . .

'Well? Do we have a deal or don't we?'

As his right hand moved between her legs two men burst through the door from the workshop, dragging a third man, bruised and bleeding.

'Junius!'

The coppersmith hammered frantically in the background. There was no rhythm to it, he was simply pounding the metal as though his life depended on it. Which, of course, it might.

'Look what we've found sniffing around the shop.' They were laughing. 'Her ladyship's dog.'

Otho grabbed hold of Claudia's hair and dragged her forward by it. 'Yours, yes?' His voice was back to its quiet, conversational menace. 'What you think this mongrel's after?'

Junius tried to struggle free, but a boot thudding into his kidneys changed his mind. He buckled to his knees. They hauled him upright.

'Leave him alone!'

Otho moved forward to look at him. 'I wonder maybe this dirty dog he cock his leg up her ladyship? What you think, boys?'

The lewd gestures sent Claudia's blood cold. 'Don't be disgusting. He's just a slave, let him go.'

The two thugs pretended to howl and bark.

'We can no do that, Claudia. You see, he been very

78

'bad dog,' Otho said quietly, fixing Claudia with his eye. 'He poke around in places that no concern him. We have to teach him a lesson.'

'He was only looking for me, for pity's sake. He'd get a thrashing if he returned alone.'

Otho ignored her. 'Show him price for being naughty, boys.'

The thugs exchanged glances and grinned. Junius's eyes pleaded with Claudia, but as she moved towards him Otho jerked her back by the hair, bringing tears to her eyes.

'You watch.' He twisted her hair round his wrist and pulled it tight.

There was nothing she could do as one thug laughingly headbutted the young Gaul on the nose, sending a stream of blood pouring down his tunic. As Junius's hands flew towards his face, the headbutter rammed a pole behind his elbows to render him helpless while the other slipped a ring of metal round his knuckles. One held the pole firm as the other systematically pummelled the boy's ribs. Claudia heard a sickening crack before they turned their attention on the softness of his stomach and kidneys. When they finally finished, panting from their efforts, Junius crumpled to the floor – and this time they left him.

'Not just dogs.' Otho ran his finger down Claudia's cheek again. 'Naughty bitches, too,' he whispered. 'So no forget, Claudia. Three hundred – by the weekend.'

He finally released her hair.

'Always a pleasure, Claudia.' When he planted a kiss on her cheek, she nearly threw up. He stood in the door-way and grinned. 'Nice tits.'

One of the thugs leaned down over Junius, who was

groaning quietly, balled his fist and slammed it into the boy's mouth. There was a series of crashes from the workshop, as they wrecked it on their way out, their laughter carried away on the breeze.

For a moment Claudia couldn't move. Breath had left her body, her knees could barely support her and she was shaking from head to foot.

'Junius, I am so sorry.' Tears were running down her face as she spoke. 'I am so, so sorry.'

Gingerly she removed the pole and used her palla to wipe the blood from his mouth and stem the bleeding from his nose. The silence seemed more terrifying than the noise and with every second that passed she flinched, half-expecting to see Otho in the doorway.

'We've got to get out of here,' she said shakily. 'Can you walk?'

He nodded, but when she tried to lift him to his feet, the effort proved too much for both of them.

'Hey, you!' she called.

But the coppersmith had had enough for one day; the workshop was deserted. At the end of the alley the crowd had dispersed, leaving her male slaves, battered and bruised and looking utterly bewildered as they tried to comfort the sobbing women. Damn you, Lucan. Damn you to hell! Claudia wasn't naïve; she knew what she was tangling with, borrowing money from scum like that, and she'd been waiting for some sort of warning. But she'd never in a million years imagined he might engineer a whole bloody riot *and* send in his heavies. You can't keep the likes of Lucan waiting for long, but the raw violence, the sheer brutality of this very first warning, was terrifying. All for two thousand sesterces. Plus four hundred in interest. Juno, the gambling had really got out of hand.

Trembling, Claudia despatched two slaves for Junius. He'd have to share the litter. She couldn't go on to the baths now, there would be too much talk, and even allowing for the riot, it didn't go halfway to explaining the state she was in. Thank goodness Gaius was away!

At the house Junius was helped into one of the guest bedrooms. It was the least she could do, give him a decent bed until his broken ribs had healed.

'Junius, I don't want you to say a word about what you saw or what you heard, do you understand?'

She'd had to wait until his wounds had been tended and he was alone before she could slip in.

The young Gaul opened his only good eye. 'I won't.'

'I'll reward you for this, Junius. Give you your freedom. I'll tell Gaius you saved my life or something. But only if you promise not to tell.'

'Promise.' He winced. 'Are you all right?'

No. That was a bloody hard crack she'd received on the back of the head, not to mention the scare Otho had given her. She was still trembling.

'I'm fine.'

His ribs had been bound, his face was already swollen like a melon and his torso was more purple than anything else. Almost as an afterthought she wondered whether he had a concubine who ought to be notified. He was a handsome enough boy, and she was pretty certain he wasn't fooling around with any of the Seferius slaves.

'Do you have a mistress, Junius?'

The eye widened in puzzlement.

'I mean, are you in love with anyone?'

The head moved slowly up and down.

'Shall I send word to tell her you're hurt?'

The head moved slowly from side to side and the eye misted with what might have been a tear.

'She already knows,' he said thickly. 'But thank you for asking.'

X

The wonderful thing about the baths, thought Marcus Cornelius Orbilio as an attendant slowly scraped his back with a strigil, was the sheer hedonistic pleasure you got in the name of personal hygiene. What other fundamental consideration dares draw such wicked self-indulgence and then presumes to pass itself off as a necessity? And it wasn't merely the physical rewards, great though they were. A whole cross-section of the human character passed through these portals; it was an education to watch. Or in Orbilio's case listen, because an ambitious investigator could learn an awful lot from a bit of circumspect eaves-dropping.

Most of it was politics – useful for pursuit of a later career, albeit of little relevance to his current cases – or else it was horse-trading. A lot of that went on here. In fact, he thought, wiping a trickle of perspiration from his eyes, more important deals were struck in this very sweat room than in the Senate itself.

'Lie down and I'll do your chest next.'

Orbilio allowed himself to be laid out like meat on a slab, closing his eyes as the attendant scraped the oil off his body. There was a saying going around, something along the lines of 'Baths, wine and sex ruins your body.' Probably started by some of the moralists trying to impress

83

Augustus, he thought, but without baths, wine and sex, what use *was* a good body? Moralists don't live longer than the rest of us, he reflected sadly. It just seems that way.

The shrill voice of the hair-plucker broke through his thoughts.

'Like your armpits plucked, sir?'

Orbilio shook his head. His eyes were still watering from the last time he'd let that little bastard loose on his body. Either the man's tweezers were misaligned or his sight was failing, but all Orbilio could remember was that it was bloody painful. Besides, he'd prefer a girl to do it. Somehow it added to the feeling of wicked indulgence.

'On your left side, if you don't mind.'

The attendant flipped him over and continued his scraping. It was a wonderful sensation, feeling the bronze blade slide over your skin. Down. And down. And down. A man was at his most vulnerable here. Deaf, dumb and blind. He was sleepy from lying so the hot, damp air could open his pores, his body was oiled and the steam itself swirled so thickly it was impossible to see the man next to you, you only caught snippets of his conversation. Occasionally it was possible to put a name to one of the talkers, but the atmosphere in the room affected your lungs and few people could produce little more than hoarse whispers.

Which may or may not have been coincidental.

'And now your right side.'

Orbilio rolled over. Baths, wine and sex. What a wonderful combination. If only he could incorporate all three at the same time it would be heaven on earth. And if

Claudia Seferius was with him . . . Cupid's darts, if he died on the spot afterwards he'd die a happy man. If, if, if. There were too many ifs in that particular scenario. As rather tended to be the case where she was concerned . . .

He tipped the attendant two asses from the bronze purse round his wrist, yawned, stretched, then decided to go the whole hog today and have a massage. He owed himself that, after the long hours he'd been putting in on those bloody murders. Not to mention the fact that the Sardinian fish-seller had left Rome, taking Vera with him, and Petronella refused to talk to him nowadays. Mother of Tarquin, a man needed something to redress the balance, and he was damned if he'd resort to common whores. So. He ran his hands through his hair. A massage it is.

The pattern on the mosaic guided him out of the stifling steam room and he took several deep breaths in the doorway to focus his senses. Stone chambers echoed with laughter, whistling, conversation and the piercing cries of vendors thronging the passageways and hawking everything from cakes to honeyed wine. Orbilio made his way between two flaxen-haired beauties lounging against the tiled walls. One raised her eyebrows in invitation, but he gave a swift shake of the head and passed on. The hot air was making him perspire again and he paused, wondering whether to take a cold plunge. Later, he decided. After the massage.

He chose Lupi, a masseur with a penchant for keeping his own counsel, because he wanted to relax unfettered by small talk and idle chitchat. He'd had quite enough of that this morning, hanging around the gossips and picking up bits here and bits there – and none of them any bloody use whatsoever. Who cared if this Senator dyed his hair or that matron padded her breast band?

'Hmmm.' Expert hands prodded his muscles. 'You're very tense today, sir.'

This wasn't much of a revelation to Orbilio. No wine. No sex. No clues. It would be a miracle not to be tense. He'd seriously considered taking refuge again in his wine, but the hangovers had been getting worse and he needed a clear head. Callisunus was already intimating that he might redirect Orbilio on to some fraud case.

'I place myself entirely at your mercy, Lupi. Do your worst.'

'Yessir!'

The masseur, a burly fellow from Dacia, grinned as he oiled his hands with a spicy unguent and began to pummel Orbilio's shoulders. Gradually the flesh yielded and the sound softened to a soft slap-slap-slapping. He knew Claudia visited these baths virtually every day and that her visits also happened to coincide with the times Gaius wasn't here. Orbilio tried to tell himself that his own decision to come to the baths today was coincidence. Seferius was away in the country, maybe she had better things to do? Maybe she'd already come and gone? Orbilio had already established she didn't spend the same amount of time on her visits as her husband.

Lupi began to knead his muscles like dough and Orbilio knew the masseur had felt the sudden pull of tension. Praise be to Mars he can't read minds, Orbilio thought, wondering why the idea of Claudia with her husband should make him jealous. Jealous? Whatever made him think of such a word? Of course he wasn't jealous!

'Harder, Lupi.'

Surprise. Interest. Curiosity, even. But no, never jealousy. It must have come as a shock to Seferius about his son, he thought. Briefly, he'd considered going round to the house to offer his condolences, but she had the temperament of a she-wolf, that woman, and she was just as likely to follow through with her threat of telling Gaius that Cousin Markie had molested her. A smile played around his lips. There were other ways of skinning a coney. Yes, indeed there were!

It had been something of a knock, seeing Claudia and Gaius together at the games. He'd seen Seferius many times, never to speak to but certainly by sight, and he hadn't thought too hard about the fellow. Rich. Fat. Middle-aged but wearing well. Then, when they were side by side, Orbilio realized that Gaius hadn't gone to seed the way he'd thought. Overweight, although only in a solid, muscular sense. A man who had, quite literally, consolidated his bulk. Systematically, too. And suddenly the thought of the big man's hands manipulating Claudia's soft, white breasts was offensive in the extreme. Orbilio remembered when she'd linked her arm into his at the amphitheatre. Admittedly, she'd done it in a patronizing manner, but the sensations it had caused still rippled through his nerve ends.

'Nearly done, sir.'

The Dacian's skilled hands had worked small wonders. When Orbilio stood up, he felt five years younger, full of life and energy. A lightning dip in cold water left him feeling vigorous enough to run up Vesuvius backwards, although Petronella's charms would have served well enough. Along the colonnaded walkway leading back to the dressing room he noticed Paternus the lawyer, head bowed in conversation with a man Orbilio didn't recognize. Thin, weedy and with a voice to match, the lawyer had a tendency to leave discretion in the changing rooms with his other valuables. Orbilio lounged nonchalantly against a column, arms crossed, staring upwards at the sky.

'. . . so I said, for twelve gold pieces it's yours, my boy.' That was the voice of the stranger.

The two men laughed.

'I recall our friend the wine merchant extricating himself in much the same manner,' the lawyer said. 'I was handling his case against that Bithynian upstart . . .'

At that point, an extrovert general who enjoyed the sound of his own voice came strolling along, belting out a bawdy ballad, and the rest of the sentence was lost. They could be discussing any number of wine merchants, the city was full of them. However, Orbilio convinced himself he had no option but to follow them.

'. . . at which juncture, Seferius clapped the Bithynian on the back and said, you obviously haven't heard about my latest . . .'

Once more the thin voice was drowned out, this time by a group of boisterous youths racing each other towards the cold pool. For a moment Orbilio was distracted, remembering the days when he, too, would rush headlong into the icy waters straight off. There was, he reflected, definitely something to be said in favour of maturity.

Oh, shit! Paternus and his companion were heading for the steam room! Orbilio ran his hand over his chin. There was no need for him to follow them. The conversation had absolutely no bearing on the case. Gaius was of no interest to him. No interest whatsoever. He'd head for the exercise yards.

'Back already?' The attendant proffered a small flask of oil. 'Glutton for punishment, aren't you, sir?'

The dense impenetrability of the steam room closed in, making him catch his breath.

'Fancied a bit of extra pampering today.' Orbilio declined the oil. Another scraping and he'd be down to bare bone! 'I'm looking for two friends who just came in. One's small and skinny, the other's—'

'That way, sir. To your right.'

Orbilio thanked him and followed the mosaic. He passed two men, groaning and grunting, and prayed they were just reacting to the oppressive air.

Paternus's voice sounded ever reedier. '. . . advise you to tread carefully. I have it on good authority – nay, the best – that Seferius has a preference for . . .'

Damn! No matter how hard his ears strained, Orbilio couldn't pick up the whispers.

'Never!' The lawyer's companion sounded incredulous. 'Gaius Seferius! Are you sure?'

'Is the Princeps a Roman? Naturally, you won't bandy this around, will you?'

'Trust me. One presumes Seferius guards his secret well?'

Paternus sucked his teeth. 'In view of Augustus's, shall we say, *sensitivity* on the issue, you can bank on it.'

There was a long pause, and Orbilio fought for breath as the steam swirled and eddied.

'To be frank,' the other man said at length, 'I also enjoy – how can I put it? – pleasures which one's wife is not willing to provide.'

The lawyer let out a weedy laugh. 'Who doesn't?' he said. Orbilio couldn't see, but he sensed Paternus had edged closer to his companion. 'My own preference—' The voice dipped to a hushed tone. After several minutes of intense whispering, at the point when Orbilio was starting to fidget, he heard the lawyer scoff.

'Claudia Seferius? Believe me, *she*'s not what she seems, either.'

Orbilio's head shot up and suddenly he was on the alert. Gossip and filth were second nature to him. He picked up all manner of information to store away in the library of his mind, calling upon it whenever the occasion demanded. It came in useful during his investigations, because faced with another's knowledge of his own peccadilloes, it was surprising how a man tended to remember events rather more clearly or how names were dropped with a greater frequency. There was an up side to everything, Orbilio reflected, especially when it allowed him to pocket the money Callisunus allocated for bribes. Thus he'd expected to routinely squirrel away this information about Seferius, but not by any stretch of the imagination had he imagined hearing Claudia's name brought up. Particularly not in such a derogatory tone.

'Bugger!' The extrovert general, blundering through the steam room in much the same way he'd charge across a battlefield, tumbled headfirst across Orbilio's outstretched legs.

Apologies were exchanged as both parties accepted the blame, but by the time the general had left so, it appeared, had Paternus and his friend.

Orbilio took another dip in the cold bath to tighten

his pores. He admired Seferius, the way he'd clawed his way up, and it must have been a proud day for him when he was finally appointed to the equestrian order. Moreover, this promotion for a man whose father had been a humble road-builder and whose great-grandparents weren't even freeborn. No indeed, it was no mean achievement, amassing the four hundred thousand sesterces necessary before you could even consider admission to the order, which in itself was no foregone conclusion. Orbilio would have liked to hear more about Seferius's improprieties, maybe drop subtle hints to Claudia? As he towelled himself dry, he began to question the ethics of stirring up trouble between husband and wife, but decided he could justify it somehow, if he put his mind to it, because the prospect of Claudia divorcing her husband . . .

'Enough of this, Marcus Cornelius,' he muttered aloud. 'She doesn't even like you, so you can rein in those thoughts immediately.'

Many a night he'd plotted how best to win her round. The quickest way, he supposed, was to solve these bloody murders and perhaps, when he stopped treating her like a suspect, she might open up a bit. Trouble was, he thought, she still was in the frame. However hard she tried those strong-arm tactics, Claudia Seferius was indeed *very much* still in the frame.

He dressed, drank a goblet of wine topped up with water, treated himself to a couple of pastries then made a beeline for the exercise yard. A workout with weights ought to sweat out his frustrations.

'Pssst!'

He stopped instinctively. Occasionally it was an

informer, most times it was for someone else, but it always paid to keep your ears open. He pretended to fix the lace on his boot.

'Pssst!'

He glanced round. There was no one there.

'Over here!'

A small face peered round the base of a fluted pillar.

'Rufus? Rufus, what are you doing here?' A grubby finger hooked itself into a gesture of beckoning and Orbilio followed, shaking his head ruefully. 'What do you want?'

The ragamuffin settled himself cross-legged behind the column. 'You know that classy tart you was interested in? Well, she's been in a right old hoo-ha this morning.'

'Oh?'

'There was a riot down by the cattle market and she was right in amongst it and no mistake.'

'Sure it was her again?'

'Yep. Can't miss that orange litter, cor, what a colour! Anyways, she tries to run off, like, and guess what? Some big geezer yanks her into a shop.'

'Rufus, are you telling me she's been kidnapped?'

'Her? Leave off! Duffed up a bit, that's all.'

Orbilio sat down beside the boy. 'Rufus, I want you to tell me exactly what you saw. Understand? Don't leave anything out, describe everything as you remember it.'

His head was buzzing. He should be chasing leads on Crassus. Dammit, he should be chasing leads on all four victims, checking accounts, grudges, lunatics, locksmiths, slaves, family, friends . . .

'Rufus, what were you doing following her?'

'I wasn't following her, I was—'

Thieving. Orbilio covered his ears with his hands. 'No, don't tell me, I don't want to know. How did you know where to find me?'

The dirty face broke into a knowing grin. Orbilio grinned back, tossed him four quadrans, then, taking pity, tossed him another four. Venus is fickle today, he thought, scratching the back of his head. There but for a handful of street yobs, Claudia Seferius and Marcus Cornelius Orbilio would have met at the baths this morning. It felt as if he'd swallowed one of the lead weights from the exercise yard. He jumped to his feet. No longer did the prospect of a day to himself appeal. The thought of ball games and athletics palled, because suddenly it seemed urgent to nail the bastard who went round chiselling eyes out of their sockets.

'Mister?'

'What?'

'Can I come along with you?'

'No, you most certainly cannot.' He wanted to say it was dirty and dangerous, but he quickly realized that that was probably all this poor kid had ever known. 'Don't you have a family?'

'Nope.'

There were so many like Rufus, he thought sadly. Despicable as the practice was, he could see the case for abandoning unwanted babies up on the midden heaps. At least it would be relatively quick, whereas kids like Rufus – who was what? seven or eight? – were doomed to die in some fetid alley without ever knowing love or warmth or happiness – or even a full belly.

'I think it's high time you had a bath, my lad,' he said, lifting Rufus up by the back of his tunic. 'Come along.' There was more than a hint of resignation in his voice. 'Let's get you fed first.'

XI

The journey to the villa was hot and dry and dusty. The wagon's wheels sought out every bump on the road, the slaves sulked and the driver remained disgustingly cheerful. Drusilla, joggling along in a specially constructed cage, howled incessant protests. Dear Diana, who deserves this, Claudia thought, gouging her initials out of the woodwork with a bone hairpin. It was all right for Gaius, shooting off in his two-wheeled car. He didn't have to contend with three obstreperous horses being wound up by a skittish fourth possessing a truly evil sense of humour.

'I suppose it's asking too much of you to get these nags to break into a gallop?'

Kano, the driver, broke off from his whistling. ''Fraid so,' he said happily. ''Cos horses is like wives, see? Give 'em free rein and a full belly and they'll serve you well enough – so long as they sets the pace, anyroad.'

'I've never heard such tripe in my life. Now for heaven's sake use the whip, man, or they'll die of old age before we reach the next changing station.'

She rolled her eyes as Kano gave a half-hearted crack of the whip. If anything, the wretched animals slowed down and Claudia vowed to have a word with the wagoner's wife when she got back to Rome. She glanced at the milestone. Actually it wasn't bad progress. A quick break for a change of animals and they'd make the tavern with an hour to spare before dusk. The cart tipped to one side as the wheels caught the camber and everyone groaned. It would have been better had Junius and Melissa been with her. They were slaves she felt comfortable with – unlike this miserable rabble. Junius, though, was in no fit state even to get out of bed and the girl Claudia had left behind deliberately, because that poxy banquet still needed to be organized, even if it had been postponed. Besides, who else could she trust to deliver the money to Lucan?

They passed a cart clanking with pottery and glassware. Claudia's eyes narrowed. A shipment like that would be worth a small fortune, she calculated, it would only be a matter of finding a buyer . . . Impossible, Claudia! Out of the question! Never in a month of Bacchanalias could you of all people hijack a load that size. Robbery needs time and skilful planning, not to mention a healthy contingent of willing, strapping men. One could hardly use slaves – what would you say? Hey you, you and you, cover your faces and come with me, we're going to hold up a wagon? Supposing in the unlikely event they got away with it, the roads were too well patrolled, she'd be lucky to get five miles. But, and this was a very big but, even if she didn't get caught, how could she offload the stuff?

Come on, Claudia. There must be smarter ways of raising two or three grand.

'Kano, exactly why are you stopping in this godforsaken place?'

'Goldie's shoe's fell off,' the driver replied. 'Won't be a tick.'

She watched him lumber up the road, collect the

horse's sandal then tie it back on, taking advantage of the break to fish out a flask of heady Judean perfume. There was, after all, a limit to what a girl could put up with.

'Mmmmmrow!'

'Drusilla, you'll have to jolly well lump it. Animal smells might be acceptable to you, but I tell you, I've had it up to here with the rear end of those bloody nags.'

'Mmmmmrow.'

'Oh, don't sulk!' She waggled her finger through the bars to scratch the cat's ear. 'Fancy this?'

Drusilla scowled at the piece of raw meat that plopped on to the floor of her cage and backed away from it, glowering.

'I see.' Claudia sniffed. 'Well, I've no sympathy for you, we're all in the same wretched boat.' It hadn't occurred to either of them that Drusilla might be left behind in Rome.

Kano resettled himself and the wagon began to lurch and rattle once more. She was in a tight spot and no mistake. Gaius did his reckonings once a month on the dot and, bereavement or no, he'd not put the job off. He couldn't fail to notice a shortfall of three hundred sesterces . . . A heat haze shimmered over the horizon, casting make-believe pools of water on the road. Bugger decorum, she thought, pulling off her stola. She only wore the bloody thing since it was deemed decent and proper to do so. Julia, being childless, hadn't been conferred one; why should she be the lucky one? You could poach to death in your own sweat in all this clothing. Her heart missed a beat as she remembered yesterday. Was it really only yesterday? Her clothes were wringing with sweat when she got home after that run-in with Otho, and one thing was sure, she'd never wear Minoan blue again. A flurry of lavender linen flew across the wagon.

And Otho wasn't the only one she clashed with, either. This is your doing, Minerva, I can smell it! Her toe thudded into the woodwork. That Minerva's always had it in for me, ever since the day I was born, and I'll bet she was chuckling her bloomers off yesterday.

It had been a real pig of a day. First she'd been scared spitless by that Thracian psychopath. (When I've paid off Lucan, I'm going to get you for that, you bastard!) Then, having sponged herself down and tidied herself up, Claudia had decided the best way to regain her equilibrium was to lose herself in the street bustle. What better way to unwind than in the cries of the pedlars, the smells of the cookshops, the banter of the street barbers urging young dandies to have their hair curled like Nerva the charioteer or dyed like Totila the gladiator? She paused to watch a cobbler astride his sturdy bench, hammering at his last, as she savoured the rich, acidic smell of the leather, when a shadow fell over her.

'Ligarius! Good grief, have you been on the sand with the gladiators?'

'Oh, this.' A huge hand gingerly explored the cuts and bruises. 'Fights come with the territory if you keep a tavern.'

Only the sort you keep.

'Well, I do hope you get better soon. Nice meeting you again, Ligarius, cheerio.' She gave him a smile and tried to move on.

'This is a quiet place. I thought we could talk.'

She felt the afternoon temperature plummet. What did

he mean, quiet? 'Ligarius, have you been following me?'

The big man shrugged. 'I only want to talk.'

'And I thought I made it plain last Thursday: I don't.'

'But the old days . . .' A hand fell on her arm. 'We had some good times, Claudie.'

Any minute now and someone would see them together. She jerked her head and ducked down a sidestreet. Behind them the clanking of the huge grinding stone of the bakery drowned any conversation from would-be eavesdroppers.

'How much?'

'Pardon?'

'Don't play games with me, Ligarius.' This was what he'd been building up to at the games, just before Marcellus interrupted. 'How many sesterces will it take before you *don't* want to talk about the good old days?'

The smell of freshly baked bread seemed horribly incongruous.

His bearded face puckered into a frown. 'Don't be daft, I'm not trying to blackmail you. This is the first proper chance I've had to talk to you face to face.'

The sound of her breath coming out nearly obliterated the creaking and thumping of the millstone. That was Ligarius all over. All heart and no brains. She wondered what or who Jupiter was thinking of when he dished out Ligarius's organs, because something had certainly distracted him.

'Hey.' He nudged her. 'We had some good times together, you and me.'

'Nonsense. You used to drool over that little scrubber, what was her name?'

'Antonia. I married her when you went away.'

'More fool you. So what's the problem? Left you, has she?'

'She died.'

'Oh!' The big ugly lump looked close to tears. 'Oh, Liggy, I'm sorry! Really I am.'

Dammit, they *were* good times. Times when she could laugh, times when she could cry, times when she could feel pain.

'Me too. Mind,' the sound he let out was half-hiccup, half-laugh, 'she could be a right shrew when she wanted. Worse than you, sometimes.'

'Watch your mouth, Ligarius. I have a serious reputation to uphold and I can't afford word getting around I'm second best.' She stuck out her tongue. 'Still as sharp as ever, see?'

'Hey, remember that striping you gave Lefty for pinching your bum when it weren't him at all? Poor sod never drank in my tavern again after that.'

'Talking of which, whatever happened to that old sea captain who used to fancy himself so much? Strutting around like a peacock – totally unaware we'd nicknamed him Bumface, poor bugger.'

'And what about that Sicilian woman, eh? Remember her? Big as a barn door, used to drink the men under the table and fight 'em afterwards. We always called her Brutus!'

'Not in her hearing, we didn't!'

'Too bleeding right, nobody dared.'

'Except Shorty forgot that night, didn't he?' Claudia stepped back and made her legs go bandy and put on a high falsetto. 'Poor old Shorty, he was walking and talking funny for a week!'

'Aye, right in the nutmegs, she got him. Ooh, makes yer eyes water even after all this time.'

They were doubled up by the time the baker's boy emerged from the shop with a tray of steaming loaves. Sobering instantly, Claudia spun round and covered her face with her pulla.

Damn you, Ligarius. You have no right to remind me of the old times, no right at all! She bit her lip. Those days were long past; she was perfectly content in the sanitized vacuum of her life today. Every day she woke in the morning knowing she could eat and drink till her belly was full, and sleep in a proper bed at night. She had clothes on her back, and damned fine ones at that. She could bathe every day, had slaves at her beck and call, wore jewels till she stooped from the weight if she wanted. And Claudia Seferius was quite prepared to take whatever steps were necessary to protect this precious existence.

The bearded giant had launched into another trip down Memory Lane, but she refused to listen. 'Ligarius, you're the only person in the whole of Rome who knows my past. I'm asking you – no, I'm begging you. Please don't ruin it for me.'

His mouth dropped open. 'I wouldn't do that, Claudie. Never! Only,' his mood also changed and a big, fat tear trickled slowly down his cheek, 'you're my only friend in the entire city.'

'We're hardly friends, Ligarius.'

'Close enough.' He sniffed loudly and wiped his nose with the back of his hand.

Juno, Jupiter and Mars! 'How long since whatsername, Antonia, died?'

'December.'

'Tell you what, Liggy. I can't stop now, but why don't I come and visit you in the tavern? Perhaps early one morning, before you open? We could have a quiet little chat?'

'I'd like that, because . . . well, you know how I've always felt about you.'

Sentimental claptrap, of course, and without Antonia to whip him into line, he'd gone soft again. Why is it people always look back and see only the good times? She turned on her heel and marched back to the house. With any luck, the packing would be finished by now, and wouldn't Gaius be happy to have her at the villa five days ahead of schedule? Damn that slimeball Lucan for diddling her out of the fun of the games!

It was only when she was changing her stola that Claudia realized she'd forgotten to ask the whereabouts of Liggy's tavern. No matter. When she blurted out her offer to call it was genuine, though in the cold light of day she realized it was folly to even think about it. Oh, he'd get over it. Hell, he might not even remember it, because she had a suspicion he'd been drinking his profits of late. The main thing was, his loyalty was firm, he wouldn't give her away. Of course, it had come as a real shock, seeing him at the games – and his shadowing of her this afternoon didn't bear thinking about. But no, she was satisfied Ligarius wouldn't spoil it for her. Unless . . . Unless . . .

'Your cousin to see you, madam.'

'Melissa, how many times do I have to tell you, girl? They're Gaius's cousins—'

'No, madam. *Your* cousin, he said. Marcus Cornelius Orbilio.'

Minerva, how could you do this to me? How could you! Otho, Ligarius and now . . . this! Well, Orbilio, you can't say I didn't give you fair warning. This time I'll suck you in then blow you out in tinksy winksy bubbles, so help me I will.

He was standing in the atrium, admiring the newly painted frieze which Gaius had commissioned to celebrate all things Egyptian. Unfortunately this afternoon he wasn't alone.

'Good grief, you *and* the oik? What a frightful combination!'

'I've missed you, too, Claudia.'

'Difficult to recognize him without the headlice. What do you want?'

'I heard you were in a spot of trouble this morning.'

'You heard wrong. Goodbye.'

He ran after her as she flounced towards the garden. 'No, *I heard right*, Claudia.'

She paused. 'Oh, don't tell me. That scruffy little tike is your chief witness? Again.'

'It doesn't matter who the witness—'

'Yep!' Rufus had run up to join them. 'I saw you. You was fighting with this real big geezer – umph!'

A hand clamped itself over the boy's mouth. 'Listen to me, you spiteful little monster. One more lie from your duplicitous lips and I'll rip your skinny liver out and serve it up for breakfast. Is that clear?'

The boy's eyes swivelled round to Orbilio, but Orbilio was giving intense study to the capital of the column beside him.

'Oi, don't get shirty, missus. Can I help if it's the truth?'

'Truth?' Claudia pinched his earlobe and dragged him

into a secluded corner of the garden. 'You wouldn't know the truth if it landed on your face and pecked your nose off. Now if I hear one more—'

'Leave him alone, Claudia.'

'You keep out of this.'

'I said that's enough. Let him go.'

She gave the earlobe a sharp tweak before releasing it. The ghastly child seemed more interested in the two adults than his wretched ear. Well, she hoped it turned black and dropped off in the night.

'The gaffer's in a bad mood,' Rufus said cheerfully. 'Callisunus raked him over the coals a couple of hours ago and, boy,' he let his breath out in a whistle, 'were them coals hot!'

'Splendid.' Claudia smiled radiantly at Orbilio. 'Now you can run along and chase criminals – and leave me in peace. Toodle-oo.'

'For heaven's sake, woman, I'm trying to catch a murderer.'

'So who's stopping you?'

'Tell me about this morning.'

She scowled at the boy, then she scowled at Orbilio. 'Very well. Claudia – on her way to the baths. Claudia – tipped out of her litter. Wee bit of a scrap. Junius – vital organs rearranged. Claudia – came home.' She held her hands out, palms upwards, and arranged her face in a smile. 'End of story.'

'Tell me about the Thracian.'

'Good heavens, man. You don't think we stopped to exchange pleasantries with them, do you? Oh, what a charming riot, but tell me, didn't we meet in Thrace a year or two back? Don't be ridiculous.'

Orbilio settled himself against the trunk of an apple tree. 'I'm a patient man, Claudia. I can wait.'

She turned to Rufus. 'You.' She jabbed him with her finger. 'Kitchen.'

He looked over at Orbilio and opened his mouth to speak.

'*Now!*'

The boy ran off so fast that had the floor been made of wood it might well have caught fire.

'And you.' A slave came running. 'Follow that urchin. Make sure he doesn't steal anything.' She clapped her hands and sent the rest of the slaves packing.

'Wine?' she asked pleasantly.

His eyes narrowed in suspicion, but finding nothing except ingenuousness, Orbilio slowly nodded acceptance.

'You're derisive about Rufus, but his testimony is reliable, I'm afraid, and since— Claudia, are you listening to me?'

'Try the figs. Come along, they're not poisoned!' She busied herself with pouring wine and settling herself on the bench, then patted the marble beside her in invitation. Seeing the scepticism on his face, she added, 'I don't bite.'

He glanced under the shrubs, but didn't sit.

'And Drusilla's indoors.'

He sat.

'Now you seem very tense today, Orbilio,' she said, patting his thigh. 'Something the matter?' She was met by a look of undisguised distrust, and she shrugged. 'Suit yourself.'

She leant backwards, picked up her lyre and began to strum. From the corner of her eye she could see he was as stiff as a ramrod.

'Tell me about the Thracian,' he said quietly. 'Who was he?'

'Have you adopted that guttersnipe?'

'What?'

'Simple question. I'm asking you whether you've adopted that little arab out there.'

'No, of course I haven't. Oh, come on, you can't believe I'm bribing the boy.'

Claudia smiled. 'As if I would. No, no. I merely wondered why he's trailing round with you. I presume you're the one responsible for cleaning him up and giving him a proper tunic?'

Orbilio's back lost some of its starch. 'I felt sorry for him. Living off scraps, sleeping in doorways. That's no life for a lad of his age.'

'And what do you propose to do with him now?'

He shrugged. 'I don't know. Give him some money, I suppose.'

'You've picked him up, washed him down, filled his belly, filled his pocket – and that absolves you of any further responsibility? Orbilio, you're a fool. You should have left him where he was.'

'I couldn't.'

'Yes, you could. It would have been kinder for the boy. Now you've given him a taste of what he can never have; how do you think he'll feel after that?'

She placed the lyre on the seat, stood up, smoothed her tunic and smiled. 'As I said, Orbilio. You really are a fool.'

With that, she opened her mouth and let out a blood-curdling scream. Orbilio sprang to his feet. 'What the—'

'Aaaargh!'

'Claudia, for pity's sake!'

'I'm sorry, Orbilio. I did warn you that if you came back, there'd be trouble. There's only one rock, you see, and we can't both be cock of it. *Aaaargh!*'

In two quick strides, Orbilio was across the garden, covering her mouth with his hand. She bit it and he let go. '*Aaaargh!*'

'Claudia, for pity's sake, what are you doing?'

He lunged towards her, but the move had been antici-pated. Claudia sidestepped him. Unfortunately, she'd under-estimated his athleticism and on the next move he'd overpowered her. Terrific, she thought. Better than I'd hoped. There can be little doubt about Cousin Markie's intentions now. Squirming free, Claudia opened her mouth to scream again. Bloody slaves. Always earwigging when they're not supposed to, never around when you need them!

From behind, Orbilio's hand suddenly clamped over her mouth to stifle the scream, and this time he'd pre-empted the bite. She tried to elbow him in the ribs, but his free arm lashed her shoulders tight against his body. Entwined, they fought and writhed until the backs of his knees collided with the seat, toppling them both back-wards into a bed of lavender and parsley. And when help did finally come, it was to find Marcus Cornelius Orbilio spreadeagled on his back with Claudia's head grasped firmly underneath his arm.

XII

It was characteristic of Gaius Seferius that, having decided to make his fortune from wine, he should do so with the same style of military precision that was proving so successful in broadening the Empire. Well-thought-out strategies, attention to detail and a modicum of luck until, day by day, little by little, the outposts of his own empire were extended to the point where it, too, became almost unassailable. For any man this was a considerable achievement, but for the son of a road builder it was truly exceptional.

Despite an outward appearance of bonhomie, Claudia quickly realized he was as ruthless as he was logical. He divorced his first wife, Plotina, because he believed her barren, and a man like Gaius Seferius would not allow fourteen years of marriage to stand in the way of what he called progress. By the age of twenty-four, he'd accumulated sufficient funds from his foray into the world of viniculture to purchase land suitable for the production of his own wine and when, at the age of twenty-eight, no heir stood to inherit his flourishing empire, he felt he had little option but to put Plotina aside. To his credit, Gaius had gone to considerable lengths to arrange a decent remarriage for her and it was one of life's ironies, Claudia reflected soulfully, that the poor woman had fallen pregnant almost immediately and then had had the misfortune to die in childbirth.

The fright that Plotina's pregnancy had given Gaius was immense. It set him questioning his own fertility until, to his utter relief, his new bride allayed his worst fears by announcing her own gravidity and when she finally produced a bouncing boy she named Lucius it coincided with Gaius's twenty-ninth birthday. In the eight years that followed she dutifully birthed several more children, three of them healthy, until she, too, was claimed by childbed fever. By then Lucius, small as he was, had been groomed to take over. Gaius had engaged personal tutors at the expense of Secundus and Calpurnia, whose upbringing he entrusted to his mother without asking or even caring, and he fostered baby Flavia out to his sister, with scant regard to either her or Marcellus who, at the time, was struggling to set up as an architect.

It was equally characteristic of Gaius, Claudia thought, that he should choose his land so carefully. Call it luck, call it fate, call it skill if you like, but the hundred hectares of fertile land he'd purchased was as good as you'd get anywhere for the price. Near a main road and with access to the sea, he could ship his wine all round the Mediterranean from the one place. You had to hand it to him, you really did. Under his shrewd and careful eye, his fortune seemed to multiply with an almost consummate ease, the pinnacle of his career, of course, being his appointment to the equestrian order.

The wagon rumbled into the farmyard after what seemed an eternity on the road, and Claudia wondered whether she'd be bow-legged for the rest of her life or whether it would pass after a week or two. Certainly she'd never lose the stoop. The scene before her presented a picture of rural tranquillity – clear skies and pure air, interrupted only by the droning of bumble bees and the warble of songbirds. Moonshine, of course. The place was a seething hive of labouring activity, with slaves of every creed and colour from every corner of the Empire working their skins off to fill a never-ending succession of barrels with the very finest Seferius wine. But that, thought Claudia, is always the case. Turbulence is invariably hidden below the surface and that, unfortunately, is when it's at its most dangerous.

Gaius ambled into the yard to greet her. She had hoped he'd be busy inspecting whatever frightful little things one had to inspect on a vineyard in the middle of July, thus giving her ample time to plaster a spot of white chalk on her face to cover the bruises and disguise the whole damn lot with a generous dollop of rouge. Isn't life a bitch?

'Good grief, Claudia, what happened?' There was no mistaking the look of genuine consternation on his face.

'It's a long story, Gaius,' she said, twisting her mouth. 'I'll tell you about it later.'

He helped her out of the wagon. 'Good journey?'

'Foul! I'm covered in dung and dust, splinters and blisters.'

'Then what you need is a bath. It's all ready.'

Claudia did something she'd only ever done twice before in her life. She wrapped her arms around her husband and kissed him warmly on the cheek. 'Bless you.'

You can shower me with gems, Gaius, but sometimes water can be more precious than gold.

'I'll come with you, we can talk.'

He looks old, she thought. The lines on his face had deepened, his eyes had retired so far that if they went much further, they'd come out of the back of his head.

'I'd prefer to be alone, if you don't mind.' It was bad enough they'd have to share a bedroom in this godforsaken dump; she didn't want him in the bath house with her as well. She'd never taken her clothes off in front of him before, why the hell start now? Besides – she swallowed a mouthful of dust – he looked so lost, so vulnerable all of a sudden, she had a sneaky feeling that, although he'd never pestered her for sex before, sweet Hymen, he might just change his mind!

She smiled apologetically and patted her stomach. 'Women's troubles.'

'Oh.' He went pink and his arm fell away from her shoulder. 'Oh. Well in that case, I, er, I'll see you later.'

Sometimes we forget how lucky we are, she thought, breaking into a whistle as she headed towards the bath house. We girls take ourselves for granted far too often, we really do.

'You know, Drusilla, I've never understood why people enjoy living in the country.'

The cat, curled into a tight ball on Claudia's lap, didn't twitch so much as a solitary whisker, even though she was far from sleepy.

'Look over there. Nothing but fields and trees, vines and hills.' She stared blankly into her empty glass. 'Turn your head the other way, and still nothing but fields and trees, vines and hills. Miles of them.'

She hiccuped.

'And what happens, eh? I'll tell you what happens, Drusilla. Bugger all.'

She picked up the jug, but it was already drained.

'Bloody countryside.'

The earthenware jug smashed into a dozen pieces as she hurled it into the middle of the yard. Drusilla, instantly on the alert, found herself being soothed back to sleep.

'Sorry, poppet, but just look at it, will you? Back home, around now,' she hiccuped again, 'the gates would be cranking open to let in the first of the carts. Yep. Lots of wagons piled right up to here with grain and fruit and wine and oil and . . . and . . . and . . . stuff.'

She clapped her hands for wine, but no one answered. It served her right, she supposed, settling down in this stinking yard. The house had been designed to face away from the farm, so who'd know she was even here? The slaves would be clustered round Gaius and his awful, awful family, who'd have finished dinner and would be sitting on the terrace, boring themselves into an early grave. Well, sod the lot of them!

'And these carts will be rumbling round the city, delivering here, delivering there, and there'd be donkeys braying and torch-bearers to light the way, and the eating houses and the taverns will be mowry and derry . . . uh-uh, rowdy and merry and everyone'll be having a wonderful, wonderful time. But here?'

She pointed at the red ball of fire slowly sinking behind the horizon.

'That, Drusilla, is tonight's entertainment. No brawls. No robberies. No accidents, no fires, not even a bloody riot to liven things up.'

Another hiccup.

'They say Rome never sleeps. Well this place, Drusilla, this place never bloody wakes up.'

The cat, hearing a rustle from one of the rectangular cottages that served as labourers' quarters, stiffened and pricked up her ears. For her the pulsating heart of the Empire wasn't Rome, it was here – with that big, fat, juicy rat!

'Mmrrr.' She crouched low on Claudia's lap.

'No gambling. D'you hear that, Drusilla? No gambling. Out here,' Claudia giggled, 'I'd have to bet with myself. Oh, to hell with it!'

The glass hurtled through the air and splintered against the cottage wall. A head poked round.

'Hey, you! Fetch some wine. And another bloody glass.'

The head hesitated.

'*Move!*'

Drusilla, unfazed by the rat's vanishing trick at the sound of breaking glass, yawned, stretched and clambered off in search of another victim to harry. By the time the slave had returned with the wine, she'd found it, in the form of a fat, hairy spider.

'I know you're going to tell me there's been a death in the family and I should make allowances and,' she gave a soft belch, 'excuse me, and you're probably right. But this place is so dull, poppet, it'd bore the freckles off a frog. Not, you understand, that that's the only reason I hate this poxy place.'

Drusilla looked round, reassured herself that it didn't matter that Claudia hadn't noticed her absence and busied herself with her quarry.

'It's that mummified bag of bones I can't stick. Larentia.'

Claudia gulped at her glass.

'Do you know what she calls me, eh?' She wagged her finger. 'She calls me a gold-digger. Me? I've never heard you complain about this life of luxury, I said to her last time I was here. You never wore rings like those when you were a navvy's wife. Insult me if you like, she says, I recognize your type. Not surprised, I said, you only have to look in the mirror, you miserable old fossil. Yes, yes, call me what you will, she says, but you can't fool me, you only married my son for his money. Ah, well, I had her there, Drusilla. Pinned like a winkle, she was. I leaned forward, till my nose was nearly touching hers. And your son only married me for my looks, I said. Which is more than you can say for your old man! Drusilla? Drusilla?' Her eyes swept the courtyard. 'Juno, even the bloody cat's gone now.'

She staggered to her feet, steadied herself against the brick wall and set her sights on the door. Cursing the threshold gods for tripping her, she kicked off her sandals and padded silently across the mosaic. What a frightful design! She'd lay money it was Larentia's choice, because what that woman knew about taste could be engraved on one of the tesselae.

'Claudia! How lovely.' Bugger. It *would* be Marcellus she ran into. 'Have you been avoiding us? I say, what happened? Looks like you've been on the sand with the gladiators.'

Claudia's senses were never so addled that she couldn't remember the things that were important. She sobered instantly. He couldn't have overheard! This was coincidence, surely. Yet – yes, those were the self-same words she'd used to Ligarius on Friday . . .

'No, Marcellus. I only wrestle elephants on my birthday. When did you arrive at the villa?'

'Came out for a breather.' He nodded towards the garden. 'Heavy stuff going on out there.'

'Hardly surprising, but—'

'It's always hard going after a funeral. Of course, Gaius's taken the blow like a man and Valeria's putting a brave face on widowhood, but as for Larentia, well – you can never tell with her, and Flavia's really cut up about it.'

'Don't be naïve, Marcellus. Flavia hated her brother, she was as jealous as sin. Tell me, when did you get here?'

'Felt dutybound to come, of course, if only to give Julia a break from being cooped up with the presence of death all the time.'

Give me strength. 'I asked when, not why.'

'Dunno. Not long. Who cares? Coming to join us?'

Not bloody likely. 'I'm tired.'

'It's early.'

'It's boring.'

Marcellus ran the flat of his hand over her shoulderblade. 'We could change that, you and I.' He glanced around. 'No one would even notice we were missing.'

'You know, Marcellus, you really are an offensive little wart.'

For some unaccountable reason, he seemed to find that funny – although not quite funny enough to leave his hand where it was. 'So why the black eye, Claudia? Did some bloke try to—'

'If he did, Marcellus, he'd be in the city mortuary by now.'

'What, then?'

She jerked away from the hand that was tracing the wound on her forehead. 'It's hardly a shiner, and you lay so much as one more finger on me, you miserable worm, I'll snap it clean off.' She gingerly rubbed the cut. 'And if you've infected this wound, I swear by all things holy you'll pay with your life.'

'Bad journey up, then?'

'Find me a good one. Look, why don't you run along and join Lucius, there's a good chap?'

'Lucius is . . . oh, very droll. Claudia, you ought at least to give you condolences to poor Valeria.'

'In the morning.'

Another day wouldn't make any difference, and what can you say to a young widow eight months pregnant with a child whose father's ashes are still smouldering?

'Ah!' There was a knowing look in his eye. 'It's Larentia, isn't it? You know, she's not so bad once you get to know her.'

'I don't want to know her better, thank you very much.' Venomous old bitch.

Claudia began to dab at the corner of her eye. 'I can't see anyone now, Marcellus. You must remember that this is . . . extremely painful for me. Why, it was only five years ago that I was in the very same position myself.'

The catch in her voice was masterful, she thought. Absolutely bloody masterful. As Mulberrychops retreated, his head bowed in shame and embarrassment, Claudia was left to ponder why her brother-in-law was suddenly making overtures lacking in both subtlety and discretion. No matter, she could sort out that smarmy reptile any old time; there were more pressing matters on hand.

Slamming the bedroom door in the face of Galla, the one who had replaced Melissa and was supposed to help her undress (because the last thing she wanted at the moment was company, especially from a girl who lisped), Claudia flung her sandals into the corner. On the whole, she thought, splashing water over her face, you've managed rather well. That exquisite soak in hot water had eased the aches and pains, the cold plunge had sharpened her wits and by the time she'd met up with Gaius again in the privacy of their bedroom, her spirits and confidence had buoyed themselves up.

Naturally he'd been flabbergasted when she told him about the riot. 'Surely you notified the authorities? Good grief, my dove, they nearly killed you!'

She'd thought about that one.

'At the time I was too concerned for the slaves,' she said. 'Then, afterwards, I was glad I hadn't summoned the police.' She patted his arm. 'You've had so much to contend with lately, Gaius, the last thing you needed was your good name dragged into a common street brawl.'

'You're a very considerate woman, Claudia, do you know that? No, don't look so modest. Most wives would have panicked and pandemonium would have been let loose. Instead, you mop up trouble like a wine spill and no one's the wiser.'

Certainly not once you've set Junius free, they won't be.

'One of our slaves – oh dear, I can't remember his name – anyway, the poor boy stepped straight in and practically saved my life. I've hinted, only hinted, mind, that you might see your way clear to setting him free as a reward for his heroism.'

'Could I do less, my brave little dove? Now, Claudia,' the furrows on his brow deepened, 'what's this nonsense about your cousin Marcus? You said he made a pass at you?'

Honestly! The best playwright in the whole of the Empire couldn't have penned a better script, she thought afterwards. The timing was perfection itself and Gaius, poor soul, fell into every trap. Now, waiting for him to come up to bed, she calculated there was no better time to play the loaded dice she had up her sleeve . . .

The oil in the lamp was burning low before Claudia, fully sober, heard her husband's hand on the latch. He dismissed the slave with a growl. Hmm. If Marcellus believed he was taking Lucius's death well, Claudia knew better. Gaius Seferius took *every* knock on the chin without obvious sign of damage. It was his way.

'You're not still awake?'

Claudia mentally rolled the dice down her arm and began weighing it.

'I was worried about you, Gaius.'

'That's very sweet of you.' He eased his tunic over his head then paused while his breath came back. 'Jupiter, I'm getting old.'

He'd been having chest pains again. She could tell by the way he massaged his breast. 'Rubbish,' she countered.

'No, no, Claudia, I feel myself teetering on the border of death—'

'For heaven's sake, Gaius, cut that out. You're fifty-three, not eighty-three.'

Grunt.

'Good grief, your mother's across the hall – she's

knocking seventy and, Gaius, I swear Larentia will outlive the pair of us, just to spite me!'

Thank Juno, he began to chuckle. Claudia shook her mental dice and decided there was no better time for a roll.

'Couple of things I meant to tell you, Gaius.'

'Oh?'

There was an unexpected edge to his voice, which caught her off guard. She propped herself up on one elbow and forced a smile.

'Yes. Business matters you asked me to handle in your absence, remember?'

'Ah.' The relief was unmistakable.

Claudia carefully recounted the gist of the meetings he'd entrusted her with, but her mind was only half on them. Something was up, she could smell it. The bed tilted as Gaius sat on the edge and kicked off his sandals.

'And, Gaius, I'm afraid I've got a confession to make.'

His eyes bored into hers and suddenly the air was so heavy you could have sliced it up and served it with honey.

'You know—' Claudia cleared her throat and started again. 'You know the shipment that was due the day you left?'

Again the ominous exhalation of breath. 'What about it, my dove?'

There was a definite smell of fish in the air, but Claudia chose to pass over it. There was an iron which needed to be struck while it was still red hot.

'The captain called at the house to collect the three hundred sesterces outstanding on the account. I'm afraid I was terribly upset about Lucius, I mean you can imagine how it brought back my grief . . .' She tailed off and sniffed. 'Five years and it still seems like yesterday!' She turned away and sobbed into the pillow.

'There, there, I understand . . . What the hell did he mean, three hundred outstanding?'

'That's the point, Gaius. I was so distraught, I paid him on the spot. Then when I sent down to the wharf for a receipt, I realized we . . . I . . . had been conned. The ship was there, so was the captain. Unfortunately, it wasn't the same man!' She flung herself face down into the pillows. 'I'm most terribly sorry.'

He was cross – Juno, was the man cross! – but thankfully not with her. Claudia let her breath out ever so slowly and peered out between her fingers. Dammit, had she known he'd take it this lightly, she'd have given Lucan five hundred. Too late now, but this was the time to get to the source of that fishy smell in the air.

'Gaius, there's something worrying you, isn't there?'

'As a matter of fact—' He stood up and began to pace the chamber. 'This is very difficult for me, Claudia, but the morning I left Rome, a letter arrived – an anonymous letter. It . . . it made some rather unsavoury accusations.'

So Gaius's secret was finally out, was it? 'About you?'

'Um, no. About you, actually.'

Once, when she was very small, an earth tremor rocked the town where she was living. Nothing serious, no lives lost, just a couple of statues which lost their heads when they toppled over and a few shopfronts which tumbled down. But during the tremor, when the ground rumbled and buildings rocked, it had scared a five-year-old girl to her marrow.

'You threw it straight on the fire, I hope. Pass me

another pillow, will you, this one's stuffed with old boots.'

Come on, Claudia. Force a laugh.

There was a tortuous silence as she forced herself to continue the feign of disinterest. Pillows were plumped, tried, replaced. Come on, Gaius, change the subject.

'It – er, it suggested you were . . .'

'Not spinning my own wool? Not sending your tunics to the fullers? Sneaking titbits for Drusilla?' Thatta girl.

He chuckled. 'Worse! It said you were – promiscuous!'

'Prom—?' Dear Diana, he must surely have heard the catch in her breath? '*Promiscuous?*' She slapped his arm and fell back in a heap of pretended mirth. 'What, when you and I don't even share a bedroom?'

'I know! The daft thing is, that damned letter had me worried for a while.'

Got *you* worried?

'Of course,' he began to sober up, 'I suppose the writer meant . . . with lots of other men.'

Deep breaths. One, two, three.

'Gaius. If you start thinking along those lines, it's a victory for the spiteful lunatic who penned the letter. Have you got it with you?'

He shook his head.

Bugger!

'When you get home, throw it away and forget it, because if you can tell me where I get the time, running a house that size, to go gallivanting with hordes of lovers without arousing a single rumourmonger's suspicions in the whole of Rome, I'll eat your best tunic with onions.'

Claudia blew out the lamp and stared up at the ceiling in the darkness. By heaven she'd have to kill that lunatic soon and put a stop to both killings and rumours. It might mean finding other means for paying Lucan off, but she'd cross that bridge when she came to it. In the meantime, unless she was careful, she'd be needing a whole sack of onions if it meant eating one of Gaius's tunics.

XIII

The face that stared back from the looking-glass was like nothing on earth. The bruises ranged in hue from yellow to green to purple, the bags below her eyes could have carried sufficient water to see a whole legion through a week's campaign.

'Ouch!'

If she'd told that stupid girl once, she'd told her a hundred times. Twist the curls to the *left*. Twist them both ways and you get knots!

'Oh, for heaven's sake, get out and leave me alone! A blind man with a broken arm could make a better job of it than you.'

The slave, the one with the lisp, the one whose name she could never be bothered with, pulled a sulky face and slunk off as Claudia slumped in front of the mirror, her head in her hands. For all her making light of last night's thunderbolt, the anonymous letter had unnerved her and no matter how many times she told herself she was hungry, she was tired, she'd had too much to drink, she was simply overwrought, nothing dissipated the deep-rooted feeling of anxiety.

All night long she'd tossed and turned, turned and tossed – but no matter how desperately she invoked it, sleep simply wouldn't come. The same questions followed in the same sequence. Who sent the letter? What did it say? What was its purpose? The night was one of the longest she'd ever known, yet no sooner had the Great Healer finally heard her summons than the most atrocious racket started up right outside the window. She was bolt upright within seconds.

'What the hell . . . ?'

'Relax! It's only the dawn chorus.'

'Well, bugger the dawn chorus, that's all I can say!'

The couch had joggled as Gaius Seferius's huge body shook with laughter. 'You lie back and get some shut-eye,' he'd said, rolling off the bed. 'I want to check the vines.'

'At this hour?'

'Why not?' He ruffled her hair. 'Don't think you've got a monopoly on unorthodox behaviour, my dove.'

Drusilla, who had been biding her time outside the window for Gaius to leave, had leapt on to the bed the moment he'd closed the door behind him, and, soothed by the cat's purring, Claudia had fallen asleep. And with sleep had come dreams. Dark, diabolical dreams. There was Flamininus, the censor, chained to the bloated corpse of Quintus Aurelius Crassus, urging her to whip harder, because he'd pay her another quadran for every strike. A quadran's not enough, she was saying; I need two thousand sesterces. Suddenly the corpse on the chain rolled over. 'I'll double that if you find my eyes,' it said. 'I dropped them with my sandals.' 'I sold 'em,' Rufus piped up, 'swapped 'em for a pig's head.' When Claudia turned to give him a clip round the ear, the boy wore Otho's scarred face and she had woken up sweating. Drusilla had snuggled closer, and thanks to her rhythmic washing, Claudia had drifted off again. This time Gaius – on his back, naked and wriggling like a big, fat baby – was crying, 'Help me, Claudie, help me,' and while she watched, doing nothing, the tears dissolved his eyes into raw, red sockets and she had woken up again, shaking.

'There's a perfectly simple explanation for all this,' Claudia Seferius told her reflection. 'You're hungry, you're tired, you drank too much last night. What do you expect, you silly cow?'

Expert fingers began to cover the bruises with chalk, drawing a thin (but steady!) line of antimony round her eyes and rubbing ochre into her cheeks and lips. By the time she'd stuck the last bone pin into her curls, Claudia Seferius was equipped to deal with any obstacle in her path, and had she come face to face with the Minotaur himself raging on the other side of her bedroom door, her stride would not have been broken. Unfortunately, as it happened, it was Marcellus she bumped into.

'Remus, Claudia, you look like shit.'

'Why, thank you, brother-in-law, you look terrific yourself.'

He was, she noticed, shifting his weight from one foot to the other.

'Did you want me?'

Marcellus flashed a lecherous grin. 'Any time, darling, any time. Although, at this particular moment, it's your old man I'm after.'

She jerked her head towards the fields. 'At dawn, would you believe? He went off to potter round his precious vines. Could be anywhere by now.'

She wondered what Marcellus wanted. In fact, she wondered why an architect embroiled in the restoration works was at the villa at all. He seemed edgy, that was certain. Claudia quickly forgot him and followed her nose in the direction of freshly baked bread.

'So you've condescended to join us at last.'

Her mother-in-law, lips pursed, forehead puckered, didn't even bother to look up.

'Larentia, darling! Lovely to see you again.'

Claudia swept over to her and planted a loud kiss on her mother-in-law's withered cheek.

'And good morning to you too, ladies.' Julia, Flavia and Valeria were also reclining in the dining room.

Larentia snorted. 'You'd best throw another salt cake on the fire,' she said to the slave hovering at her shoulder.

'I've already put one on today, madam.'

'I know,' Larentia replied dryly, darting a reptilian glance at Claudia. 'But Vesta will need a damn sight more than that to appease her.'

The slave bowed and went off to toss another offering on the sacred flame. Claudia inspected a pear and, pretending she'd missed the jibe, turned to Valeria.

'How are you doing, kid?'

'Can't complain.' The girl patted her swollen belly. 'This baby's been thumping half the day and all of the night since Lucius died.'

'You'll call him after his father, I presume?' Julia stared at the bulge under Valeria's tunic.

'Not if it's a girl,' she replied with a chuckle, 'and besides, I never cared for the name. Antonius has a nice ring to it.' Flavia's expression darkened, so she added quickly, 'As has Sylvanus.' She turned to Claudia. 'That was my father's name.'

'I like that, Sylvanus.'

Pulling off a chunk of bread, Claudia decided Valeria

didn't strike the traditional pose of a grief-stricken widow. It was common knowledge, of course, that Gaius had arranged the marriage purely to advance the Seferius cause, though Lucius and Valeria seemed to have knuckled down and made the most of it, as indeed most young couples did. Uppermost in both their minds was the provision of an heir, and this was their fourth try. The tally so far ran to two miscarriages, plus one stillborn.

'I wouldn't call my son after my father.' Trust Flavia to muddy the waters. 'Anyway, I've told Antonius, I don't want babies.'

'Flavia!'

Julia was scandalized. It wasn't something you ever said aloud, even if you meant it. Times were hard enough, as Valeria could testify, and the Empire sorely needed more stout citizens. Wasn't Augustus imposing financial penalties on couples having less than four children or on men who remained single?

'I think your aunt is trying to tell you that a global shortage of babies is something to be deplored, rather than encouraged.'

Flavia turned to her stepmother. 'Well, I don't want them, so there. What's more, I shan't sleep with Antonius—'

The slap that rang out stopped everyone in their tracks, including the slaves. Flavia blinked at her aunt in momentary disbelief, then burst into her usual flood of tears and ran out. Surprised and mortified by her unaccustomed outburst, Julia apologetically gathered up her skirts and went after her. Larentia chewed her lower lip as she stared at Claudia.

'Don't look at me, Larentia. You can't be putting the right cakes on the fire.'

'They're the right ones, just not enough of them when you're in the house. Didn't have no trouble till you arrived.'

Claudia rolled her eyes and turned to Valeria. 'So you think the little one might come early?'

'Yes, and it wouldn't surprise me a bit if—'

'My daughter was right, though. You *will* call him Lucius.'

Both women's eyes turned to Larentia, who was presiding over the dining room like a judge over a trial. Valeria, Claudia noticed, had turned quite pink. No doubt without her husband to stick up for her, she'd been in for a rough ride of late.

'She'll call her baby what she damn well pleases.'

'Got nothing to do with you, keep your stuck-up nose out of my family affairs.'

'Valeria's her own woman, let her make her own decisions.'

'She's carrying my great-grandchild and if it's a boy she'll call him Lucius, won't you, Valeria?'

'Oh, for heaven's sake stop bullying the girl. Valeria, why don't you lie down, love?'

Valeria flashed a brief smile of gratitude and tottered off. Claudia pitied her, poor little bitch, suffering six years under the same roof as this imperious old cow, and if Gaius was entertaining any thoughts about inviting his mother to live with him in Rome he could damned well think again!

'Ach, there's always trouble when you're around.'

Claudia settled herself deeper into the couch, concentrating on the new frieze whereby each wall represented a different season. If that scraggy old bag of bones believed she could cower Claudia Seferius with her poisonous tongue she was in for a surprise.

'Don't think I don't know what you're up to, either.'

Claudia continued to ignore her and broke off a piece of crumbly yellow cheese.

'You won't get away with it.' She spat the words out, syllable by syllable.

Slowly Claudia laid down her goblet and dabbled her fingers in the bowl of water. 'Something on your mind, Larentia?' she asked sweetly.

'Bitch!'

Claudia smiled. 'Don't suppose you could be a little more specific?'

Of course! She hadn't considered this old harpy when she was looking for the writer of a poison pen letter, but who else? Weren't anonymous letters always written by women? And who better equipped with venom?

'Whore! You're nothing but a vain, idle, good-for-nothing, gold-digging harlot!'

Unless Julia watched her ways, she'd end up the very image of her mother in thirty years' time. Crabbed and bony, with claws for fingers and only spite to keep her going. With a jerk of her head, which sent two curls loose from their moorings, Claudia indicated to the slaves in no uncertain terms to get lost and stay lost.

'What really interests me is did you write it yourself?'

A puzzled frown bit into the old woman's forehead. 'Write what?'

'Come, come, Larentia. I know. And you know. And Gaius knows. But he's thrown it away. Thinks it's a load of old codswallop, if you must know. Doesn't believe a word of it.'

'Thrown what away? Codswallop? What are you going on about?'

'Don't play games with me, Larentia. I simply wondered whether you wrote it all on your own, or whether you brought in a third party to write it for you.'

Everyone knew Larentia had very little schooling, and what she had she wasn't very good at.

'Don't try and sidetrack me, you scheming hussy. It won't work, I tell you. I know what you're up to, and I'm warning you here and now, you won't get away with your nasty tricks any longer.'

'You're terrifying me.'

'Think this is funny, do you? Well, you'll laugh on the other side of your face when they throw you to the bears, my girl. And guess who'll be there to cheer them on?'

Good heavens, the old duck was senile! She wondered whether Gaius was aware of it, and, if so, how far down the line she'd gone.

'Well I'll be sure to blow you a kiss, Larentia.'

At least when Gaius realizes what she's like he won't give another thought to that bloody letter. Dreadful coincidence, though. Larentia accusing her of promiscuity.

Claudia pushed her plate away and prepared to leave.

'Not so fast, my girl.' To her surprise, Larentia's claws closed over her wrist. 'I want to hear what you plan to do now.'

Claudia sighed. 'Very little, if you must know. I hate the country, there's sod all to do here.'

'Don't mess with me, you scheming slag. You know damned fine what I'm talking about. Believe it or not, I'm giving you a choice. Disappear now, or I'm going straight to Gaius and the authorities.'

'Magic's not my strong point, Larentia.'

'Lying bitch. Sleight of hand's what you're best at. Poison, accidents, what next, eh?'

A chill wind seemed to have infiltrated the room. Claudia concentrated on the spring frieze. Was that a myrtle wreath round her head?

'Oh, that's got to you, hasn't it? All ears, aren't you, Claudia High-and-Mighty Seferius?'

Maybe Summer was prettier? No, she was worse. Had a bit of a squint, did poor old Summer. 'Are you insinuating—'

Larentia laughed. 'Insinuating? Bit late for that, isn't it? You've murdered three of my grandchildren . . . oh, not personally, no. You wouldn't sully your dainty little fingers, would you? But because I'm old doesn't mean I'm stupid. Think, woman. Think where Gaius got his shrewdness from – and I'll give you a clue, it wasn't from his father.'

That's right, he built roads all his life.

'I didn't suspect, not at first. Not with my beautiful Calpurnia.' The old woman's rheumy eyes began to fill with tears. 'Lovely child, she was. Sent by Venus to bring joy on earth. My, I had such plans for the girl . . . until you killed her.'

Claudia lolled back in a show of indifference and picked up a small bunch of red grapes.

'Calpurnia died of a fever, Larentia. F-e-v-e-r, fever.'

'That's what you wanted us to think. Thought yourself clever, didn't you, but you're rumbled. Who else caught that fever, eh? I'll tell you who else, no one, that's who. Just my lovely Calpurnia. And what a coincidence she was on the brink of marriage.'

The old girl sniffed and blew her nose.

'The key word here, Larentia, is *coincidence*.'

'Huh! And was it coincidence that her brother fell under the wheels of a grain wagon?'

'He was steaming drunk by all accounts, and it was midnight, when only full loads are rolling into the city.' The grapes had turned to ash in her mouth, but Claudia kept on chewing.

'Drunk, my arse. Secundus was pushed. Which left Flavia and Lucius between you and my son's fortune, didn't it? How many times had you tried before you were successful, eh?'

'You're raving.'

Colour flooded Larentia's gnarled old face. She jabbed Claudia on the breastbone with her index finger.

'Well, you left it too late, you gold-digging bitch. That child of Valeria's will inherit jointly alongside Flavia. Or did you plan to murder them both?'

'I know who I'd like to murder.'

The old woman cackled. 'Go ahead, let them catch you in the act. I've had my day, I'm willing to make the sacrifice. But you can't do it face to face, can you? No. You pay people to do your dirty work for you. Scum, prepared to slip a poison to a fifteen-year-old girl and watch her die in agony, scum who don't mind pushing a total stranger under a heavy cart just so long as they get paid. How much did it cost you to poison Lucius?'

Claudia stood up. Funny. Her knees suddenly seemed to find the weight too much for them and idly she wondered whether Larentia could hear them knocking.

'I've had it up to here with you, you fossilized old bat. One more slur from your venomous mouth and I'll have you buried alive so fast you'll be chewing worms within the hour. Do you hear me?'

Larentia curled a lip. 'You and who else? Think your threats can touch an old woman? If you're so innocent, why don't we lay the evidence before Gaius, see what he makes of it?'

'Leave my husband out of this. He's had enough on his plate lately.'

'Worrying himself sick about your debts, most like. Ho, ho, that took the wind out of your sails, didn't it? Thought because I was stuck out here I didn't know what was going on? Well, I told you before, Larentia Seferius is nobody's fool. Two thousand sesterces you owe. Is that how much it cost to murder my grandson?'

Claudia's teeth were clamped together so hard her jawbones were hurting. She forced herself to take several deep breaths.

'Larentia, you are one sick woman.'

'Oh, you're the one who'll be sick. Sick as a parrot. You under-estimated me, daughter-in-law, and now you're going to pay the price. I'm going straight to Gaius, then I'm going to the authorities.'

Claudia made a great show of rearranging her tunic, flicked several imaginary crumbs off her bodice, then walked slowly but purposefully towards the door. Precisely how much this old trout knew and how much of it was guesswork remained to be seen.

'Nothing you do, Larentia, either interests or concerns me. Now if you'll excuse me, I've got a very busy day ahead.'

XIV

In a narrow alley, less than fifty paces from the banks of the Tiber, a young slave girl cowered against a wall that reeked of dog piss and cabbages. The moon was not yet up, leaving the alleyway plunged into the colour of estuary mud. Nearby a tavern door opened, spilling light as well as two drunken oarsmen on to the cobbles. The girl flattened herself against the stonework, but the men, arms round each other for mutual support, wove their way down to the river, too engrossed in bawdy song to notice.

In the street at the end of the alley, creaking wagons made their deliveries. She could smell the oxen, hear the bark of directions as loads were hoisted off or on to the carts. Perhaps she could wriggle under one of the sheets? Hide in an empty wooden crate? Escape the city and . . .

And what? Head north? How? At sixteen, with virtually no money, no friends, no allies, how could she hope to survive?

Again the tavern doors threw a yellow oblong of light into the dingy street and three men tumbled out. Within seconds knuckles were cracking off jawbones, noses squelching under fists, shards of smashed drinking vessels skimming over the cobbles. The girl flinched as a small piece of pottery flicked against her calf and she covered her face with her hands. A yellow-haired whore jeered from the doorway until the tavern keeper threw a bucket of water over them all, including the woman, and suddenly the four were comrades again. The door closed and the alley fell silent once more, with only pools of wine and water to bear witness to the brawl.

She could hide on one of the carts, only . . . suppose they were being searched? Tears trickled down her cheek, cutting a path through the grime. Even if she escaped the city, she had no real idea which direction to take for home. There were mountains to cross, she knew that. Bleak, bitter mountains, where the wind howled like a wolf and the snow never melted. And what after that? The journey that had brought her to Rome had taken weeks. Months. She could never find her way back without help.

Suppose she slipped on to one of the boats? She shivered in the darkness, recalling tales of horror at what befell stowaways. She was desperate now. She had no one to turn to. She daren't return to the house to collect her paltry savings, for they would be waiting, with their lies and their accusations.

She drew up her knees, wrapping her arms round her body for comfort. Why were her gods punishing her like this? It had been a normal working day and she'd simply been going about her business. Then, quite without warning, a man she'd never seen before, a man with a limp, had rounded on her and publicly branded her a thief. A crowd had begun to gather. She hadn't understood. There was no reason for it. He had no grounds, no evidence, but the man insisted on sending for the police.

Then she heard the word 'murder'.

Murder?

As the crowd's interest turned to the arrival of the soldiers, she had seized the moment to run and run and run. Ten hours of running and hiding and crying and whimpering already seemed like ten days. Ten years.

She wanted to go home.

Home was where blue-white frosts sharpened your senses. Home was where soft summer rain whispered into the broad leaves of the trees. And home was where those very same leaves blazed copper and bronze and gold after the harvest. There was no dry, dusty wind to choke your lungs up there. Nor a sun which thickened and darkened your skin like leather. Home was kind, benevolent. It would welcome her back to its bosom.

Wiping her eyes with the back of her hand, the girl picked up the shard that had scratched her leg. She stared at it long and hard for several seconds, then slashed it deep across her left wrist before plunging it into her right.

Now I am going where they can't hurt me, she thought. Now I am going home.

XV

By any standards, the journey back to Rome was a damned
sight better than the journey out, despite Kano's continued
reluctance to chivvy up those foul-smelling nags, and Claudia thought that if she saw one more swish of a tail after
this she'd scream till she exploded. Not that she ought to
complain, she decided. She was going home, and in less
than no time she'd be rolling around theatre aisles, cheering military parades and living it up at the Circus, you
just try and stop her, because in the end the threat to her
cosy existence hadn't come from Larentia, or from the
crazed killer whose elimination was imminent. The threat
had come from tedium.

Quite why ordinarily level-headed people scuttled to
the hills in summer was beyond her. Try the freshness
of the air, Gaius suggested, which shows how much *he*
knew, because you couldn't smell a damned thing in the
air, not one damned thing. Good life in Illyria, there were
only so many times a girl could inspect the beehives or
wander round the orchards or potter in the winery, and
you simply couldn't stay indoors. You either ran into that
poisonous old dustbag, Larentia, or else you were faced
with poor Valeria's pregnancy problems, Julia's nagging
or Flavia's geyser. Claudia would have sold her soul for a
party, but it was out of the question, Gaius explained. Not

only was the villa isolated, but this was the busiest time of the year for everybody. Thus July fell quietly upon its sword and August showed no signs of improvement as talk continued to revolve around wine and hay, peas and beans. She was pig sick of it.

Take last week, for instance. Gaius was making his way down from the threshing floor as Claudia stepped off the verandah. He looks his age, she thought. He really looks his age and despite being flanked by slaves he had every appearance of being utterly alone.

'How safe are the roads around here?'

'Huh?' He was a million miles away.

Claudia shrugged impatiently. 'The roads. How many men do I need for a bodyguard?'

Gaius looked confused. 'Five, six, I suppose.'

'Then I'll take six. See you later.'

'Wait! Wait.' He was slowly coming back into focus. 'Where are you going?'

Claudia looked round sharply. 'Nowhere, of course. I'm going for a walk.'

Gaius's jaw dropped. 'A what?'

She patted his cheek and smiled. 'There's a first time for everything. YOU!' Her voice stopped a Nubian in his tracks. 'Pick five others, arm yourselves, then meet me at the main gate in ten minutes.'

The negro, who was pushing a loaded barrow across the barnyard, glanced fearfully at his master as Claudia flounced off.

'Do as she says,' Gaius said wearily, shaking his head. 'Just do as she says.'

He was right to look startled, she thought, as Galla laced up her stout boots. I've never been for a walk in my life, but there can't be much to it. Follow the road for an hour, turn round and follow it back again.

'We'll need water, wine, and I daresay something to eat as well. Figs, pears, peaches and raisins. I like raisins.'

She held up the other boot for lacing.

'Throw in a couple of chickens, something to go with them, say, onions, leeks, a few eggs, and perhaps a rabbit. I think I smelled honey cakes cooking in the kitchen, so they'd go down well, oh, and some almonds. What's the matter?'

The girl quickly shook her head. 'Nothing, madam.'

'Then wipe that stupid look off your face.'

'Yeth, madam.'

Bloody girl! Why couldn't they find her a slave who didn't lisp?

'And if there's any pecorino cheese floating round the kitchen, pack that, too – it's my favourite.'

'Yeth, madam.'

'And apples. Don't forget the apples.'

Claudia tested her boots for comfort and found them wanting. I'll get blisters, I know. Bloody countryside. Trees and sky and hills and whatnot – dull as a dolphin's dongler. Now then. To wear a pulla, or not to wear a pulla, that was the question. Not, she finally decided. The girl could carry it.

'Galla, aren't you ready yet?' For heaven's sake, what was keeping her? 'Dear Diana, what's *that*?'

'We'll need the donkey for the food, madam.'

'Galla.' Claudia crooked her finger. 'Galla, come here, I want to explain something to you. We're going for a walk, not a bloody route march. The moke stays.'

'What about—'

'You're not listening to me, Galla. The ugly sod stays, that is my final word. What the—'

Flavia was shouting and waving from the doorway, apparently signalling to Claudia to wait for her, she was coming with them. Claudia wrinkled her nose.

'Second thoughts, Galla, the donkey's fine. Gee up, boy.'

She set a cracking pace and when she looked back Flavia was still in the yard flapping her arms and looking for all the world like a windmill with sacks for sails.

Blisters. Donkeys. No doubt she'd get bitten to bits by gnats and midges as well. Juno, Jupiter and Mars! To think people actually put up with this in the name of enjoyment! Oh well, the big Nubian seems happy; that's something, she supposed. First she tried counting vines, but, since they spread as far as the eye could see, she gave that the elbow in favour of a succession of nonsense. Spotting roadside flowers. Birds. Not stepping on the cracks between the octagonal slabs. Composing idiotic rhymes. At the fourth milestone, she spun smartly on her heel and marched home, tutting as her bodyguard tripped over both themselves and the donkey at the suddenness of the turn.

'Good walk, my sweet?'

Gaius and Rollo the bailiff were deep in conversation when the sorry procession straggled through the gates.

> 'The sun was too bright,
> The breeze was too slight,
> The hills were too steep,
> Now I'm going to sleep.'

Her husband blinked and she thought he muttered something about the heat getting to her.

'And you. Yes, you, girl.' Galla limped over. 'What's the idea of packing so much stuff? Can't you see that wretched animal's wilting?'

'You said—'

'You should never have allowed it out in this heat. Give that poor creature water at once.'

Now, as the heat haze danced and glimmered for the first time over the seven distant hills that were Rome, Claudia decided it was difficult to see why people took to this walking lark – after all, it wasn't as though there was anything to see. Still, never let it be said of Claudia Seferius she wasn't willing to try out new experiences.

Gaius had taken the two-wheeled car, which made better time, but Claudia was happy just to be home. The comforting street cacophony, her own room, her own bed, even her own maid. Galla's irritating lisp was grinding her nerves to pulp; it would be a relief to return to the rhythm of Melissa's unassuming ministrations. Oh yes, it had been an uphill struggle at the villa, especially with Larentia, although luckily the old cow hadn't been anywhere near as sure of herself as she'd made out. No accusations were made publicly and the constant sniping at her son's wife had effectively served to alienate Larentia from Gaius, although she hadn't noticed until it was too late.

'I'll see you get your come-uppance, you conniving bitch.' She'd finally bearded her daughter-in-law in the bath house the day before she was due to leave.

Claudia stretched. 'Maybe you will, maybe you won't,' she said, rubbing oil into her thighs. 'But if you have any sense, you'll take a word of advice from me.'

'Never!' The old woman spat the word out as though it were a glowing ember burning through her tongue.

Claudia smiled slowly, her eyes glistening. 'Take it or leave it, Larentia, but if I were you I'd certainly be careful what I ate from now on.'

'Why you ... you ...'

Revelling in both physical and psychological superiority, Claudia stood up and proceeded to oil her breasts.

'Hedonistic whore?' she asked sweetly.

'... grasping bitch,' snapped Larentia. 'But you'll pay. And when retribution comes I'll be there, in the front row, you just wait and see. You won't get a quadran of Gaius's money.' Her mouth fell open as the colour drained from her face. 'Merciful Juno, that's your game! You're poisoning my son!'

Claudia shot her an amused glance. 'Ah! So you've noticed the haunted eyes, the lacklustre expression, the dark circles? I wondered how long it would take you.'

The horror on Larentia's face aged her ten years. She looked like a walking skeleton.

'I must warn him,' she said breathlessly. 'I'm going straight ... straight ...' She was panting and wheezing, gulping for air. 'I ... I ...'

She began to sway and clutch her throat. Claudia caught her before she hit the tiles. Dammit, the old bat didn't even have the decency to die! Claudia sighed, threw a towel over herself and called for assistance, ensuring Larentia's seizure was passed off as a fainting fit and that no talk of collapse came to Gaius's ears.

As the wagon rolled downhill, she threw a fig in the air and caught it in her fist. If nothing else, this wretched sojourn has cleared my mind and brought matters into perspective. Lucan. Otho. Junius. Larentia. Anonymous letters. Murders. Accusations. Gaius. Orbilio . . . Oh yes, she was feeling confident again now. Gaius had finally lost patience and Flavia's wedding to Scaevola was firmly fixed for the beginning of September, which was a niggling weight off Claudia's mind. Larentia's seizure would put the old fossil out of action for as long as it took for counter-measures to be set in motion. She'd had an idea about Lucan, and Otho could be dealt with any old time. Junius would be a loss, because, without him, who could she trust to place bets discreetly? And as for that other nasty business, whoever the bastard was his days were well and truly numbered, Claudia reckoned she'd have him nailed within a week, two at the outside.

'Life is wonderful, don't you think so, Galla?'

Sulky cow.

At long last the shimmering haze became solid walls, which in turn became roofs and streets and columns and arches. The lifeless road turned into a clamour of men and women, children and oxen, beggars and pedlars. There were shopkeepers shouting, dogs snapping, slaves yapping, porters rumbling amphorae over the cobbles. The smell of hard-earned sweat mingled with charcoal, animal ordure and dusky, musky scents. Graffiti on the walls, sacred fires outside the temples, deep shadows cast by the mighty aqueducts which straddled all Rome. You could practically smell the steam from the baths as the cart joggled past, hear the babble of gossip echo through the vaulted chambers.

Claudia thought of Gaius, of the weight that had fallen away, of the breathing problems that had been plaguing him of late. Almost overnight he'd become an old man.

She was slumped into her cushions, chewing her thumbnail and calculating how long before Gaius Seferius left a grieving widow, when the wagon finally drew to a halt outside the house. There was a song on her lips as she lifted the flap of Drusilla's cage.

'Home, poppet. Home with a vengeance.'

Gaius's banquet had been rearranged for this coming Thursday, with Melissa sorting out all the tedious chores. Acrobats, dancers, you name it, she'll have them lined up, and Verres would have had his dainties worked out ages ago. The Wine Festival starts on Saturday, but let me see, today's only Tuesday. What's on tomorrow? Isn't there a hearing in the Senate House she could toddle along to?

Leonides, the household steward, was hovering in the atrium beside the bust of Gaius's father.

'I wonder if I might—'

'Not now.'

'It's rather important, madam.'

Claudia twisted her lip. 'Leonides, if you wish to keep your ears attached to your neck – and I fully understand that you might not, because they don't seem to serve you particularly well – but *should* you want to keep them, I suggest you listen more closely. When I said not now, I meant *not now*.'

The lanky Macedonian coloured, nodded and retreated hurriedly. Her eyes scanning unsuccessfully for Melissa, Claudia dismissed Galla with a wave and marched towards the garden. She could catch up on the banquet details later; right now a glass of wine among the roses and lilies was just what the doctor ordered!

'Gaius? I thought you'd be working.'

'I'm entertaining a house guest.'

Not another of those boring colleagues of yours, I can't stand it.

'Splendid. Have I met him?'

'Indeed you have . . . cousin.' Orbilio's curly mop peered round a laurel shrub. His face had a schoolboy grin plastered all over it.

'Gaius . . . !'

'Calm down, my sweet, let me—'

'Calm down?' She grabbed hold of her husband's arm, jerked him to his feet and dragged him aside. 'Gaius, that monster tried to rape me!'

Fat fingers patted her shoulder. 'He's explained that.'

She shot a glance in Orbilio's direction. The bastard was watching a butterfly flitting round the lavender as though this was no concern of his.

'Said he had no idea re-enacting those childhood wrestling matches might be misconstrued, so make up with your cousin, Claudia. Tell him you're sorry.'

I am not sorry, Gaius. I am incandescent. In-can-bloody-descent!

'Marcus! What can I say?' There was more honey on her tongue than in those twenty beehives up at the villa. 'What a silly, silly goose you must think me!'

Orbilio covered his mouth with the back of his hand to stifle what might have been a cough.

'Oh, boys will be boys.'

'Ha, ha. Absolutely.' Her mouth was beginning to ache. 'And why did you say you were here? I think I missed that.'

'His house burned down.' Gaius brushed specks of dandruff from his shoulder.

Claudia turned to Orbilio. 'Tragic, Cousin Markie. Absolutely tragic!'

'Weren't it just?'

A second, smaller head popped up. It looked better nourished than on previous occasions.

'Oh no! Don't tell me that filthy little arab is staying here as well?'

She shot Orbilio a look which said, What the hell are you trying to do to me?, but he pretended he hadn't noticed. The next look told him she'd flay him alive for this, and he pretended not to notice that, either.

'Try to be charitable, my sweet. Marcus plucked this poor child from the gutter, we owe him our support, what?'

'Like hell.'

'Ah ... well ... I daresay it'll only be for a week or two, eh, Marcus?' Gaius ruffled the urchin's hair. 'Come along, Rufus.'

Claudia felt the colour drain from her face to her toes. 'You're not ... you're not going out?'

The boy's face lit up. 'Yep. Master Seferius has promised to show me his warehouse.'

He glanced up at Gaius, then signalled to Claudia by drawing one finger across his lips and winking that it was all right, he wouldn't say a word about that day in the Forum. Claudia rubbed her forehead. There must be something she could do to stop them.

'I'll take him out,' she said.

'You?' It was a joint male chorus.

'Yes, me. You'd like that, wouldn't you, Rufus?'

'Nope. I wanna go with the gaffer.'

'Then I'll come with you.'

Gaius frowned. 'Claudia, you ought to stay here and keep Marcus company.'

Rufus repeated his I-promise-to-keep-my-mouth-shut gesture, but she ignored it. 'Let's all go.'

Orbilio shrugged. 'Suits me,' he said, but Gaius aimed a mock punch to the child's chin.

'Ah, we'll keep it the two of us, eh, lad? Have fun, you two.'

Wonderful! Absolutely bloody wonderful! Claudia slumped on to the bench while Orbilio leaned back, draping his elbow over the ridge of the seat with the air of a man expecting to be crucified but who'd got away with a tongue-lashing instead. She poured herself a full glass of wine and swallowed it without stopping for breath.

'I won't ask why,' she said wearily. 'I'll just ask when.'

'When did I arrive? Yesterday.'

'I see. And how long do you estimate before your house will be . . . habitable again?'

'As long as it takes, Claudia,' he said so quietly she almost missed it.

It felt as though snow had suddenly fallen.

She pursed her lips. 'Is it better than sex, prying and spying in other people's underwear?'

'Claudia—'

'I'm serious, Orbilio, I want to know. Do you get off on this lark?'

'For pity's sake, woman, can't you get it through your thick skull, I've got a job to do? Four men have been butchered, their eyes chiselled out of their sockets, and it would be naïve in the extreme to imagine the carnage has stopped—'

'Stop right there.' Claudia held up a hand. 'Let me ask

another question. Do you suspect me of killing them?'

'Don't be daft.'

'So what's stopping you from packing up this very minute? And spare me that hogwash about your roof still smouldering. You've poked and prodded in every little corner, what's keeping—'

'You're wrong.'

She gave a half-laugh. 'Still a few nooks and crannies left, are there? I do so admire a man who's thorough!'

Orbilio rubbed his chin as though checking for stubble. His eyelids, she noticed, were blinking rapidly and he was avoiding her gaze. So this pondscum had a conscience, did he? Or was it pure embarrassment, finding a collection of whips and manacles in her bedroom? If challenged, she'd say it was strictly between her and Gaius what they got up to, and if he drew a comparison between her paraphernalia and Crassus, so what? Her client list – their names and proclivities – she kept in her head, he couldn't prove a damned thing. No, it wasn't that which troubled her. It was the fact that someone had violated her privacy by systematically rifling through her personal belongings. That the man who had laid her soul bare happened to be Marcus Cornelius Orbilio was neither here nor there, she told herself. Neither here nor there.

'It didn't seem . . . decent to ransack the place in your absence.'

The wine spilled over the table, forming a dark red pool which she made no effort to mop up. 'Are you seriously expecting me to believe you've spent two days under my roof without making a search?'

Rivulets of wine trickled across the wood to drip noisily on to the tiles below.

He puckered his lips. 'Believe what you like,' he said. 'You asked and I answered.'

The snow melted, the sun came out, birds began to sing.

'Oi!' She clapped her hands. 'Clear up this mess,' she commanded the slave who came running. 'Fetch another jug – and be quick about it.'

Orbilio brushed a fly away from the sticky puddle. 'You ought to know, however, that I do intend to search this house. Ideally with your permission and you can be present, by all means, but if I have to get written authority from Callisunus, so be it.'

Claudia filled both glasses from the new flagon. 'Why this house?'

'I've got a hunch,' he said simply.

'Never mind, dear.' She patted his knee. 'There's a way of hanging the toga that'll disguise it completely.'

What the hell? Let him search the bloody place! She'd have ample time to move her knick-knacks in the course of his ferreting.

The corners of his mouth twitched. 'You can be a real pain in the backside at times, Claudia Seferius.'

'I simply take the shortest route to your brain, Cousin Markie.'

His eyes twinkled as he topped up his glass. 'We could go out together this evening, just the two of us.'

'We could, yes. Alternatively you could go to hell all by yourself,' she replied companionably, 'and I know which I'd prefer.'

Orbilio laughed aloud and for several minutes they sat in silence in the garden, sipping wine and listening to nothing but the drone of bumblebees heavy with pollen and the hiss of water, foaming white as it hit the marble fountain.

'There's one thing I discovered,' he said at last. 'You and Gaius have separate bedrooms.'

'He snores.'

'Come off it, Claudia. He's on the opposite side of the house. In fact, it's a separate bloody staircase.'

She shot him a look out of the corner of her eye. 'Don't tell me, let me guess. You just happen to be installed in a bedroom on my side, right?'

'Wishful thinking, I'm afraid. If you want me, you'll have to tiptoe past your husband's door.'

She smiled. 'You couldn't afford me, Orbilio.'

'Wanna bet?'

Any time, lover boy. 'One million sesterces.'

'What is?'

'My price. One million sesterces.'

His breath came out in a whistle. 'A million?'

'A million.'

'Then I suppose there's little point in leaving my door unlocked tonight?'

'You suppose right, Orbilio. However, while we're on the subject of accommodation, I have something to say and I'll make it plain. I don't want you in my house. You've wormed your way round Gaius, so it looks like I'm lumbered, but the oik goes.'

'That's unreasonable, he's—'

'I'm an unreasonable person, Orbilio. Get rid of him. Tonight.'

'I can't.'

'Tonight!'

'Claudia, this lad's got the chance of a decent, healthy

life. Schooling, a trade. What am I supposed to do, throw him back to starve in some alleyway? Is that what you want? Have him die of the flux, like half the other gutter-snipes in Rome?'

Claudia ran her finger round the rim of her glass until it produced a high-pitched humming sound. 'What you do with him, Orbilio, is your concern, not mine. But take my word for it, that boy leaves this house tonight. Either you tell him or I do, it makes no odds to me.'

'For pity's sake, woman, he's only seven years old!'

'Try eleven.' She flashed him a glance. Life on the streets stunts your growth. Believe me.

He hurled his glass across the garden. 'You're a hard-hearted bitch.'

Claudia smiled a brittle smile. 'I take it, then, that you'll be telling him yourself?' She stood up and shook her tunic into its folds. 'Oh, don't trouble yourself with the splinters, I'll send a flunky to clear up.'

XVI

Orbilio ran so fast to catch up with her that he skidded, lost his footing and collided with a pillar. Why was it called the funny bone, he wondered, when it hurt like hell? Not that she'd got very far. That poor beanpole of a steward was the one taking the brunt of her anger this time.

'I will not tolerate you hovering in the shadows, Leonides . . .'

'I need to speak to you—'

'You are not paid to hover. The best thing to be said in your favour is that for most of the time you are blissfully invisible.'

'It's a matter of some urgency, madam.'

'Unless you wish to seek other employment within the hour, I strongly suggest you melt into the background immediately.'

'But—'

'Butts are for billy goats, Leonides. Shoo!'

Standing by the kitchen, rubbing his elbow, Orbilio thought he had never seen her looking so lovely. When she was angry, her eyes flashed like water in the sunshine. She'd stick her chin out, as if to say 'just you try it', and curls would tumble loose. Thick, springy curls, with terracotta tints that made a man want to bury his face and hands in them. He couldn't begin to describe the sensations that consumed him once he discovered Gaius didn't sleep with his wife. Verres the cook had proved most garrulous when it came to domestic gossip and he was quite adamant on that score. Seferius never touched her, never went into her room. Probably not allowed to, he'd joked, digging Orbilio in the ribs – a gesture he'd never dare make sober – but privately Orbilio disagreed. As strong as Claudia was, in matters of policy Gaius Seferius's word was law.

Lying awake at night afterwards, his arms folded behind his head as he stared at the ceiling, Orbilio had gone back over the times he'd seen them together and decided Verres had the situation sussed correctly. There *was* no visible sexual chemistry between husband and wife, which in itself isn't unusual, but in Seferius's case he seemed to treat Claudia more like a daughter than a lover. A blind man could see Gaius was proud of his wife, but it was eating away at Orbilio why this wealthy wine merchant should pick such a magnificent, hot-blooded woman . . . and not make love to her. It wasn't natural. Was it size? Orbilio knew of bigger men than Seferius who were at it like rabbits. Children, then? So desperate was the Empire to breed strong, healthy citizens that Augustus was paying families to have babies. But Gaius had fathered four and Claudia was supposed to have had three. (Would you credit it? A figure like that, after three kids!) Perhaps they'd both had enough? Cupid's darts, there were simpler ways to prevent pregnancies than abstinence! What, then? Impotence?

As Leonides sloped away, ruefully shaking his head, Orbilio stepped in front of her.

'I'm sorry.'

'Sorry enough to pack up and leave?'

He gritted his teeth and pressed on. 'You're entitled to have who you like in your house. I had no right to foist Rufus on you.'

'Yet you have no qualms about foisting yourself on me?'

Chance would be a fine thing. 'That's different. That's business.'

He'd had to tell Callisunus his reasons for infiltrating the Seferius household as a last-ditch attempt before being taken off the case. Callisunus was becoming increasingly exasperated with Orbilio's dead-end leads, especially since it was his personal belief the killer was a maniac who selected his victims at random. Confiding his hunch was a risk Orbilio had taken very, very reluctantly, but on the strength of it Callisunus had granted him a week's extension. Seven days but no more, he said, and Orbilio was no fool; he knew an ultimatum when he heard it.

'Claudia . . .' He linked his arm through hers to draw her away from the prying ears of the kitchen. 'Claudia, I would very much like us to be friends.'

And more, Claudia. Much, much more. You don't know how I ache for you, long to hold you in my arms, lay you on my wolfskin cloak and kiss your lips, your hair, your breasts. To make love to you in the lapping waters of the ocean . . .

'Friends?' She shook her arm free. 'As Cleopatra might have said, kiss my asp.'

'I understand why you're so tetchy about the boy—'

'You know nothing.'

You think not? 'Rufus is all right, he's as streetwise as

they come and won't have let anything slip.'

Dammit, she wasn't listening to a word he was saying! That Gaulish boy of hers had come limping into the atrium, and although he hadn't said a word or moved so much as one splendid muscle, Orbilio sensed communication between them. He felt his stomach churn. Mother of Tarquin, no! Not Claudia and *him*! Professional eyes swept over the slave. Tall, rugged, strong. Not exactly drop-dead good looks, but for a non-Roman he had That Certain Something, Orbilio conceded, bristling at the way the boy's eyes smouldered at Claudia. And it would pay you to remember Junius isn't a boy, Marcus, my lad. He'll never see twenty again, that was for sure.

So they wanted to talk, did they?

Orbilio excused himself and headed up the stairs, whistling under his breath. Claudia, he noticed, drifted nonchalantly towards the peristyle and although Junius turned his back and walked off towards the kitchen, Orbilio wasn't in the least surprised that a convoluted route just happened to bring the young Gaul into the garden. By this time, however, Orbilio had staged himself behind the household shrine. He mightn't be able to see, but he could hear.

'How are the ribs now?'

As her perfume, rich, exotic and spicy, drifted over, Orbilio closed his eyes and inhaled.

'So-so, thank you, but I wanted to warn you. That investigator, the one who pretends he's your cousin, he's been questioning the servants.' Junius lowered his voice. 'That fat slob Verres has a loose tongue, and some of the women, too. Orbilio's very generous, though. Gave me a whole denarius.'

The sun was beginning to set, throwing a rich cloak of molten fire over the garden.

'In exchange for what?'

'Nothing. I told him nothing!'

Orbilio heard the boy spit, then he heard Claudia's laughter ring out.

'Did you catch that, Cousin Markie?'

Bugger! Well, there was no point in pretending he'd been pouring a libation at the shrine or tying his laces . . .

'Most of it,' he said casually, wondering whether his face was as red as it felt. It was difficult to decide whether he'd been seen, which might have influenced the conversation, or whether it was an out-and-out set-up. He wouldn't put it past her.

'I heard about your part in the riot,' he said to Junius. The official version was that he'd stepped in to save her from harm. 'Very commendable, I must say.' Rufus's story, on the other hand, contained a few marked differences.

Claudia and the Gaul exchanged glances.

'You may go,' she told him, and Orbilio was surprised at the speed with which the boy took off, limp or no limp.

'Shouldn't you be out catching killers, or don't you work of an evening?' She looked Orbilio over long and hard.

He was tempted to say I am working, but held his tongue.

'I suppose you're going to tell me you have skivvies running all over this city, lifting up stones and delving into slime, why dirty your own hands?'

That was true, as well. 'Can't a man have a night off occasionally?'

'Supposing . . . Now what the hell is that?'

The garden, normally a peaceful refuge, was suddenly invaded by a knot of people pressing forward. Leonides, skipping backwards with his hands outstretched, was telling someone they couldn't just barge in here like that, whilst at the same time trying to suppress the intrusion by using a guard of male slaves.

Both Claudia and Orbilio were on their feet in seconds.

'Claudie! Claudie, it's me, Ligarius. They wouldn't let me through the front door, I had to push my way in.'

Despite the slaves' manful efforts to restrain him, the giant was shaking them off like raindrops. The liquor on his breath would have felled an elephant.

Leonides cast a pained expression at Claudia. 'That's one of the things I was trying to tell you,' he said in between struggles. 'This man's been shouting your name outside the door for three nights running.'

'Claudie, you said we could talk. You promised, Claudie, you—Unk!'

There was a crash as he fell headlong on to the floor.

'I hope I didn't hit him too hard.' As Orbilio inspected the chair for damage, a leg dropped on to the floor with a clatter.

She looked as white as his best toga. 'This lunatic's been muddling me up with somebody else. Last time my brother-in-law sorted him out.'

'Not well enough, it seems.'

Orbilio turned to the goggling slaves. 'Toss him into the street, he can sleep it off outside.' He brushed his hands together. 'Not that I'd fancy *his* headache when he wakes up!'

They grabbed hold of the bearded giant and staggered off with the lifeless body, cursing and grunting under the weight.

'Thank you.' He noticed she didn't actually look him in the eye when she said it.

'All in a day's work—'

'Ahem!'

That was Leonides. He seemed to be indicating towards the corner. Orbilio looked round to see a soldier with a rather sheepish expression hovering patiently. He recognized him as Timarchides, also employed by Callisunus.

'You've a message for me?' he asked.

'If you're Marcus Cornelius Orbilio, then, yes, sir, I have.'

Neither Claudia nor Leonides made an effort to draw away, and for Orbilio to request privacy in another person's house was too disrespectful to contemplate. He waited to the point of rudeness before saying, 'Well, spit it out, man.'

Affronted, Timarchides stepped stiffly forward and stood to attention, fixing his eye on a point somewhere over Orbilio's left shoulder.

'That matter of the missing slave, sir. Reporting to say—'

'What missing slave, Timarchides?'

His mind was still coming to grips with the intrusion of the big, ugly lug he'd just brained with the chair leg, but before the soldier could refresh his memory, Claudia had inserted herself between them.

'This is not a police station, Orbilio, or an army barracks. If you wish to chase runaways, kindly go elsewhere to conduct your enquiries, because I will not tolerate this house being used as a garrison night and day.'

'Oh no, madam. This is part of the murder inquiry.'

The earnest expression on Timarchides' seasoned features inspired her to raise an encouraging eyebrow.

'The girl was caught red-handed hocking the victim's property—'

Orbilio silenced him with a look and the soldier's complexion darkened. 'You've got her, then?'

Timarchides made a great show of fluffing up the plume on his helmet. 'In a manner of speaking,' he said, his eyes riveted on the bronze cheekpiece. He didn't much care for the impatient clucking sound in his superior officer's throat, it made a trickle of sweat run down his nose, nor did he like the way Orbilio snapped, 'Explain!' but there was no alternative. He'd have to tell the truth and hope to Hermes the blame wouldn't land on him.

'I wasn't there, of course' (that was clever of you, lad; clear yourself right at the outset), 'but it seems the silversmith recognized the piece she was trying to sell, sent for the police and in the confusion of the gathering crowd somehow the little bitch gave them the slip.'

'Yes, I *know* that,' Orbilio said patiently. 'What I'm asking you, Timarchides, is this: is she or is she not in custody?'

The soldier grunted noncommittally. 'She's been found . . .' He left it trailing.

'Where?'

'Near the river. I reckon she'd seen how carefully we'd been searching wagons and carts and decided her only escape route was over the Tiber. Except she wouldn't have counted on so many soldiers patrolling the bank. So yes, we've found her all right. Only trouble is,' he crossed his fingers behind his back, 'she's dead, sir.'

'You're joking! How?'

'No other way out so she slashed her wrists. Sir.'

Orbilio waved a tired hand. 'Give the "sirs" a rest, Timarchides, just tell me whether you've made a positive identification.'

It was obvious the soldier wasn't going to be caught napping a fourth time. First, he didn't know whether it was his place to step in and help break up that brawl, then he was berated for not delivering his message in public, and finally he was made to shut up when all he was doing was explaining the situation to Mistress Seferius. Not for all the women in the Docklands was he going to cop it again!

'Oh, it's definitely her, sir. No question. Still wearing the clip.'

Orbilio's mouth turned down. 'And you're absolutely sure it's the same girl?'

'The slave catchers found her, sir, and them slave catchers don't make mistakes.'

That's true. They're mean sons of bitches and no mistake. Orbilio perked up. 'Right, Timarchides, what's the address?'

The soldier's face puckered and he jerked his head sideways, twitching his nose.

Orbilio hadn't time for games. 'Minerva's magic, man, it's a simple enough question.'

Again the histrionic facial expressions.

'Speak up, for gods' sakes, I can't hear you.'

The legionary cleared his throat and squared his

shoulders. 'I said, she lives here, sir. Goes under the name of Melissa.'

Claudia was the first to break the silence. Never had she heard so much tosh in her life, she said. Melissa was here . . . maybe not here at this precise moment, but she was certainly around, wasn't that correct, Leonides? The steward took one pace forward, held out his hands palms upwards and shrugged. Actually, no, he mumbled, Melissa hadn't been around for a while, he'd been extremely concerned. It was one of the points he'd been trying to make since madam came home. He did stress it was a matter of urgency, he said, but was withered by a look before he could finish his explanation.

All this Orbilio absorbed through his pores. Lips were moving, voices were heard, but it was happening as though he was outside looking in, distanced from the whole affair. The sun was sinking fast now, casting long shadows across the peristyle. He could smell fish cooking in the kitchen, felt the first faint chill of the evening, heard the delivery wagons clatter along the street in the distance, yet still he hovered above it, his mind whirling. He heard a man's laugh – and started when he realized it came from himself. Dismissing Timarchides, he strode off to the slave quarters, aware of Claudia in hot pursuit. She looked pale, he thought. Vulnerable.

The cubbyhole that was Melissa's was better than most, he noted absently, undoubtedly reflecting her position in the household, but it was still little more than the size of a packing crate. For furniture, it contained a bed and a table and no more. A small looking-glass sat on the table. An oil lamp in the shape of a ram, which he lit. A pot of cream. Some hideous heathen medallion. A bottle of perfume. Without thinking, he lifted the lid – and his eyebrows arched. It was rich and exotic and spicy.

'What did you expect? That I'd put up with the chit hanging round me all day reeking of cheap scent?'

The rims of her eyes were red, he noticed; embarrassed, he turned his search towards the rest of the room. Clean underclothes. A spare tunic, showing Melissa could turn a neat needle. He knelt down and searched under the bed. One small ivory-handled knife.

'What are you looking for?'

Orbilio leaned back on his haunches. 'I'm not sure,' he said slowly. 'Something to connect her to the others, I suppose.'

'Like what?'

He weighed the knife in his hand. It could scarcely have peeled a peach, a flimsy thing like this.

'I don't know. I really don't know—Jupiter!' He'd thrown back the bedcovers automatically. 'Claudia, take a look at this!'

Exposed under the mattress was a beautiful cotton tunic, brand new by the looks of it, in the most stunning shade of apple green. He let his breath out in a whistle.

'Well, well, well.'

He had a feeling it sounded smug, but who cared? Smug was definitely how he felt. Glancing up, he saw the expression on Claudia's face was one of sheer incredulity.

'She had Crassus's obsidian brooch, you know.' Orbilio straightened up, feeling for all the world like a dog with two tails. 'Had the gall to wear it in the street, brazen as anything.' He clucked his tongue. 'Greed's what tripped her up, she was trying to sell it when the silversmith recognized it and sent for the police. In the confusion she gave them the slip.'

Once the search was complete, he rolled up the tunic, whistling as he worked. Claudia had gone.

'I thought you'd be here,' he said gently.

The house was too brightly lit, she could take refuge in the darkness of the garden. Heady floral scents drifted in the night air, although the sibilant hiss of the fountain failed to drown the sound of her sobs. He eased himself on to the seat beside her, tossing up whether to chance his arm by slipping it round her shoulders on the pretext of offering her comfort. Maybe later . . .

'I didn't realize it would upset you so much, this Melissa business, but look on the bright side—'

'A sixteen-year-old girl slashes her wrists and you think there's a bright side?'

Yes, Claudia, yes I do. Orbilio could barely contain his joy. It means you are in the clear. Completely and utterly exonerated! He wanted to sing to the heavens, dance till he dropped.

'You can see what happened, can't you? Oh, I'm not suggesting she deliberately set out to impersonate you, I'm sure she saw you as a role model.'

'Orbilio, you don't seriously expect me to believe Melissa murdered four high-ranking officials?'

In the dark he reached out, snapped off a spring of lavender and ran it through his fingers. 'No.' It was a grudging admission, but it was the truth.

'Huh! After seven months I'd have thought you'd be delighted to have your scapegoat.'

'My interest lies in the guilty, not the innocent. And no, it wasn't Melissa.'

Orbilio began stripping the lavender of its florets, one by one.

'For a start, this is a man's crime. A woman *might* be capable of driving a blade into a bloke's heart with that degree of force and accuracy, but . . .'

Together they watched the tiny blue specks blow away into the night.

'But what?'

'In my opinion, precious few women are equal to gouging out the eyes of their victims while they're still warm. There's an awful lot of blood and stringy bits and . . .' The denuded stalk dropped to the ground. 'Precious few men, come to that.'

'So where does Melissa fit in?'

Orbilio chewed his lip. He couldn't confide in her, it wouldn't be fair. 'I'll tell you that,' he replied, 'when I find where she's hidden the money.'

'What money?'

He leaned forward and lowered his voice. 'Claudia, there's something I need to—'

He was interrupted by a small head which poked itself round the pillar behind him.

'Wotcha! Heard about Publius?'

'Rufus, this isn't the time. Publius who?'

'Publius Caldus the banker. Dead as a herring, he is.' The boy made a gleeful gagging sound in his throat. 'Dagger through the heart and his eyes dug out, same as the rest of 'em.'

XVII

'Were someone to ask me to write it down, I honestly wouldn't know where to start,' Claudia told Drusilla.

She'd barricaded herself in her room; it was the only sure way to get peace and quiet these days.

'The House of Seferius has turned into Pandora's Box and had the very gates of hell been thrown wide I swear Jupiter wouldn't have more turmoil to contend with than I have.'

'Ffffrow.'

'Yes! As for you, you little hussy!' Claudia's fingernails raked up and down the cat's backbone. 'Don't think I'm fooled by this extra podge.' She gave Drusilla's tummy a gentle prod. 'I know you're carrying kittens in there.'

Not one to miss an opportunity, the cat flopped over, squirming from side to side as Claudia's fingertips tickled her soft cream underbelly. Her front claws began kneading the air. This was the time of day she liked best, when she'd had her supper and the light was failing. Moths would come out, and although she was particularly partial to moths nothing could beat cuddles with Claudia, because once she, Claudia and a jug of wine got together, Drusilla knew she was in for a session and a half. Her blue squinty eyes closed in excruciating ecstasy.

'Broop.'

'The trouble is, poppet, everything's spiralling out of hand. The minute I think I've got one aspect licked, another horror pops up. Look at this.' Claudia's hand reached out for the letter on the table. 'From Lucan, waiting for me when I got home. Very polite, he is. Requests five hundred sesterces before Wednesday. What am I supposed to do, eh?'

She crumpled the parchment into a ball and lobbed it neatly out of the window.

'I fobbed him off, of course. Sent him an equally polite letter back, enclosing fifty with the possibility of another fifty next week. I mean, you can't say fairer than that, can you?'

Sneaking fifty out of the banqueting fund was a doddle.

'I had such grand plans for raising the whole wretched sum, until Gaius scuppered it.' Claudia changed hands; her fingers were aching. Drusilla continued to knead bread in the air. 'It was that line I fed him about the galley captain which inspired me. I thought, why not put the trick into practice? Heaven knows, there are enough gullible bods in this city, I felt sure we could milk a handful without pushing our luck. And what did Gaius do?'

'Brrrr.'

'Gaius, the man who plays everything so close to his chest it gives him blisters? He blabs to the entire contingent at that bloody banquet last night how he, Gaius Seferius, wine merchant of repute, had been conned out of three hundred sesterces!'

'Brup, brup.'

Bloody banquet. A veritable farce if ever there was one. Claudia's eyes rolled at the memory. Melissa's suicide

left all manner of nightmares in its wake, not least the fact
that she'd left no notes of the arrangements she had made.
Or, to be more precise, the lack of! Consequently, of the
dancers only six Syrian girls bothered to turn up, forcing
Claudia to put them through their paces so many times
their ankles buckled under the strain. The tumblers didn't
arrive until midnight, the fire eater didn't arrive at all, nor
did the poet or the comedian or the snake charmer. The
acrobats were atrocious, and Claudia had had no qualms
in docking their money and putting it towards paying off
Lucan, but the musicians, to give them credit, excelled
themselves. It was just a pity no singers turned up to
accompany them.

A lesser woman would have spent the evening squirming with embarrassment. Not Claudia. The minute she
realized the banquet would be a fiasco, at least from
the point of view of entertainers, she announced to the
assembled party: this was to be a night of comedy.
Imagine, if they pleased, the type of revelry they could
expect if the *hoi polloi* were left to organize it. She congratulated herself, because appealing to their obscene
snobbery was an instant success. The worst thing imagin-
able was for their cosy patrician/equestrian world to be
invaded by the Great Unwashed, and so to watch the same
old dance troupe perform endlessly, hear music without
song or poetry and not even having the satisfaction of a
bawdy female impersonator went a long way towards
bolstering their own superiority. And the supreme irony
of it was, she reflected happily, none of the arrogant sods
was even remotely aware they'd been sent up!

Had it not been for Verres's genius with the feast, of
course, she'd never have got away with it, but there you

are, that's life for you. Some you win, some you lose, and that boar stuffed with live thrushes took their gluttonous breath away. As did the peacocks and cranes, the lampreys and oysters. Tomorrow, being Saturday and the Wine Festival, she could afford to give him a day off as a reward.

Another uplifting point was that although Gaius had invited Orbilio, luckily the odious little ferret had been too bogged down with Caldus's murder to attend. The immediacy of the banker's death meant that questions about alibis became a trifle touchy, but she'd handled it rather well, she thought. At least having Orbilio under her roof she'd been able to extract that poor old Publius copped it some time between five and seven, so it was relatively simple to say to her punters, hey, I waved to you in the Forum yesterday, must have been around six o'clock, why didn't you wave back? With the wine flowing plentifully and everyone having a jolly time, it was instinctive for them to reply, Me? You made a mistake, I was at such-and-such at six, or whatever. Not one of the seven hesitated . . . which meant the list was narrowing nicely.

Claudia mentally stropped the dagger which would kill the killer.

'Not that everything ran smoothly.'

'Prrrrrr.'

'Guess who found herself lumbered next to Ventidius Balbus all night, but I have to say there was nothing by way of entertainment which might have nudged his memory back to Genua. I mean, how those elephants dare call themselves dancers, I've no idea! And then demand a triple fee for it. Just because you danced non-stop, don't think you can con *me*, I told them. It's quality not quantity that counts in this household.'

'Mmmrow.'

'Balbus? Oh, you remember him, poppet. Puny little weed, eyes like boiled gooseberries. Dull as chastity, too. Spent the entire evening banging on about how he's divorcing his wife, and all I could think was bloody good luck to the little woman.'

Drusilla set one long, elegant back paw to check an itch inside her ear. Claudia was uneasy, she could tell, so she pushed her wedge-shaped face into her friend's.

'Now don't start worrying about me, Drusilla. Oh, I won't deny it wasn't harrowing, spending six hours beside the one man in Rome who might yet ruin everything, but I'm sure as eggs is eggs he didn't make the connection.'

All the same, it does no harm to avoid the boring old sod wherever possible. She drained her glass.

'But what about Junius, though? Dear Diana, you wouldn't credit such imbecility, would you?'

It had put Claudia right off her food that evening – and they were in the middle of a particularly succulent duck, too. Gaius announced, very matter of factly if you please, that he'd spoken to Junius and thanked him for saving his wife's life, et cetera, et cetera, et cetera. You're a free man, he told him, promising to draw up the paperwork, and then asked Claudia to guess what. What? she'd asked, spearing a mushroom. Well, Gaius had said, you could have blown him down with a feather, the boy insisted he didn't want his freedom. Naturally Claudia hadn't believed a word of it. Gaius was behaving oddly of late, he was getting very muddled, poor soul. Don't be absurd, she'd said. Every slave in the Empire wants his freedom! Yes, that was the point, said Gaius. It was rather rum, what? Rum, she'd muttered, was an understatement.

Was the boy simple or what? No matter. She carved herself a juicy piece of duck and slipped half to Drusilla. She'd sort out this Gaulish oddity later; there was no point in letting good fowl go to waste.

'Apparently he'd rather have the money.'

Damn!

'How much money?'

'I've given him a thousand.'

'Asses?'

'Sesterces.'

The duck stuck in her throat, and when her coughing fit eventually subsided, Gaius had actually asked:

'I think that's fair, don't you?'

She'd give Junius fair when she got hold of him! A thousand sesterces, indeed! What was wrong with the boy? She'd promised him his freedom, and instead he's copped enough money to pay off half her debt to Lucan and he's *still* hanging round the bloody house. Oh, she'd give him fair, all right.

As if I need this hassle, either. Claudia ticked the problems off on her fingers. My husband's cracking up, babbling away to himself, forgetting to do things like washing or attending his business meetings. My clients are being picked off one by one by a lunatic. I've driven my own maid to suicide, and now the whole household's jittery in case they all get punished for it. My in-laws are giving me hell on all sides, I risk exposure by a bland little civil servant with a propensity for drivel – and now Junius starts playing up. She drained the jug.

'Oh, poppet, I do feel wretched about Melissa!'

Contrary to what Orbilio had assumed from her tears, she'd neither liked nor disliked the girl, but she had trusted her. More to the point, Melissa had most definitely trusted her mistress, and it was that trust which had killed her. It was a gut-wrenching, stomach-churning sensation, knowing you and you alone bear the responsibility for the death, in some stinking alleyway, of a sixteen-year-old girl who has known nothing but misery. The days were bad enough, but at night the guilt takes on monstrous proportions. It torments you in your dreams, then it prods you awake. As there was no end to it, neither was there an answer. No refuge could be found in tears of self-pity. No amount of recrimination could bring the girl back. This was a burden Claudia would carry for the rest of her life.

'Not that the silly cow is blameless, you understand. I told her to burn those clothes, but no, she decides to make herself a tunic out of that cotton. It's her own silly fault.'

The words, she felt, might have carried more conviction had they not been hampered by sobs.

'Oh, sod the lot of them! Gaius, Balbus, Melissa, Junius, Ligarius – you heard about him, didn't you? Another one completely round the bend. According to Leonides, he's still prowling around, except at least the big ugly lump has the sense to keep his mouth shut.'

Refreshed by the tickling, Drusilla sat bolt upright and began to wash her face.

'Juno, I'll have his balls, so help me I will, if Liggy makes trouble.'

'Mmmrow.'

'Yes, and talking of trouble, that venomous old bitch Larentia isn't letting up, you know. The latest news from Rollo is that she's paralysed down her left side, and when she isn't babbling incoherently she's shouting how that filthy, gold-digging whore is trying to kill her. I tell you, Drusilla, it's like walking on splintered glass at the moment. Avoid one obstacle, and you run smack bang into another.'

Clean, invigorated, happy but sensing an end to this session, the cat stretched first the front half of her body, then the back half and leapt noiselessly down on to the rug.

'That's it, poppet, you go off and inspect your territory. It's a beautiful night, warm, the stars are out, there's a lovely half-moon and just the hint of a breeze.'

Drusilla paused on the windowsill, sniffed the air, then effortlessly launched herself into the void.

Oh, to be a cat, Claudia thought, pulling off her tunic. What a wonderful, wonderful life!

Poor old Publius. Discovered in his stables, Orbilio said, and Claudia found it difficult to keep her face straight. The happy-go-lucky banker would have seen the joke there, because he was, as everyone knew, mad about his horses. Only Claudia, however, was privy to the extent of his obsession. She'd meet him in the stables, where he'd be waiting eagerly with his clothes off (a sight not recommended for the squeamish) and a nosebag over his face. She'd slip a specially crafted bridle over his head (heaven knows what the manufacturer thought when Publius gave him the order), then the banker would go down on his hands and knees for Claudia to put him through his paces like the animal he pretended to be. Once he was well and truly fired up, she would slide a spike round the inside of each ankle, sit astride the banker's back and spur him on to victory, so to speak.

Ah, well. To each his own, she thought, climbing under the bedclothes. To each his own.

She couldn't hear it, she couldn't see it, but Claudia knew. Somebody was in her room. The hairs on her neck prickled. Gooseflesh crawled over her arms and thighs. Instinctively her body stiffened, her ears alert to pick up the slightest movement. And then she caught it. Heavy breathing followed by a long, low chuckle.

'Is no good enough, Claudia.' Whisper or no, she had little difficulty placing that voice. 'When Master Lucan ask for five hundred, he mean five hundred. He don't mean no piddling fifty.'

There was garlic on his breath.

'How did you get in?'

'Tch, tch, tch.' She saw the glint of white teeth in the darkness. 'You no ask questions like that to a man in my business.' Otho moved closer to the bed and hunkered down. 'Five hundred, Claudia. By Monday.'

Her breath was coming short and shallow. 'All right, all right. Tell him . . . no problem, he'll have his damned money. Now get out of here!'

'I do hope you no lie to me, Claudia.' A hand reached out and touched her cheek. 'Such smooth skin, it be shame to spoil it.'

The silence seemed eternal, but she couldn't bring herself to break it.

'You maybe want to deal, yes?'

'No.'

He let out a soft, sibilant chuckle. 'You no mean that,

Claudia. You have no money. I know this. You no have the five hundred.' He clambered on to the bed beside her. 'So I ask again, you want to deal?'

'I'd rather die first.'

'Suppose we talking, maybe ten sesterces?' He leaned over her. 'Ah, you push me away. That mean no, huh? Then suppose we say fifteen— *Aieeee!*'

Suddenly the huge Thracian was screeching like a banshee, clawing frantically at his face. Blood poured into his eyes.

'*Aieeee!*'

Drusilla had returned from her night patrol.

'Get it off!' he shouted, his arms flailing. 'Call your demon off.'

Claudia was still pinned beneath him, her fists pummelling his chest, when the door burst open. Light flooded the room. Strong hands clamped round Otho's throat, hauling him on to the floor. Redundant now, Drusilla leapt lightly on to the windowsill, from which vantage point she could oversee events, ready to step in again if necessary.

'What's happening?' Now Gaius's huge frame was blocking the doorway. Behind him, half the household slaves had mustered. 'Claudia, are you all right?'

Having easily overpowered the Thracian since he'd caught the man off guard, Orbilio began to truss his prey. 'Looks like this great ape was trying to rape your wife.'

'Rape, my arse! This bitch invite me, you ask her, she—'

Otho was silenced by a fist slamming into his mouth. '*Are* you all right?'

It was clear Orbilio wasn't talking to Otho and for

the first time Claudia realized she, too, was covered with blood.

'It's his,' she explained. 'I'm fine.'

'She bring demons of underworld on me,' Otho mumbled through the stream of blood pouring out of his mouth. Claudia calculated he'd probably lost a few teeth with that punch.

'No demon,' she said sweetly, brushing her hair out of her eyes. 'Just one little pussycat.'

'Demon,' he insisted. 'Torn my face to shreds.'

True, true. But don't fret, Otho, I shan't bill you for the improvement, you can just thank me later.

'Well, chum. Care to tell me who you are and what you're doing here?' Orbilio heaved the Thracian to a sitting position by the neck of his tunic. 'We'll find out sooner or later, you might as well make it sooner.'

Otho used his shoulder to wipe his mouth. 'I work for Lucan the moneylender. This bitch owe many thousand sesterces, I come to collect.'

'Is that true?'

That was Orbilio.

'Of course it's not!'

That was Gaius.

'No one collects debts at three in the morning by forcing themselves on decent, respectable, defenceless matrons.'

Matron? *Matron?* Still, she could overlook the description, she supposed, seeing as how Gaius was so valiantly sticking up for her.

'Is true, you ask Master Lucan. He confirm.'

Claudia's eyes darted from Gaius to Orbilio and back again. Orbilio, she thought, was inclined to believe the thug, circumstances or no circumstances, because hadn't Rufus blabbed about her and a big Thracian geezer on the day of the riot? Two big Thracians in a girl's life was stretching coincidence, and she knew damned well how Orbilio felt about coincidences. In Gaius's life, however, Thracians were spread particularly thin on the ground . . . She flashed her husband a look of utter helplessness and waited.

'What say we geld the bastard on the spot, Marcus?'

Bless you, Gaius!

Orbilio gave a half-smile. 'Sorry,' he said. 'This charmer goes for trial.'

'Why waste public money? Together we could—'

'No.'

'That's not fair, he's—'

'Gaius, if life was fair we wouldn't need trials in the first place. This scumbag goes to court and that's final.'

A public airing? Juno, I need leprosy more than I need that!

'I've got an idea,' she said. 'Why don't we—'

'My sweet, your cousin's quite right. Regrettable as it is, I agree we ought to hand him over.'

'But—'

'Now don't distress yourself, Claudia. I give you my word, nothing like this will ever happen again. I'll mount a permanent guard on the doors . . .'

He didn't come in through the door, Gaius!

'. . . get a dog, even.'

Cover your ears, Drusilla.

'Oh, Gaius, you're wonderful. Thank you so much.' She turned to Orbilio. 'You, too, Cousin Markie,' she added through her teeth. Dammit, twice in four days! She really had to break this habit before it went to his head.

Otho was bundled unceremoniously out of the room by the slaves, supervised by Junius, she noticed. Looks like he managed to wangle himself a promotion into the bargain, the sneaky little sod.

'Leave that,' she commanded the girl mopping up the blood. 'We'll sort it out in the morning, when the light's better.'

In truth she was feeling too weak and jittery to want a servant hanging around. What she needed was a glass of wine and a good kip!

Orbilio combed his hair with his hands. 'See you in the morning, then.'

Not if I see you first!

'Look forward to it, Marcus . . .'

Oh, shit. 'Gaius, are you all right?'

His face was contorted with pain, he was clutching his chest.

Claudia was out of bed in an instant, slipping and sliding in Otho's blood as she ran across the room, but Orbilio had beaten her to it.

'Sit down,' he was saying, leading Gaius towards the bed.

Claudia held the lamp nearer his face. Shit. It was grey. Spasms of pain wracked his huge frame.

'*Junius?* Oh, there you are. Junius, fetch a doctor, the master's ill.'

XVIII

For centuries, the Roman people had revered their gods through propitiation, be it the sacrifice of a pregnant sheep, the donation of valuables, a hefty tithe or simply the pouring of a libation to remind the immortals they had not been forgotten. From the mighty Jupiter to the humblest guardians of the storecupboard, the underlying factor was fear. And the message? Anger the gods at your peril. So with this so firmly instilled in his fine patrician blood, Orbilio couldn't fathom why Claudia's performance at the household shrine didn't so much as break his stride.

'You miserable sons of bitches,' she was saying. 'Every single day for the past four and a half years you've had more bloody attention than a bride on her wedding night. You've seen this shrine doubled in size, rebuilt in the finest Carrara marble money – and try telling me you've seen carvings to match and I'll call you liars to your faces.'

She made a great show of pouring the libation.

'Saw that, did you? Right. This is your *final* warning! I've done my bit, it's about bloody time you started doing yours, do you hear me?'

Orbilio reckoned every deity in existence probably heard her – and was undoubtedly quaking in their celestial shoes with it. 'Have you considered the possibility they've already fled in terror?' he asked mildly.

'Better still! If Gaius's ancestors were half as bad as the present lot, good riddance.'

'Not ideal, then?'

She snorted. 'His mother's a viper in human form, his sister's got feathers for brains and his daughter would try the patience of Poseidon.'

'I hear she's marrying Scaevola next month.'

'Damn right.' She sounded relieved.

'Is he the one with the weak chin and gappy teeth?'

'No, that's Marcellus, the one whose hands cover more ground than a legion on the march.'

'At least that's a problem I don't have to contend with,' he replied. 'In-laws, I mean, not your brother-in-law's wandering hands.'

In many ways, he rather wished he did have an in-law problem, because once the notion of remarrying had entered his head there seemed little he could do to dislodge it. Petronella had come round eventually, as he knew she would, but it wasn't what you'd call a satisfactory encounter. Physically, maybe (although even then he felt it was a question of going through the motions), but spiritually these casual encounters were turning more and more into emotional suicide since Claudia Seferius had crashed into his life. Like it or not, she was part of him now. Day and night she walked beside him, he saw her face in every mental picture, heard her voice in every conversation. His stomach lurched at the memory of her the other night, hair tumbling over her breasts, the moonlight on her face. In a pretence of questioning the Thracian, he'd bent over her bed to drink in the smell of her. The crumpled pillows, the spicy perfume, the brush of fine linen against his hand . . . those memories would take a long, long time to fade. Assuming he ever allowed them to.

'You'd been married, though?'

His pulse quickened. So she'd been interested enough to find out about him?

'Long ago, yes. She ran off with a sea captain and the last I heard they were holed up in Lusitania with three plug-ugly kids and a herd of goats. Or maybe it was the other way around?'

Mother of Tarquin, he loved it when she smiled. Her eyes were the colour of beechnuts, her cheeks as soft as sealskin. Orbilio folded his arms across his chest to stop himself reaching out.

'Hardly a love match, then?'

'She was a flighty piece to start with, despite her patrician blood. Frankly, I was glad to see the back of her.' He wondered why he was telling her this. More to the point, he wondered why she was listening. 'But it was the old, old story. Her father, my father, a good marriage contract. Of course, it all blew up in their faces when she ran off.'

Everyone knew Roman law and the role of the father in the family, but suddenly it was important to tell her that his own father no longer had a say in what Orbilio did.

'Her father demanded the dowry back, my father refused and so it went on. The case went to court, but unfortunately the strain was too much for the old man. He collapsed and died.'

Could he make it any plainer without shouting it out? My father's death releases me from the burden of arranged marriages, Claudia. Do you hear what I'm saying?

'Don't let Flavia hear that story; it might give the little madam ideas. Her opinion of Gaius is extremely low at the moment.'

He paused. 'And you?'

'Scaevola is an excellent choice,' she replied emphatically, leaving him with the feeling she'd deliberately misinterpreted him. 'However' – there was a flash of emotion in her eyes that he couldn't define – 'never let it be said I tried to influence the child in the matter of her marriage.'

The atmosphere had changed. A second ago it had been joky and relaxed, suddenly it was taut. He had the impression she was telling him something. Something important. But for the life of him he didn't know what. Orbilio the star-crossed lover vanished; Orbilio the investigator was pricking his ears, alive to the slightest nuance. She was polishing a spot on the marble with the hem of her tunic.

'How's Gaius?' he asked, forcing his eyes not to stare at her bare leg.

If she was surprised by the question she didn't show it. Orbilio had not only helped to carry Seferius across to his own room, he'd sat up while the doctor made his examination.

'Oh, you know my husband. The quack told him to take it easy, but Gaius went off anyway, swearing he wouldn't miss the Wine Festival yesterday, not for all the mud on the Nile. Orbilio, my patience with you is running out. Could you please explain what you're doing in my house?'

This second change in tempo threw him completely. He should have known, he thought, she was always doing this. Yet every time he found himself caught on the wrong damned foot.

'I'm still your guest, remember?'

'Uh-uh. You moved out.'

'I what?' He looked round wildly. 'Claudia, you haven't thrown my stuff into the street? Please tell me you haven't thrown my stuff into the street!'

Four days had passed since Rufus had brought the news about Caldus, four days and nights in which Orbilio had been chasing his tail following every single lead. He'd eaten when he'd remembered, slept where he dropped, practically. His eyes were gritty, his limbs where leaden, in fact he was almost dead on his feet, but, by Jupiter, he was *this close* to solving this bloody murder! The last thing he wanted to hear, when it boiled down to it, was that his clean clothes had been trampled by oxen then stolen by beggars.

'What did you expect? We'd heard neither hide nor hair of you for a week. This isn't a common tavern, you know.'

'It's been two days, don't exaggerate. And you missed me every single hour of them, admit it.'

He wanted to scoop her in his arms here and now. Whirl her round and round until they were dizzy. He wanted to pull the pins from her hair in that little pool of morning sunshine over there. Then he'd slide her rose pink tunic down – over her shoulders, her breasts, her hips. To a backdrop of splashing fountains he'd ease off her breast band, untie the tiny thong that hid her delicious feminine secrets and together they would dance under the open sky, laugh as they kissed, cry as they loved . . .

'Don't be absurd! I've got better things to do than

moon after some little upstart masquerading as a relative.'

Dammit, Claudia, you don't have to be so bloody brutal!

'Oh, stop sulking, Orbilio! I haven't thrown *all* your stuff out, just the oik. Seeing as you weren't here to do it.'

Rufus? Oh shit, he knew there was something he'd forgotten! Even as he was dashing out on Tuesday night, he had a feeling there was something he'd forgotten to do. Well, he was buggered if he was going to apologize. She was being totally irrational about the kid, anyway. Irrational *and* unreasonable!

'How did he take the eviction?' Funnily enough, he'd grown used to the lad's chirpy banter and his wily ways. He didn't like to think of Rufus fending for himself again.

'I believe he muttered something about it being my gaff, I could do what I liked in it and sodded off without another word. You could do worse than learn from him, Orbilio.'

He didn't know quite which way to take that and decided the best course was to stay silent. Watching her yawn and stretch, thrusting out those splendid breasts, he found his mouth had gone dry. Absently he sipped the wine Claudia had poured for her husband's ancestors.

'By the way, the Thracian escaped,' he said nonchalantly.

She flashed him a look. 'Why?'

Mother of Tarquin, Claudia, you're wonderful, you really are! Is it surprising no other woman matches up to you? I tell you Otho's escaped, yet you don't ask how. You don't gasp or clap your hand over your mouth in horror. You don't scream and say we must post a guard in case he comes back. You don't panic and cry What shall I do? What shall I do? You ask why.

One delectable eyebrow rose slightly. 'Orbilio, we are talking about the same gorilla who broke into my room the night before last? The one you half-strangled? The one who was reeling from that punch in the mouth? In fact, the one you personally trussed tighter than a boiling fowl?'

Orbilio spread his hands and shrugged. 'So I need more practice tying knots.'

'Well, you needn't have bothered on my account, the oaf was lying through his teeth.'

'Skip it, Claudia, you don't need to pretend with me. Whatever he was up to when I burst in, his original purpose was to deliver another warning. Am I right?'

'Tripe!'

'Notice I say another warning. I know all about the riot, Claudia. In fact,' he added quietly, 'I know just about everything.'

Melissa had been whoring, he knew that now, hence his thorough search of her room. She'd have her money stashed somewhere, that was certain, and the chances are it would be under this roof. But she'd need a pimp. Who would steer her towards these high-ranking officials? There could be only one answer, it was just a question of proving it. There *were* a couple of points that bothered him, such as why, for instance, did nobody see the killer? How could he slip in and out without attracting attention? Also, a man covered with blood would not be difficult to miss – unless his toga covered the stains. But these were minor quibbles; his curiosity would be satisfied at the confession stage. And, by Jupiter, he had no worries about extracting one. Not with the case he'd so painstakingly built up! His hardest task had been unearthing a motive. Without it, of course, he had no killer, but once he'd found the motive, Minerva's magic, it had been plain sailing all the way. One more interrogation was all he needed to clinch it.

She stared at him long and hard for at least a minute. There was a twinkle in his eye, he couldn't help it, because he knew, he just knew, she was dying to ask. She wouldn't be able to resist. Who? she'd say, and that's when Orbilio would come into his own. He'd been preparing for this moment. Nothing could throw him, not at this stage; he was ready for anything. Or was he? As an impish smile spread over her face, he had an uneasy feeling in his gut.

'You will let me know,' she said sweetly, 'when you've quite finished drinking that sacred libation to our household gods?'

Without a breath of wind in the air it was simply too hot to sit in the garden, and her bedroom was stuffy. Unfortunately, to tackle the task she had in mind privacy was crucial.

'Hey, you!'

A snap of the fingers brought a small slave boy running. Born to one of the kitchen women, Claudia had never thought to enquire who the father might be. Quite often, she thought, it was best not to know these things.

'Send Cypassis to me at once. Tell her to pack a picnic, some raisins, a dish of almonds and a bowl of plums. Oh, a flagon of wine and a glass. Hurry, now.'

The little lad beetled off, his pudgy legs stumping this way and that as he ran. Claudia's nose wrinkled. Surely the father couldn't be anyone in this house! She resolved to give the men a closer inspection in future, because if they were going to breed, for heaven's sake, they really oughtn't be allowed to spawn such ugly sprogs. She'd have to have a word with Gaius, really she would. She tucked a roll of parchment into the folds of her stola. It was high time, she decided, to make a written list of her clients because, thanks to the deluge of other problems, her mental resources had become decidedly stretched of late and it was a simple enough task on the face of it. Who's dead, who's in the clear . . . and who's still in the frame?

Her litter, its distinctive orange canopy attracting curious glances wherever it went, set her down in one of the public gardens in the Field of Mars. Once a swamp more or less encircled by a great loop of the Tiber, it had been transformed over the last ten to fifteen years into one of the most beautiful spots in the whole of Rome. Adorned by temples and baths and flanked by hills that ran down to the water's edge, the Field was all things to all men. A peaceful haven to read or gossip. A place to work out, with ball games and gymnastics. Space for chariot practice, military exercises, horse races and all manner of outdoor athletics that could be grouped under the general heading of Showing Off. Claudia settled herself on the steps of the small but elaborate temple to Anna and chewed the end of her reed pen.

The first list was simple enough. There was Tigellinus, in charge of Juturna's sacred pool. Horatius, the aedile responsible for the Megalesian Games. Fabianus, the jurist. Crassus the retired senator. And now Publius Caldus the banker. Five men who had met with an undeserved and grisly end; steps urgently needed to be taken to ensure the tally stayed at five. Not out of sentiment, particularly, but before Gaius discovered the link. Amiable as he might appear on the surface, rumour spread like a forest fire in this city and it would need but one small whiff of misdemeanour and Claudia would be out. O-U-T, out. She bit an almond in half and flicked the rest into a clump of pinks. A person had to watch their step with Gaius Seferius. Yes, indeed they did.

Glancing up, she was met by the comical sight of Cypassis staggering under the weight of a silver tray piled high with fruit and wine, a monstrous fan of ostrich plumes trailing across the grass behind her.

'You don't have to bring everything at once,' she said.

Cypassis smiled. 'Saves a second trip.'

'A longer tunic, my girl, and you'll have a different kind of trip. Now for goodness' sake, drink some of this wine and stop wheezing. No, no, you can start fanning when you've got your breath back.'

She'd found Melissa's replacement at the slave auction on Wednesday. The oil merchant's widow who Cypassis had served for the past three years was selling up and going to live with her daughter in Capua, and Claudia snapped up the bargain. Gaius expressed surprise at her choice of this big-boned girl from Thessaly, but Claudia had warmed to her instantly, attracted to her wide smile and obvious desire to please. She suspected that had Cypassis been left to her own devices she'd have tumbled not only every boy in her own village but neighbouring villages and surrounding farms as well, leaving them with smiles on their faces and warm memories in their hearts. Maybe it was something to do with the dimples in her cheeks, or maybe it was her bosom, which resembled two diving otters desperate to surface for air, but whatever the reason, Claudia reckoned those memories would have lasted them a lifetime. Reluctantly she returned to the task in hand.

List three, the list of suspects, remained depressingly long. Although she'd questioned several punters over the last few weeks and cleared them of any involvement, there always seemed to be someone she'd forgotten, another contestant for the title 'Maniac of the Month'.

'I brought you some cheese, madam.'

'What? Oh, it's pecorino! That's—'

'Your favourite. Yes, I know, madam.'

Claudia nodded appreciatively. This girl had potential, she really did. Within the space of an hour, Cypassis had made the house her home, her eyebrows twitching a come-on to the male slaves, her dimples instantly diffusing jealousy among the women. Another almond shot into the pinks. Assuming those broad hips intended to fulfil the promise made in her eyes, Claudia might need to teach her maid some tricks about contraception, because she was damned if she was going to lose this gem to childbed fever!

The gentle waving of the ostrich plumes sent ripples of pleasure down her backbone. She leaned back, closed her eyes and began to hum. It was her own special song, the one she had composed years back in Genua, plaintive, haunting, blatantly sentimental, the perfect accompaniment to the languorous dance with which she always finished her act. Or, to put it more bluntly, the perfect way of ensuring generous tips.

There was one further nominee for list three, a name she'd been reluctant to add. That of Antonius Scaevola, dammit. She liked Scaevola. For a start they enjoyed a different arrangement, since he was no pervert wanting to be trussed up and beaten, or clamped and humiliated. His was a healthy, energetic libido, all bounce and chortle. But for all that, his two previous marriages had failed to provide him with an heir, leaving him with a zest for procreation, even in middle age. Claudia bit clean through her pen and spat out the tip. Scaevola was pivotal in her plans; she couldn't think of him as a crazed killer. Dear Diana, what am I thinking of? In less than a fortnight he'll be married off to Flavia and if he doesn't get her pregnant on her wedding night he will by the second, I'll lay odds on it.

'Good morning, my sweet!'

'Gaius!'

Juno, Jupiter and Mars, look who was with him! Of all people, it was that pasty-faced twit, Balbus, staring at her with a strange half-smile on his face. The sort of half-smile that is remembering a tune and can't yet place it . . .

In her haste to stand up, the parchment fell to the ground. Faster than she could have imagined, Gaius swooped to pick it up.

'What's this, then? You? Writing a letter?'

She could barely speak, her legs had turned to aspic. 'Oh. Yes. You remember Octavia?'

He looked blank.

'Octavia whatsername. Husband's big in olive oil. Lives up on the Palatine. Seven children. Mother's a cripple.' What on earth's making her trot out this drivel? 'Well, she's sick – thought I'd drop her a note, cheer her up. Usual thing.'

'Very thoughtful. What's wrong with her?'

'VD.'

Claudia, shut your mouth before you swallow your foot altogether!

'So what brings you this way, Gaius?' She snatched the list out of his hand, surreptitiously glancing at Ventidius Balbus, who was still smiling blandly. Please, please, please don't let him make the connection!

'Oh ... things. Business ...' Gaius trailed off. 'Bumped into Balbus, you remember him?' he added by way of belated introduction.

I do, Gaius, I do. The question is, does he remember me?

'You are indeed looking lovelier than ever, Claudia.' There was little enthusiasm in his voice, but his eyes bored into hers and she decided no, she wouldn't have slept with him back in Genua. Starving and desperate she might have been, but never suicidal.

There was a brief lull, then Claudia's prayers were answered when a short, bald-headed man came puffing up.

'Ventidius, what luck! I was just on my way to your office.'

Apparently some property that Balbus had been interested in purchasing had suddenly come up for sale, and so linking her arm through Gaius's, as much for her own support as for his, Claudia made what she hoped were polite noises at Balbus's departure. As she fell into step with her husband, she thought again he looked old. Really old. His eyes were sunken, his cheeks seemed to have collapsed and several times recently she'd stumbled upon him sobbing like a baby.

'You look tired, Gaius. I think you overdid it yesterday.'

'Oh, don't fuss. It was only a mild seizure, the doctor said so. Besides, what would people think if I missed the Festival of Wine? What good would that be for business, eh?'

'Seferius wine tells its own tale, Gaius.'

'Yes, but to miss the augur pronounce the vintage? Claudia, how could I not attend?'

She snorted. 'With Flavia's wedding coming up, you should take it easy, conserve your strength . . .' She paused as a thought struck her, and indicated to Cypassis by a gesture to hang back so she could speak more privately. 'Gaius, exactly *what* are you doing out here this morning?'

'The, er, library, my dove—'

She stiffened and snatched her hand back. 'Liar! You've been to one of those foul little backstreet parlours, haven't you?'

'Don't look at me like that, I've been discretion itself. We agreed—'

She made no effort to hide her contempt. 'Don't tell me what we agreed, Gaius, you conned me into marriage.'

'Hardly conned, Claudia. I didn't realize you wanted children, I thought after three you wouldn't want any more.'

'They died, Gaius.' Dammit, now she couldn't even remember how old this fictitious brood was! 'Of course I wanted more.'

Tears filled the big man's eyes. 'My son – my babies, Claudia. There's only little Flavia left. You can surely forgive a man his pleasures now and again?'

Claudia scrunched her list into a ball and pummelled it.

'Your letter . . . Claudia, what about your letter?'

'What about it?' she snapped, hurling it into a grove of lotus trees. 'Couldn't stand the woman, anyway.'

If Orbilio was half as clever as he made out, she wouldn't need the bloody list. She'd kill the bugger long before it got to the confession stage, even if it meant poison.

Gaius stood staring at her, his face haggard but his jaw set. 'I'm sorry you feel I've let you down, but this is the way it is, Claudia.'

'I accepted that long ago, but if I find it's anyone I know' – the unspoken name hung in the air between them – 'a day won't pass when you don't live to regret it, Gaius, you have my solemn promise on that.'

XIX

Paternus the lawyer was dictating to his scribe when the stranger arrived.

'I bring a message from your brother, sir. Says it's a matter of exceptional delicacy and under the circumstances he would be obliged if you would treat it with the same confidentiality you bestow on all your cases and mention it to no one.'

The messenger then coughed politely. 'Including your scribe, sir.'

Paternus leaned back and rubbed the furrows in the bridge of his nose. He didn't recognize the messenger, but then again he rarely did. This one wore the long, dark hair of a Cretan. He didn't like Cretans.

'You purport to be from Caius Paternus, is that correct?'

'Yes, sir.'

'Are you employed by him?'

'Oh, no, sir. Freelance. The name's Milo, should you ever need my services. No message too complex, no distance too . . .'

The look in the lawyer's eye quelled his sales pitch.

'Well, Milo,' Paternus's reedy voice made the name sound unclean, 'perhaps you would be so kind as to furnish me with the address from which you were dispatched?'

'The large red house up on the Aventine, sir. The front part is let as a poulterer's, there are two—'

'Yes, yes, that's quite sufficient.'

So it wasn't an error. Paternus chewed the inside of his lower lip. Would wonders ever cease? he asked himself. He hadn't heard from his brother in – what? – oh, it must be seven, eight months now, that's right, December. And now, like one of Jupiter's thunderbolts, he sends a message out of the blue. Well, Caius can go to hell, he thought. That business over the slander case had driven such a wedge between them that, personally, he'd be quite happy never to see or hear from his brother again.

He looked down his long nose at the Cretan, treating him to one of the interminable silences for which he was famous in court. At the same time he could sense, rather than see, his scribe's interest picking up moment by moment. Should he decide to despatch the fellow, no doubt he'd have his wretched ear to the door, given half a chance. Servants are like that these days, no breeding, no dignity. In court, Paternus's silences were tools to impress and unnerve. Today, however, he was thinking. In particular, he was thinking about Publius Caldus, the latest official to fall victim to this crazed killer. Outside he could hear the chants of children reciting their alphabet, the rattle of a chariot on the stones, the crush and chatter of the market. The sweet smell of fruit ripening in the hot sunshine filtered in through the open window. It wasn't wise to be left alone these days, he thought. Not wise at all. On the other hand (and he was a lawyer, after all), it had to be argued that Caldus had been killed just days previously and the last murder was how many weeks ago?

Five? Six? Paternus pursed his lips. Why not take a chance? Good heavens, the man was hardly likely to pull out a dagger and kill him in his own office, was he? He smiled to himself. Ridiculous, he thought. Utterly ridiculous. Yet it was a sad reflection that a man grows wary of venturing out alone and has to think twice before being left with a stranger. It was all very well Callisunus giving assurances that it was only a matter of time. What consolation was that to the banker's widow, or indeed the hundreds of law-abiding Romans holding down responsible posts who were unable to sleep at night for fear of a maniac? Overreaction was becoming the norm.

'There are some papers to collect from old man Roscius,' he said to his scribe, finding a certain pleasure in watching the fellow's face fall. He glanced at the messenger. He can wait, he thought. Let him sweat. Paternus himself waited until his scribe had not only left the room but crossed the Forum and passed under the Arch of Augustus before turning to the Cretan.

'Very well, then,' he said wearily. 'Let's have the message.'

Milo was used to waiting, it was part of his routine. The fact that this snotty-nosed lawyer was trying it on didn't bother him one bit. He was only one of the equestrian order, after all, and although Milo himself could never hope to aspire to the ranks, nor in all probability his son, his grandson – the third generation freeborn – might manage it. So this clever dick didn't bother him one iota.

'First, your brother said to give you this.'

Slowly – almost insolently – he reached into his pouch,

drew out a seal and passed it across to Paternus. When the lawyer realized what he was holding he sat up straight and looked the messenger in the eye.

'You know what this is?'

Milo nodded. 'Yes, sir.'

Paternus wiped his bony hand across his mouth. Remus, this was the sphinx. The seal of the Princeps himself! My, it must be a serious matter indeed for Caius to be involved at this exalted level. And just what was the extent of his brother's involvement? As an aedile, he organized some of the games. Had Augustus approached him that way? Or could Caius, out of charity and brotherly love, have dropped his name into the Emperor's ear? Paternus nodded slowly. Maybe it wasn't such a bad time to bridge the divide. After all, they were kith and kin, weren't they? And to be honest, when Caius accused him of pocketing half the damages on that wretched slander case, one couldn't say he was totally wide of the mark.

'And the message, Milo?'

Oh, attentive now, are we? When the Emperor's involved! Suddenly the name Milo isn't so offensive to your fastidious tongue.

'The message, sir, is could an envoy of . . . the owner of the seal meet you in your house at noon? You will understand the sensitivity of the issue, your brother said. Would you please dismiss your slaves and leave the side door unlocked for the envoy to slip in.'

Paternus glanced at the seal. No doubts concerning its authenticity. Only Augustus used the sphinx and the penalty for forgery was . . . death.

'Naturally. Anything else?'

Poor weedy sod was actually licking his lips. 'Yes, sir.

You must be certain not to speak of this to anyone, even your family, and I am to deliver your assurance back to your brother forthwith by returning the seal to him.'

'Then, Milo, you must give him that assurance.' Paternus passed the seal back, watching it disappear into the messenger's pouch. 'Tell him – oh, tell him my lips are *sealed*. It's a joke, man. Sealed? Seal?' Remus, these Cretans had no sense of humour. 'Great heavens, it's nearly noon now.'

He stood up and reached for his toga.

'Yes, sir. Will that be all, sir?'

Damn the fellow, he was hinting for a tip!

'Yes, Milo, that will be all.'

Bloody money-grabbing Cretans, all the bloody same.

'No, wait.' Paternus pressed a silver denarius into the man's palm. If, as he suspected, the Princeps needed legal assistance outside his usual sphere – and this implied fraud (or worse) within his own household – then the name of Paternus would be on everybody's lips and he didn't want to acquire a reputation for being a skinflint. A denarius was excessive, he knew that, but the alternative was a measly couple of asses; it was all he carried.

'Help me on with this, will you?'

'Of course, sir. Thank you, sir!'

Milo's estimation of the man hadn't altered, he still found the lawyer an arrogant, pompous snob, but a denarius was a denarius. He could still afford to help this little worm with his toga before delivering the necessary assurance to the man's brother with time to spare, and hopefully – you never know – generosity might be a family trait.

Once the Cretan had left, Paternus hurriedly tidied his

office, rolling up his papers and locking them in his private chest. It was always possible, of course, the word envoy was a euphemism . . . ? He toyed with the idea of leaving a note for his scribe but decided against it. What was an hour or two out of the office? The scribe could handle the next client, he'd probably begin work on the Roscius case without being told, anyway.

Paternus was whistling by the time he'd dimissed his slaves, going so far as to slip them a few quadrans each so they could pass the time shopping, because he could afford to be generous; this commission would set him up for life. He changed his tunic, slapped on some of his wife's perfume – lightly, of course – and laid out wine and fruit in readiness. Simple pleasures for the Princeps, he remembered. Nothing fancy, nothing showy. Not that he expected Augustus to turn up in person, but it never hurt to be prepared for every contingency. He began to pace the atrium. The Princeps would approve, seeing that the décor was in keeping with the African campaign. Was it noon yet? Couldn't be far off. He glanced out of the window. The street was teeming, as usual, nothing out of the ordinary. But then again, if the Emperor was planning a low-key visit, there wouldn't be anything unusual, would there? He checked the bedroom. Ridiculous! As if his wife had crept back unannounced! Besides, she was always at the baths until one. He thought he heard a noise and darted back into the atrium. Nothing. Must be noon. Must be! Now, why did he need to check the boys' room? They were both at school. Jupiter, he'd never seen the house so empty! A man can hear his own footsteps; hell, he can even hear his own breathing. Should he have worn a toga, as a mark of respect? It was customary for a man to dispense with the formality under his own roof, so might not Augustus think he was overdoing it? No, the clean tunic was fine. It was well after noon now; what had happened? He could feel the sweat on his palms, down his back, between his toes. Well, he'd just check there was no one left hanging around in the kitchen.

'Jupiter, you made me jump!'

He hoped the flatness in his voice was attributed to nerves, rather than the disappointment that he felt on not seeing the Emperor in person. However, an envoy was still an envoy, and – oh, for pity's sake, what was the man's name? He shouldn't have let the fellow walk in without being greeted with the honour due to him; what was the matter with him? So absorbed in the Princeps and possible reasons for the visit, he wasn't paying attention.

'Welcome, sir, to my humble—'

'Ssshh!'

The visitor put a finger to his lips. Paternus had spoken to him often enough, he was a client, for heaven's sake, albeit some time back, but for the life of him the name eluded him.

'Ah!' His voice dropped to a whisper. 'You've come about the . . . delicate matter?'

The man nodded and glanced round. 'Where can we talk?'

Paternus ushered him into the small dining room, the most opulent room in the house with its walls of pink marble and a hunting scene mosaic. He could feel his face flushing with pleasure at being picked for this most supreme honour. Just as well he'd followed the instructions to the letter. Had but one slave been in evidence, the Princeps would have written him off as indiscreet. Paternus rubbed his hands together. He always knew he'd make it big one day. How many times had he told that disbelieving wife of his that he'd make the big time soon?

'So what is it?' he asked, reaching for the yellow glass flagon. 'Fraud? Theft? Adultery?'

Oh yes, adultery! Julia, the Emperor's daughter, had been making such a spectacle of herself lately. That would be it. He'd be looking for someone with a low profile but a good track record to handle the case.

'In a manner of speaking, yes.' His illustrious visitor divested himself of his toga.

'Julia's?'

The man smiled. 'No,' he said, rolling an apple in the palm of his hand. 'Yours, actually.'

Paternus had been too busy pouring wine to notice the flash of blade. He felt what seemed like a punch to his chest, felt his heels lift clean off the floor with the jolt. His mouth dropped open and only when he looked down did he see the handle of a dagger protruding from his breast. Stunned and helpless, he pitched forward on to his knees. Somewhere in the back of his mind it registered that the envoy had now divested himself of his tunic and was standing stark naked in front of him. Then the pain hit him, surging through his body like white lightning. Relentless, remorseless.

'Not my eyes,' he gasped. 'Please, not my eyes.'

''Fraid so, old chap,' his murderer said pleasantly, smiling down at him. 'You've seen her, you see. Can't have that, can we?'

Paternus could feel the room spinning. Ineffectively he clawed at the dagger, felt a strange gurgling sensation in his throat, a ringing in his ears. The wine he'd been pouring had spilled over the mosaic, dribbling among the ridges of the tesselae. Soon, he realized, his blood would be mingling with it. How could he, Paternus, the lawyer of all people, have let himself be duped so easily?

'Pity. Have pity!'

The room was growing dark. He could barely distinguish between the lion on the mosaic and the wine spill. Mighty Mars, take this life of mine as sacrifice and strike the bastard dead on the spot! Don't let him take my eyes. Mars the Avenger, I implore you now. Take vengeance for me!

'She's only a wh-wh-whore.'

The envoy had to lean forward to catch the words. 'Claudia Seferius? Oh, Paternus, that was a very foolish thing to say. You *can* hear me, can't you?'

Paternus nodded. His sight might be failing, his strength almost gone, but his hearing was intact, and the pain no less excruciating.

'Take . . . the . . . dagger . . . out.' It was his only hope now. Hasten his death, put an end to this agony. 'P-please.'

Never before had he put so much of himself into one small word. The man would be inhuman to sit and watch him die like this! Paternus knew about the other murders. A quick thrust to the heart. Instant death. And if it wasn't immediate – well, the moment the blade came out, it was all over and done with.

He heard the man suck his breath through his teeth. 'Can't do that, Paternus. Not when you've called the woman I love a whore.'

'S-sorry. I'm s-sor-ry. D-didn't m-mean it.'

The searing pain in his chest had spread to his head. 'T-take the b-blade out. P-please!'

He could feel tears burning a path down his cheek. Surely no man, even this lunatic, could feel anything but pity now? A man crying and begging for his life? He realized he would never see his boys again. They'd grow to manhood and he wouldn't be able to steer them through the pitfalls of adolescence, he wouldn't be able to arrange decent marriages for them, he'd never know what it was like to play with his grandchildren.

'See this, Paternus?'

In his closed dark world of pain, he managed to make out the glint of a blade. Mercy! He'd been released from his torture. Then his breath caught in his throat. This was a different, smaller blade. Used for cutting fruit.

'Your heart's in a different place from the others,' the voice went on, calmly and pleasantly. 'Divine intervention, don't you see? You called her a whore, Paternus, and for that you must pay. Yes, indeed. You do know how, don't you?'

Numbly the lawyer shook his head.

'No? Come, come, think, man!'

But Paternus couldn't think. Pain was searing every muscle, every sinew, every blood vessel. He squeezed his eyes tight with every agonizing wave – and then it dawned on him what this maniac meant to do.

'*No!* For gods' sakes, man, no!'

He didn't think he had the strength left to scream. In fact, he didn't realize he had strength left at all until he felt the ice-cold metal brush against his cheek and the sound of inhuman laughter echo in his ears.

XX

Callisunus was waiting for him in the underground temple of Consus, his florid cheeks redder than usual, the fury on his face etched deeper from the flickering torchlight. Orbilio wasn't late for the appointment, far from it, yet he had a feeling that whatever was bothering Callisunus would be dumped upon his own shoulders as sure as the cock would crow in the morning and dogs would bark in the night. It was turning into that sort of a day.

His footsteps echoed in the dank, hollow chamber as the sacred attendants paused to scrutinize the intruder, resentment bouncing off them in waves. Who could blame them, he thought. Overhead a small army battled to prepare the Circus Maximus for the chariot races tomorrow, while below they were still eons away from digging out the altar. He wanted to shout at them, tell them to put their backs into the job, because they were shovelling soil as though they were a bunch of lovesick maidens mucking out pigshit, but he couldn't, of course. Not in front of Callisunus. And especially not today. With a muted sigh Orbilio saw the little man was drumming his fingers against his thigh – always a bad sign – and wished the omens were more favourable for the extension of time he needed to ask for.

It seemed an odd choice for a meeting, underground,

during the annual excavation of the altar before its ritual reburial. Furthermore, Callisunus had no connection regarding tomorrow's festival, so why pick this place? Privacy couldn't be a factor. A portent of new communication lines reflecting Rome's increasing addiction to intrigue? Orbilio ran one hand through his hair. He thought not. In fact, so strongly did this smack of celestial involvement, he could almost hear the conversation. There was Jupiter, picking ambrosia out of his teeth.

'Terrific wheeze, having that Orbilio chappie brought to book at two shrines in one day, don't you think, Juno?'

'Not half, darling, and if you hang on just a minute I'll see if I can't round up Apollo, he enjoys these gags.'

Come to think of it, Orbilio decided he wouldn't be surprised if Venus, Diana and Neptune didn't tag along as well. They could make a whole bloody picnic of it.

'Made the arrest?'

Beads of sweat broke out on Orbilio's forehead. The ignominy of drinking the Seferius libation was shame enough, but did she really have to laugh quite so enthusiastically? Mother of Tarquin, the more he squirmed the more it amused her, until in the end tears were streaming down her face. Marcus, you can be such a bloody fool at times, how can you ever hope to—

'Pay attention, man! I'm asking you whether you've got a confession yet.'

'What? Oh, sorry, sir, I was, er – I was just wondering whether they need help digging out the altar?'

Say no! Please say no! If you say yes I won't have time to wind up the case, and you'll never give me another day's grace, I know it.

The little man's manner seemed to take a swift upturn.

'You know, Orbilio, that's an extremely generous offer.'

Bugger.

Callisunus tapped the side of his mouth with his finger. 'Though I think, on balance, it won't be enough. I'll need to bring a slave gang in.'

Orbilio's head was buzzing. His mind, already a seething cauldron of logic and emotion, torn as it was between concentrating on his case and brooding about Claudia, was suddenly thrown into utter confusion. *I haven't heard right. My boss – and let's be clear on this, we're talking about the Head of the Security Police, here – is involving himself with . . . harvest rituals? Can't be. No way! I'm cracking up.* His mouth was dry, he needed a drink. In fact, he needed several drinks.

'I will not allow it, Paulus.'

Orbilio turned round. *What the . . . ? There were two of them, for gods' sakes. Two Callisunuses? No, no, pull yourself together, man.*

'I simply cannot permit a bunch of heathen slaves down here when I am trying to prepare my sacrificial rites.'

Holy shit, Callisunus was talking to himself. Or rather, he was talking to the second Callisunus, the one dressed in a thick woollen cloak and wearing a pointed cap on his head.

I am, I'm going mad. Marcus Cornelius Orbilio won't be remembered as the chap who solved those gruesome murders, he'll be known as the chap who couldn't handle the pressure and ended up a headcase. Stark, staring bonkers. Spends all his time locked in his room, poor fellow. Really? Oh yes, tragic case. Had such a bright future at one stage, too. Orbilio pressed the heels of his hands into his eyeballs. Jupiter, unless he pulled himself together, and he meant right now, he could kiss the Senate goodbye, that's for sure.

Callisunus – the Callisunus he was familiar with, the one drumming his fingers – turned to the other Callisunus, the one who was dripping with sweat and had his hands on his hips.

'Marius, you arsehole, at the rate you and those other fairies are digging there won't be a fucking sacrifice.'

'There is no need to be offensive!'

Orbilio blinked, and blinked again. I'll be damned, he thought, blowing his nose to cover his laughter. Twins. They're bloody twins! Keeping his handkerchief over his mouth, he studied Marius, the brother. Same squat build, same piggy eyes and wonky nose, and yet there was an ocean of difference between them now he looked carefully. A sensitivity in the priest's face which was lacking in the policeman's; a shrewdness in the policeman's, which was lacking in the priest's. And suddenly the comedy opened his eyes to a world he'd not previously entered. The world of illusion. What you see isn't necessarily what is real, he thought with a start. The dank humidity began to cloy as the most significant piece of his puzzle, leastways as far as he was concerned, slotted into place. His very blood seemed to congeal and he decided the taste in his mouth owed nothing to the acidity of the earthy air around him.

'You've dug yourself into this hole and if I'm to bail you out, you brainless cretin, I'll be as offensive as I fucking well like.'

The pointy hat drooped slightly to the left. 'Is it my fault I get the date wrong?' Marius threw up his hands. 'I have not been well lately, but do you care? My own brother, and he ignores me.'

He turned to Orbilio, who forced himself to follow the conversation as though nothing had turned his world upside down.

'Do you have brothers?'

He was given no chance to either nod or shake his head.

'Do yours leave you at death's door? I should say not. You know, I could have *died* the other night.' He lowered his voice and whispered, 'It was the fish, I swear it—'

Callisunus grabbed his brother by the shoulders and shook him. 'Marius, you self-absorbed prat, I suggest you take that fish and shove it right up your arse.' He marched towards the steps to the Circus, jerking his head to indicate Orbilio should follow him. 'My own brother, can you believe it? Jupiter, he really pisses me off at times!'

Callisunus human at last? Could it be? Encouraged by the sudden (not to say unexpected) uplift in his fortunes, Orbilio raced up the steps after him, eager to capitalize on the moment. He was aware of Marius following in his wake. The glare of the late afternoon sun made him squint as a pungent smell of horseflesh slammed into his nostrils.

'I need another day, sir.'

The Head of the Special Police stopped in mid-stride. 'Tell me I didn't hear that.'

'One more day, that's all.'

Callisunus barged aside a charioteer. 'We've been through this, Orbilio. Tomorrow you start work on the Verianus fraud case.'

The cracking pace he set down the length of the racetrack presented no obstacle for Orbilio's long legs. Behind them, however, the priest was rapidly losing ground. His thick cloak flapped like heavy flightless wings, his conical hat wobbled precariously. Callisunus glanced round, tutted and stopped short.

'My brother is a right pain in the arse,' he said, casting his eyes over the seats banked up the side of the auditorium. 'But tomorrow a quarter of the city's going to pack itself into this place, including my good self, so if Consus doesn't get his honouring of first fruits, it'll fuck things up good and proper.'

The priest of the festival was wheezing like a pair of bellows and had to support himself on the low wall which divided the track down the centre. When he realized the dark stains he was leaning against were dried blood, he quickly jumped away again.

Orbilio felt his moment melting away. It was now or never. Callisunus would not have the patience to grant his request after another round with his brother.

'One more day, sir, and I'll tell you why.'

'Forgive me, Paulus, it was not my intention to annoy you. The slave gang will be fine, honestly.'

Callisunus looked from one to the other, using the same expression of exasperation for both men. If he chose to hear his brother, Orbilio was sunk, his rosy future little more than mucky brown, and for the first time he began to realize what it must be like for a defeated gladiator to beg the crowd for pardon. For Callisunus to turn to him would be the thumbs-up, while if he turned to the priest . . .

The Head of the Security Police had no problem deciding which irritant to brush off first. 'Marius—'

It really was turning into a pig of a day.

'Marius, where the fucking hell do you think I'm going? I'm on my way to organize your fucking slave gang, so go back and fucking dig, will you? Because if by tomorrow morning every fucking flower and fruit known to man isn't garlanding your altar, your fucking head will be. Got it?'

The priest smiled ingratiatingly, and as he did so the spiked skull cap plopped into the sand. Swooping down to retrieve it, the bronze buckle holding his cloak fell off, and the moment his fingers closed round the clasp his woollen cloak slid into a pile of steaming horse dung. Callisunus closed his eyes and shuddered.

'Oh dear, oh dear. I do hope I am not embarrassing you, Paulus.'

Callisunus could take no more. He shook his head and began to march down the track in the direction of the Tiber, the lengthening shadows implying a deceptive cool-ness in the air. Orbilio kept pace in silence, and when he glanced back he noticed Marius was still encountering difficulty with his priestly garb and wondered how he coped when he had to wear the laurel wreath as well. The god of the harvest store deserved far better, he thought. Of course, Marius would only have landed the job because of his brother's influence, the same as this oily bastard only landed his own job because he'd fawned and flattered every rung of the ladder. For a man of the equestrian order, however, the position was nevertheless a remarkable achievement – even for a fathead like Callisunus, doggedly maintaining the killings were random in spite of the evi-dence laid before him. He sighed in the deepening gloom. Not that Callisunus, whose breadth of vision extended little further than the tip of his pug nose, looked upon these conclusions as evidence.

'Bollocks!' he'd said, when Orbilio had finished outlining his case. 'Gossip, hunch and innuendo, the lot of it. You mark my words, this is the work of a maniac, picking his victims at random, and at the end of it you'll find he's been hearing voices urging him to do it. Divine retribution or some such shit, see if I'm not right.'

Orbilio supposed that having expressed this opinion so often and so vehemently to the Princeps when he made his weekly report Callisunus was hardly likely to retract without cast-iron proof. Which could only come in the form of a confession. Well, he was buggered if he was going to be sidelined on to some damned fraud case for the sake of one lousy interview, and if this quick-tempered, foul-mouthed, narrow-minded weasel thought he could brush Marcus Cornelius Orbilio aside just like that he had another think coming. The Senate beckoned . . . and competition was stiff. Unless he solved this bloody case, he might as well forget it.

At the obelisk at the end of the track, Callisunus stopped abruptly. 'I don't need a bodyguard, Orbilio. Even this lunatic wouldn't pick on the Head of the Security Police.'

'He's not a lunatic, sir. Leastways, not in the sense you mean. Another day and—'

'Orbilio, watch my lips. You are off the case. Finished. End of story. You've even put in your report.'

'Only verbally.'

'Yes, and I warned you about that, too. I don't want to see these scurrilous lies on paper, do you understand? For your sake, as much as mine. I told Seferius what you said—'

'You what?'

Anger boiled through Orbilio in a way he'd never imagined possible. The bloody imbecile! 'This was supposed to be a covert operation, sir.' How many more had he blabbed to, for heaven's sake?

'Oh, come on, man, what did you expect? You've been masquerading as his wife's cousin, how much longer do you think before he found out? What is it with you and her, anyway? Got your leg over?'

Orbilio's fist thudded into the palm of his hand. 'No, sir,' he said quietly, 'I have not. I told you before, I had a hunch about the house and forgive me for saying so, but that hunch proved correct.'

The sun was sinking fast now.

'The little slut Melissa, you mean?' Callisunus gave a snort of derision. 'So she'd been giving Crassus a bit of hanky-spanky, nothing wrong with that. Partial to a spot of it myself sometimes. You just remember, Orbilio, her involvement was only discovered because the greedy bitch tried to sell that poor bugger's clip, not through any cleverness on your part.'

'I understand that, sir. But—' Should he or shouldn't he? Hell, at this stage he had nothing to lose. 'There's something else.'

Callisunus chewed his thumbnail. 'Oh?'

'I believe there's a series of murders going on in the Seferius household.'

'Don't fuck with me, Orbilio!'

Damn! It sounded so utterly inane when you said it like that.

'Please, sir, hear me out. First it was his eldest daughter, then his two sons. Now his new granddaughter is dead.'

'Seferius is full of this shit at the moment, you shouldn't listen to him, it's pitiful coming from a man like him.'

Callisunus swatted away a troublesome wasp.

'The babe was an abomination. They put it out of its misery—'

'Who, sir? *Who* put it out of its misery?'

'Oh, get real, Orbilio, the child was malformed, they killed it. Happens all the time. Now will you clear the hell out of my face!'

'No, sir!'

'I'm warning you, Orbilio. One more word and I'll have your balls for subordination.'

Have them, they're no bloody good to me.

'If you would listen to the full story, sir—'

'If, if, if! The world's full of if's, haven't you noticed? Well *if* you have reasonable grounds for opening a case, and by Jupiter I do mean reasonable, then put them in writing, to me, and I will consider them.'

Callisunus skirted the obelisk and set off towards the gate.

'Does that mean I can work on the case, sir?'

'What case, Orbilio? There isn't a fucking case, I haven't had your fucking notes yet. And even if there fucking was, you won't be fucking working on it. Do I make myself plain?'

There was a shout from behind, different from the cries of the charioteers and the slaves working in the Circus, which made both men turn. Orbilio recognized the man running towards them as Timarchides.

'Sorry to interrupt, sir, but you ought to know. Paternus the lawyer's been found dead in his home.'

'Shit!' Callisunus glanced towards the underground shrine. 'Timarchides, organize a slave gang to dig out the altar. About ten men should do it. Oh, before you do that I want you to brief Metellus about the lawyer.'

'Metellus?'

Timarchides was looking from Callisunus up to Orbilio and back again.

'Deaf, are you? Yes, Metellus. He's working this case from now on.'

Callisunus turned to Orbilio. 'And you. Get some sleep, get laid, get whatever you want, but get the fuck out of my sight. Tomorrow's the Consualia and I'll be holding my idiot brother's hand, but the very next day I want your views on the Verianus business. Tuesday morning, is that clear? And in writing.'

He stumped back up the track, muttering to himself.

Timarchides twisted his face. 'Off the job then, sir?'

'Looks like it,' Orbilio said, narrowing his eyes. 'Unless I can work two cases at once.'

Timarchides smiled. He'd worked with this investigating officer for the past four days and his opinion of him had softened considerably since he'd brought the news about the slave girl to the Seferius house. He'd watched the professional at work, seen more dedication from one man in those few days than in as many years from some of the men he'd served.

'I'd give it my best shot, if I were you, sir. Two murders in six days, looks like the killer's getting daring.'

A warm glow began to spread through Orbilio's veins. 'And daring, Timarchides, means careless.'

'Precisely, sir. And I'll tell you something I didn't have a chance to tell the gaffer: Paternus was still alive when his eyes were gouged out. There was blood everywhere; it must have been one hell of a struggle.'

He saluted and ran back up the track in the direction Callisunus had taken, his figure quickly swallowed by the deepening twilight. Orbilio ran his hand over his chin and headed for the nearest exit. He didn't need sleep, he was too worked up. He couldn't get laid, the very thought of touching any other woman was becoming more abhorrent by the minute. But, by Jupiter, he could get drunk. Oh yes, mind-bending, brain-numbing, sick-making drunk. He turned out of the Circus and towards the river. There was a good tavern down on the waterfront. The men were rough, the whores were raddled, the food was rubbish. But the wine was strong. Minerva, yes, that wine was strong.

'Marcus!'

Head down, thinking about the evening ahead, he hadn't been looking where he was going and of all the people he'd rather not have bumped into, Gaius Seferius headed the list. Dammit, he liked Gaius. He wished he didn't, but he just couldn't help it.

'What brings you to the Aventine?'

'I'm going to get pissed,' he said simply. 'Rip-roaring pissed.'

Seferius smiled wanly and clapped him on the back. Even after Callisunus had blabbed that Orbilio wasn't his wife's cousin, it didn't seem to bother him. In his book, a friend was a friend and Orbilio felt disgusted at his own treachery. How would Claudia explain it, he wondered, cursing himself for forcing her into such an invidious position. But then she'd think of something outrageous to pass it off, she always did. It was one of the reasons he loved her.

'You know, Marcus, I think that's the best suggestion I've heard all week. Mind if I join you?'

He looked at Seferius. Poor sod looked seventy, not fifty, and it was all very well for Callisunus to shrug off his theories, but Orbilio believed it when Gaius said his babies, as he called them, were being picked off, one by one, like ripe fruit from a tree. He didn't believe in coincidence at the best of times. Certainly not when three of a man's four children meet untimely deaths and his baby granddaughter – healthy, kicking and thumping to get out by all accounts – is suddenly pronounced malformed and hideous and gets put to the sword. Not when there's a fortune at stake. Gaius was right, Orbilio was convinced of it. Someone was murdering his family.

He wished his own father had been more like Gaius. Jovial, loving, dedicated. But more than that, he wished – Juno, how he wished – that he could hate this man who had married a red-blooded vixen with skin like thistledown and eyes the colour of beechnuts. No doubt if he thought the man's big hands kneaded Claudia's magnificent breasts on a regular basis it would be a different matter. In fact if Orbilio thought of him between her thighs, grunting and groaning, his huge belly pressed into her soft flesh, quite likely he'd kill him.

'Why not, Gaius?' he said at last, wrapping his arm round the big man's shoulder. 'Why the hell not?'

XXI

The familiar sensations returned with a vengeance. Even after an absence of several weeks where, for one reason or another, the games and the races had been out of reach, Claudia felt the age-old tingle of excitement, the rush of colour in her cheeks, the rapid heartbeat long before the first blast on the trumpet or the first beat of the drums. With half of Rome scurrying to escape the punishing summer heat, you'd think there'd be more empty seats, but the place was practically full. Something to do with celebrating a good harvest, she supposed. Which was all right if you were into peas and beans and olives and things and enjoyed watching that half-baked priest make a fool of himself. Idiot! Tripping over his cloak and knocking himself out on the underground altar, right under the noses of the Vestal Virgins, too. Claudia would lay money that next year Consus's festival runs as smooth as a water-clock . . . without the interference of that bumbling dwarf in the silly hat.

She watched the nobles take their seats, the best in the Circus to befit their status, her eyes automatically sweeping to see where Orbilio might be sitting. Not that she was interested in this particular patrician personally, but if he was attending these wretched races, it would do no harm to avoid the irritating little tick, would it? A hush settled over the auditorium. Some puffed-up little state official, feeling superior in his purple robe and gilded laurels, thought he could brook convention by making a speech. The crowd quickly taught him otherwise and, crestfallen, he dropped his white napkin sullenly into the sand, and that was it. Business began in earnest!

Claudia tapped her foot. The preliminaries were entertaining, she supposed, on a superficial level. If you enjoyed this leaping from horse to horse lark or riders standing on their heads, fine; it was all very clever, except it lacked the element of chance to which she was addicted. Junius, thank heavens, was stationed in his usual place, though for once she hadn't given him any money to bet with. She'd regret it, she knew she would, but she simply had to knuckle down and do things by the book for a while. What the hell? It wasn't as though playing the dutiful wife was a novelty, she'd kept up the pretence for virtually the first year of her marriage; the discipline would do her good.

So why, then, was her mouth so dry?

Junius hadn't turned out to be the problem she anticipated. Suspecting blackmail, she tried wheedling, she tried bullying, but eventually came to the conclusion that she might have done the boy an injustice. Whatever motive kept him under the Seferius roof, it was a mighty powerful one, because the young Gaul was adamant. He did not want his freedom, thank you all the same. It rankled like hell that he'd pocketed a grand merely for the privilege of having his ribs cracked, and had it been left to Claudia she'd have given him his marching orders and no messing. Unfortunately, she did say the boy saved her life, and it only goes to show, doesn't it? Liars get what they deserve.

She glanced across at him, hoping to find his eyes sweeping the seats in search of the lover he'd told her about. But no, his eyes were fixed on his mistress, loyal as ever, dammit.

She drew a deep breath. Most people in this stadium supported a particular faction, be it red, blue, green or white, which often erupted in fights, even riots, as one group of supporters taunted a rival team. For Claudia Seferius, the races represented an altogether different excitement and she knew, she just *knew*, the big Libyan from the red stable would win the first race hands down. By betting twenty sesterces on Red, she could place her winnings on White in the subsequent race; no one handled a team of four the way that wiry Rhodian did. Then she could . . .

'Having fun, love?' Marcellus slid into the seat beside her.

'Not any more.' Good life in Illyria, if she moved any further to the left, she'd be sitting in her neighbour's lap.

'My money's on the Blue, what do you think?'

Claudia twisted her lip. 'I'll wager one hundred sesterces Red wins by – oooh – three lengths. Are you on?'

Claudia, are you *mad*?

Her brother-in-law gave a nervous laugh. 'Shame about Valeria's baby,' he said.

'Heart-rending. A hundred on the big Libyan, what do you say?'

He fiddled with his toga, avoiding the directness of her stare. 'Gaius is absolutely devastated, I hear.'

'Gutted. Marcellus, they're lining up. Are you game or not?'

He made a vague gesture with his hands and gave a

false laugh. 'I . . . well, no. Not at the moment. I've been a bit strapped lately.'

'Nonsense, you're loaded. Julia's always bragging about it. Now watch this Libyan, Marcellus. See the way he stands? Firm as a rock, you won't catch him overturning on the bends.'

They were two-horse chariots in the first race, and what magnificent beasts they were. Pearls in their manes, ribbons in their knotted tails, charms and medallions blazing from their breastplates. In terms of splendour, the drivers came a very poor second.

'Julia's a snob, just like her mother. The fact is, Claudia, I'm stony broke.'

'You're an architect, for heaven's sake. Rome's positively ringing with the sounds of hammers with this massive restoration programme. You can't possibly be broke.'

The four charioteers had completed the first lap and were manoeuvring on the next turn. It was going to be tight. Claudia could feel her nails biting into the palm of her hand.

'Ah! Well, that's the rub. I've made one or two foolish investments and I was wondering – I don't suppose you could see your way to loaning me a quadran or two, just to tide me over?'

A collective gasp went up from the crowd as Green misjudged slightly. The horse on the inside stumbled, the chariot rocked. By the time Green had adjusted his reins and rejoined the race he was at least two lengths behind. A quarter of the crowd began to boo, while the remaining three factions heard rousing cheers to spur them on.

'Categorically not.' Was he kidding? When she owed Lucan two grand? 'Have you approached Gaius?'

Gaius, she knew, had been injecting capital into his brother-in-law's business for some time.

'Ah. Bit tricky, that. You see, since last November I've been dipping into Flavia's allowance, and last night didn't seem appropriate.'

On the fourth circuit, Green was still trailing, Blue was encountering difficulty on the bends, so it was neck and neck between White and Red. Claudia's heart was pounding, it was all she could do not to jump up and cheer the Libyan.

'I mean him rolling home, drunk as a boiled owl. Not like Gaius, is it?' The pock-marked face leaned closer. 'Or is it?' he whispered. 'Is that why you sleep in separate rooms?'

'Marcellus, if you don't get your tongue out of my ear this second, you'll be sleeping in separate rooms – a different part of you in each one. Now MOVE!'

'All right, all right, I'm just trying to be friendly, that's all. Remus, Claudia, you and I could make a great team—'

'I'm warning you. If that hand goes any further under my stola, you can kiss your nutmegs goodbye right here and now.'

He was getting progressively worse. Last night he actually tried to kiss her in the garden, and his hand slid over her breast as she passed him in the dining room. Both sent shudders of revulsion through her body every time she thought about them.

The charioteers were on the final straight now, and this is where the Libyan knew his stuff. With a toss of the head he straightened his knees, cracked his whip with a flourish and his steeds surged forward. By the time they'd passed the finishing marker, Red was declared the winner by three and a half lengths. What a bloody waste, she thought. That could have been another hundred for Lucan.

The thought of that little bloodsucker left a nasty taste in her mouth. Not only had Gaius come home rolling drunk, he'd brought that ferreting investigator back for dinner. It was supposed to be a quiet family affair to discuss the finer points of the wedding and suddenly Gaius, in his cups, starts banging on about extortion and brings up that wretched Otho business.

'I'm determined to get to the root of this, you know.' He was slurring his words badly. 'This is the second time in a month someone's tried to extort money from my wife.'

Unbelievably Orbilio turns round and says, 'Oh, I checked Otho's story out. Pack of lies, old chap. Not one copper quadran owed, according to Lucan.'

Claudia wondered what she owed the miserable little ferret for covering up. It was patently obvious he'd believed Otho's story, even at this time, and then he'd let the Thracian escape to what? Spare her blushes? Or maybe spare Gaius, because these two seemed to have grown close of late. Damn you to hell, Marcus Cornelius Orbilio. Now you're off this case, I hope I never see you again. Do you know that for one minute yesterday you actually struck a chord? There I was at the household shrine and you were betting I'd missed you every single hour you'd been away. Well, I'll admit that maybe, just for a little while, the house *had* seemed depressingly quiet, but after your magnificent performance last night I can put my hand on my heart and say the emptiness had nothing to do with you. Nothing whatsoever, so you can get that idea out of your arrogant head for a start.

'Funny business last night, wasn't it?'

Claudia pretended not to hear – though funny wasn't the word she'd have chosen.

'About Flavia and your cousin, I mean.'

Dammit, Marcellus, I know what you mean.

The second teams came into the ring, the Rhodian by far the smallest of the lot. This time there were a dozen chariots in the race, three from each faction, and he almost disappeared under his helmet, his white tunic like a handkerchief compared to the massive tunics worn by the others. Her pulse was racing. No one else would have put money on him, it would have been a walkover! With a yelp, the rope went up and they were off.

Marcellus leaned across. 'I suppose it's because he was drunk.'

The pair of them were drunk, the very worst kind of drunk, too. They were maudlin.

By the time the sixth circuit had been completed, the wiry white rider was way out in front and Claudia was gnashing her teeth. When the seventh lap marker signalled the finish, he was streaking home to riotous cheers and whistles and Claudia hated every inch of his little Rhodian body. Mulberrychops finally got the message that she wanted to neither lend him money nor discuss Orbilio and Flavia, because, come the interval, he stood up and excused himself. He had to get back to the house, he said, and by 'house', she knew he was referring to her house. Julia and Flavia had got into a terrible argument last night which had boiled over into this morning and now Scaevola was round adding his two asses' worth. Someone ought to be there to keep the peace, Marcellus was saying, because Gaius certainly wasn't up to it.

She refrained from suggesting that if they'd done the decent thing and gone home last night instead of staying over and getting under everybody's skin, life would have been a whole lot more pleasant for all concerned.

'I mean, have you seen Gaius today? Pissed out of his skull, he is, crying like a baby. It's pathetic. Well, love,' he managed to plant a wet kiss on her cheek, his hand skimming the inside of her thigh, 'I'll see you later.'

Wiping her cheek with the back of her hand, Claudia watched him fight his way towards the exit. Obnoxious little toad, she'd get him for that, he could bet his balls she would. She signalled to the young Gaul.

'Go home, Junius. The master's not well, apparently, and from what I gather of events there, it might well bring on another seizure.'

'I'm not sure I'd be much help, madam.'

'Probably not, but at least you can run like the wind for a doctor.'

He seemed a little nonplussed at the oddity of the request, and hesitated, his mouth open slightly.

'Well, go on, then. Shoo.'

Junius glanced over his shoulder. 'I don't like to leave you, madam. Not when . . . not when that thug Otho's hovering.'

'Otho? Here?' Juno, Jupiter and Mars! 'Where is he?'

'Right behind you, Claudia.'

The thick accent startled them both.

'Otho, I'm warning you, start anything here and I'll kill you.'

She teased a dagger out of her tunic just sufficiently to show him she meant business. Junius stepped forward, his eyes betraying the anger his face was masking. The Thracian held up a hand and smiled. She was right. He had lost a couple of front teeth the other night. Perhaps Orbilio had some uses, after all.

'Claudia, Claudia. Is no need for violence. I bring message from Master Lucan.' His face was criss-crossed with livid lacerations.

'I've already had two of his messages, thank you very much. Tell him to send a letter next time.'

'Is good message, Claudia. I deliver it personally, though. And' – his sibilant voice hardened as he turned to Junius – 'in private.'

She shrugged and the Gaul backed out of earshot. What the hell? Otho was hardly going to beat her up here and – incredibly – she was becoming inured to his threats. Surprising what you get used to, really.

His eyes lingered on the fullness of her breasts. 'Master Lucan say you very lucky, Claudia. Your debt, it has been settled, yes?'

What did he mean, it had been settled? Who by? She glanced over at Junius, whose teeth were bared. Whether in fear, anger or pleasure it was impossible to tell.

'Of course it's been settled, you big oaf. Ages ago.'

Dear Diana, nobody knew about the problem but her. Why should another person cough up two grand? Claudia's chin went up a fraction higher. She'd die rather than ask this pig who was responsible.

'Then is pity we can't get together, Claudia. Maybe some day, yes?'

Claudia smiled sweetly. 'Go fuck your mother, Otho.'

His eyes flashed and his lips went white, but all he said was, 'Nice tits,' before melting into the crowd.

Junius came bounding over. Either his hearing was

above average or maybe he could lipread, but he'd certainly caught the gist of Otho's message. The relief on his rugged face was undisguised.

'You'll be all right on your own, now.'

'Of course I will, Junius. Now sod off home, will you?'

XXII

A blast of silver trumpets signalled the end of the interval, but Claudia barely noticed the twelve chariots that came thundering out of the stables kicking up a cloud of yellow sand in their wake. Even when Blue lost a wheel on the third bend she didn't turn a hair. Who knew about her and Lucan? Nobody, she thought. Nobody, nobody, nobody! Which is obviously baloney, a small voice answered. Some-body obviously does, so think.

Well, there was Junius. But Junius was a slave and slaves don't have money. Hang on a mo, what about that grand Gaius gave him? Oh, come on, Claudia, why should the boy settle your account, it doesn't add up. Who else knows? Larentia, of course. Her spies had reported back about the debt, almost to the last quadran, but of all people in this world, her mother-in-law was the last person with a desire to make life easy for Claudia Seferius!

The roars of the cheers around her were deafening. It had turned into a two-chariot race, between Red and Blue, both equally matched at handling a team of four. They were approaching the last and final turn, a test of nerves and skill which would decide the race. At a glance, Claudia knew it would be Red, from the way he leaned back against the reins. He was luring Blue into cutting the corner. They charged towards the posts, enveloped by clouds of dust and sand. Too close and the chariot would swing into the centre wall. Too wide and the game was lost. Distractedly she saw Blue dive into the spot Red had left, realizing too late the trap he'd fallen into. Unable to squeeze through, the inside horse pulled towards the middle and from a jumble of hooves and wheels Blue was somersaulting through sand. Red punched the air with his whip and surged on to victory. Absently Claudia thought of the laurels that would be his later. Rich wines, rare aromatics – and a choice of girls in his bed.

Gaius knew, because when Otho was captured in her room he wasn't slow in broadcasting the purpose of his visit. However, Gaius wasn't a likely contender for paying off massive debts out of hand; he would certainly have taken his wife to task about gambling away two grand in as many months. Naturally, Claudia had a perfectly plausible answer sitting right on the tip of her tongue. Blackmail, she was going to tell him. Simple as that. An anonymous (what else?) blackmailer had demanded hefty payments to ensure her husband's secret remained safe; what could she do but pay? Gaius would swallow that. He was pretty gullible on some things, but he was definitely not the type to pay off Lucan on the quiet. Besides, only last night he'd announced his intention to get to the root of the matter.

Which left Marcus Cornelius Orbilio. His was a fine patrician family whose ancestry could be traced right back to Apollo, by all accounts. Wealthy, too. (By necessity she'd had to do her homework on him, seeing that he was Adversary Number One in this sordid business.) Not necessarily super-rich, but this boy wasn't stuck for an ass or three, that's for sure. But why would Orbilio settle her debt?

'Excuse me.'

The gentle tap on her shoulder made her jump. A small child, clean and reasonably well dressed, was standing behind her, holding a scroll in her little fat hand.

'Gentleman said to give you this.'

Claudia took the letter. 'Which gentleman?'

The small face screwed itself up and the tiny shoulders shrugged. 'Don't know,' she said quietly.

Claudia smiled and passed the girl a peach, which was instantly pounced upon. Freeborn she might be, but you had to have a lot of money in this city to afford a peach of that quality. She watched the child skip off to rejoin her family, gleefully waving her trophy. She pointed towards Claudia, who waved back, but when she tried to show them who had given her the letter in the first place, it was clear the child could neither remember nor spot him in the crowd. Too bad. Claudia ripped open the seal.

I love you.

She turned it over. Was that it? I love you? No endearments, no flattery, no compliments, no signature? Just a bald I-love-you?

More equestrian prowess, this time in the form of bare-back riding, swooping down to collect trophies from the sand. The riders could fall off and get trampled to death, for all she cared. Had the author of this feeble missive settled Lucan's bill? Why should the two be connected, anyway? Hell, she'd had more love letters than glasses of Seferius wine, and the fact that she was married didn't mean a damned thing, either. She'd lost count of the number of young bloods falling at her feet, swearing undying devotion and threatening suicide. She'd had poetry written for her, plays staged in her honour, more songs about unrequited love sung than you could tally.

Claudia stood up, straightening her back, smoothed her curls and ran her hands down the side of her body. Slowly. Very, very slowly. I know you're watching me, you bastard, so take note. She let splayed fingers glide down her neck, pausing tantalizingly at the neck of her tunic. With her eyes on the racetrack, she twisted her head this way and that, tossed her curls, stretched and yawned. Let this be a lesson to you. Claudia Seferius is a sophisticated, sensual woman – she held the parchment high and tore it slowly and deliberately into a dozen pieces – for whom three poxy words on a page isn't enough. Fragments fluttered away on the breeze. Got it?

Smiling to herself, she sat back in her seat. And next time, you can damned well put your name to it.

Whoever the author, one thing was certain. It wasn't Cousin Markie! Dammit, for a while she'd had to watch herself, because whenever Orbilio was around the air seemed to crackle between them. It wasn't anything he said – his words were professional enough – or in his facial expressions, which he masked more often than not. But his eyes. Dear Diana, his eyes! They twinkled and danced and laughed and blazed, telling more stories than a minstrel. Oh, yes. There was sin in those eyes.

The feelings he'd dredged up, feelings she thought she'd left long behind, were too dangerous to dwell on. It was nothing deeper than sexual chemistry, any fool could tell that, but she'd be damned glad when he disappeared back into the hole he crawled out of and left her in peace.

Weary in spite of the races, Claudia made her way

towards the exit at the Appian end. What the hell's wrong with you, anyway, wasting time on that two-faced, smooth-tongued, womanizing bastard? He's got nothing other men haven't got. You need your head testing if you think his attentions meant anything special. Did they hell! So long as he was on the case and had his famous hunch about apple-green cotton, he was as charming as they come; the minute Callisunus puts him to work on something else, we see the little weasel in his true colours, don't we?

She slapped one of the race attendants out of her way.

So much time wasted! The catch in her breath every time she saw him. The way he walked. His famous half-smile. Oh, she'd like to bet he practised that one in the mirror of a morning.

'Bastard!'

The janitor's eyes popped out of their sockets in surprise.

'Not you, you imbecile. Now open this bloody door, will you?'

The heat outside was intolerable. Far too hot to walk! Well you've got no one to blame but yourself, Claudia Seferius. You made this choice. You were the one who said it was too hot for the litter-bearers to hang around all day and sent them home again. If you'd stuck inside the Circus as you'd planned, you wouldn't have to walk home, would you? Not you, though. You decide you've had enough by midday. Well, you'll have to bloody well pay the price, won't you?

She'd taken the best part of a hundred paces before she realized she was stomping up the wrong hill. Swearing loudly, she turned round and stomped up the right one.

Why on earth did they have to build Rome on seven bloody great hills? She glanced down. These were not the sandals she would have chosen for walking in, either. Bugger, bugger, bugger. Over the heads of the crowds, Claudia caught a glimpse of bright orange. Terrific! Her very own litter was beating a path through the throng – then suddenly she realized it was a cheap imitation. She ducked into a doorway as it went past. Sweet Jupiter, it was Marcia, the linen merchant's widow. Claudia kicked the doorpost. They say imitation is the sincerest form of flattery, but she'd be damned if she'd let that little cow get away with this. First thing in the morning she'd have her own litter re-upholstered.

She paused to let through a consignment of timber, recognizing the portico as one of her brother-in-law's projects. Strange, Marcellus being on his uppers. What did he call it, a few unwise investments? Serves him right, she thought. Gaius had been carrying him for years. The lazy sod never put much effort into anything, and that included his marriage. She wondered how far Julia's awareness stretched. Did she condone embezzling Flavia's funds? Did she even know about it? One thing was sure. If Gaius finds out he'll hit the roof.

The last of the timber rumbled past as Claudia wondered why Marcellus was so keen to talk about Orbilio's behaviour at dinner last night. Until Gaius came home, the five of them – Julia, Flavia, Antonius, Marcellus and herself – had been discussing the banquet for the wedding. Mentally Claudia had been counting off the days (fourteen, to be exact!) when her husband and so-called cousin had come rolling arm in arm through the front door. Orbilio was singing at the top of his off-key voice, something to do with the sexual adventures of a particularly well-endowed youth called Varex, if her memory served her correctly. Strangely enough, she'd got a fleeting impression that he wanted to rush over and kiss her; not a peck on the cheek, but the sort of kiss that lasts for ever. Which only goes to show how stupid you can be at times.

They'd all trooped upstairs to the dining room (that was where Claudia's breast assaulted Marcellus's hand), kicked off their shoes and reclined in preparation for eating. Except for Flavia. Until then, Claudia had been only vaguely aware that the girl's sulky expression had vanished, but in the dining room the child turned into . . . well, what could, quite honestly, only be described as a tramp. With a sensuality Claudia could never have imagined in the child, she slipped off one sandal (showing far more leg than was decent), then the other, and instead of filling the gap between her aunt and her betrothed, the little trollop slid slowly between Marcellus and Orbilio, wriggling her adolescent hips in a thoroughly vulgar fashion. Claudia felt Antonius stiffen with rage, although at this stage Julia and Marcellus were embroiled in the trivia of the wedding arrangements and Gaius was staring solemnly into his glass. His eyes dancing with mischief, Orbilio gave one slow, blatant wink at Claudia as Flavia nestled closer and after that – well! It was sickening to watch them. The little hussy giggled and fawned and made doe eyes at him all bloody night and he was no better, flattering her on everything from her fingertips to her toes.

It took a few quiet words to calm Scaevola, whose face was positively suffused by the time the first set of dishes was cleared away. Claudia barely touched her own food. Orbilio's plate, on the other hand, was littered with chicken bones. That idle strumpet grew bolder and bolder with every course and Orbilio positively lapped it up. She was shoulder to shoulder with him after the eggs and lettuce, and by the time the fruit was wheeled in, she was running her little fat ankle up and down his calf and lifting his tunic with her toes.

At one stage, Claudia had to put her hand on Scaevola's arm to steady him when he growled: 'What the fuck's her game?' and began to clamber to his feet.

Quick thinking was called for. She promised him it was the usual case of pre-wedding nerves with dear little Flavia testing her fiancé to see whether he really loved her, which she could only prove by making him jealous, couldn't he see that? Naturally she also assured him her cousin's affections were firmly engaged elsewhere, it was something of a family joke, ha, ha, ha, but on this occasion he had to agree to conspire with the bride-to-be on such an important issue, surely Antonius could understand that? From the look he shot her, it seemed unlikely Antonius was convinced on any point, but at least he calmed down sufficiently to continue the meal without making a scene in front of Gaius who, by now, had tears rolling down his cheeks and was mumbling to himself. He needed to buck himself up, he really did. It was bad enough at the villa, though Rollo and the huge amount of work seemed to hold him in check, but since coming home he'd fallen apart. If he wasn't slobbering in his cups he was wailing to everyone and anyone who happened to be passing that his babies, his babies, look what was happening to his babies. His mother was dying, his children were dead, his grandchild, they were all dead. Dead or dying.

Sod that for a game of knucklebones, she thought

now, dodging a small boy playing in the gutter. Gaius had precious little time to pull himself together. The business was falling apart; he wasn't meeting clients, he was negligent about deliveries, sloppy over pricing. Heaven only knew what muddle poor old Rollo was having to contend with, but the main thing was, in thirteen days' time, Flavia Seferius was marrying Antonius Scaevola. If he hadn't slapped himself into shape by then, by Jupiter, Claudia would bloody well do it for him.

For all the hordes crammed into the Circus Maximus, the streets were no less of an ant's nest. A builder's wagon, one of the few vehicles allowed into the city during the daytime and that only due to the urgency of the work, was blocking one of the narrower streets and causing chaos. People were trying to clamber over the cart, marble and all, as the driver was torn between fighting them off and goading his oxen, the same oaths encompassing both. Claudia decided to avoid the route in case the weight of the people on top of the load collapsed the axle. Too many crushed limbs for her taste.

As she rounded the corner she collided with a soldier, whose nailed sole ground into her toe. He quickly apologized, but the string of obscenities with which he was greeted fairly took his breath away. She swerved round porters' poles, shoved a beggar out of the way, heedless of upturning his bowl in the process, and elbowed aside a juggler in mid-juggle. It was truly a pleasure to turn into her own street, away from the congestion, knowing that, inside, the fountains and frescoes, marbles and mosaics could soothe away the foulest of tempers. There was something wonderfully refreshing about the pale blue frieze with its long-necked cranes and elegant panthers – the whiteness of the ostriches, the grace of the antelope – which was missing in almost every other house she'd visited.

The minute she crossed the threshold she realized something was wrong. For once the usual criss-crossing of slaves was absent. There was a strange hush in the air. Her eyes sought Leonides, but it was Junius who shuffled forward to meet her.

'It's Flavia, isn't it?' She could tell. 'Don't tell me! She's run off with that snake Orbilio, am I right?'

Ashen-faced, the young Gaul shook his head. 'No, madam. I'm sorry, but—'

'But what, Junius? I haven't got all bloody day, spit it out.'

'It – it's the master.'

She noticed his eyes had flicked to Gaius's bedroom. 'Oh, no, not another seizure. Have you fetched the doctor?'

She flew across the atrium towards the staircase, but Junius ran after her. Strong hands on her shoulders stopped her from going any further.

'Don't go up,' he pleaded.

From his tunic waistband he drew out a letter, sealed with wax and imprinted with Gaius's own private seal of two leaping dolphins. She noticed the boy's hand was trembling.

'He's dead, madam.'

Colour flooded Claudia's face. 'Juno, I knew this would happen! That bloody child and her tantrums! How dare she! Where is the little bitch? I'll give her a seizure, you wait and see.'

She tried to wriggle free, but his grip merely tightened. He smelled of roses. Must have been out pruning. He was the only one in the house she could trust to look after them properly.

'It wasn't a seizure,' he said quietly. 'The master committed suicide.'

'Suicide? Gaius? Don't be ridiculous. Gaius is the last man in the world to top himself. Must have been an accident.'

The boy's fingers dug into her shoulders. 'It was no accident, madam. Master Seferius fell on his sword.'

XXIII

Claudia's litter set her down outside the modest white-fronted house sandwiched between a butcher and a wig-maker on the lower end of the Esquiline near the old temple of Juno. Opposite, a goldsmith calmly pounded his precious dust, impervious to the cries of the pedlars, the beggars, the children pressing in around him. In spite of the circumstances, Claudia hadn't forgotten her promise to herself, and the litter no longer sported the ostentatious orange so envied by that little copycat Marcia but was draped instead with the palest blue any mercer could lay his hands on. Every spot would show, of course, but that wasn't the point – was it, Marcia?

Waiting until it was confirmed the master was at home before dismissing her entourage, Claudia stepped into the atrium. One thing about these patricians, they had taste, she thought, looking around. The frescoes were quieter, the shades subdued, radiating calm even in this bustling corner of the city. The predominant colour was ivory, contrasting spectacularly with maplewood inlaid with tor-toiseshell and the occasional hint of gold. Vesta's sacred flame burned in the centre of an intricate mosaic depicting the wanderings of Odysseus. Low fountains gushed in the corner. Even the servants oozed tranquillity. A mournful-looking Libyan with perfect Latin informed her politely he was extremely sorry, the master was engaged with a visitor at present, would Milady mind waiting? No, Milady would not, nor would she care for any refreshment, thank you, or company, or fanning, or entertainment and, no, she was perfectly happy here, rather than in the peristyle. The servant glided away, leaving the atrium once again the peaceful haven expected of it as Claudia's fingers traced the carved lion that comprised the arm of the chair.

She'd far rather have married into one of the patrician families, she thought. Class had been bred into them; style and elegance came naturally. Her mouth twisted at one corner. Alas, so did suspicion. Forged pedigrees aren't commonplace, but then again they aren't such a rarity that the patricians don't make assiduous checks into a person's background and Claudia had to admit that, had Gaius been more thorough, she'd never have got past the first post.

Poor old Gaius! To her credit, Cypassis had known how to organize a decent funeral, thanks, largely, to her having gone through the whole palaver quite recently when her old master the oil merchant popped off. The mourning women were that professional you were left with the serious impression Gaius had been closely related to every single one of them, and the dirges – oh, the dirges were sung with such a depth of feeling it left your gut churning. Oh yes, the funeral had been a tremendous success, apart from one thing.

Without doubt it turned out to be the splendiferous occasion Claudia had wanted it to be, the funeral that eclipsed all others when it came to being talked about in years to come. It simply hadn't been in the way she'd either planned or expected . . .

Despite Junius's insistence that she be spared the sight of her husband's corpse, still *in situ*, on Monday, Claudia lost no time reminding him who was in charge here and marched up to see for herself.

Dear Diana, it was a depressing spectacle.

The heat of the day had intensified the sickly combination of blood and wine, of body odour and bad teeth. Black and green flies had already begun to cluster. Worse, the huge figure of Gaius Seferius seemed to have shrunk by an alarming degree and the bald spot he worked so hard to conceal was shining like a frypan in the midday sun. Quietly Claudia closed the door behind her.

'Gaius, you silly daft sod, what did you do this for, eh?' She stroked the hair back over the glistening dome. 'In this scruffy old tunic, too. You should be ashamed of yourself.'

His neck, twisted and turned inwards, ended in a face which, though waxen, seemed placid enough, and the eyes, thankfully, were closed. She wiped her cheeks with the back of her hand. It was obvious what had happened. He'd sat in the chair, positioned his sword – that splendid symbol of his rise to the equestrian order – then lunged forward. Her eyes roamed his bedroom. Rarely, so very rarely, did she enter his private domain yet how familiar it seemed. Every piece of furniture, every knick-knack, every picture on the frieze screamed of Gaius. From the redness of the décor to the heavyhandedness of the silverwork, from the marble statuary to the leopardskin on the floor, it reflected his flamboyancy, his extravagance, his love of the good life and, perhaps most importantly, the fruits of his labours. Slowly her hand travelled across his writing table, over his rolls of papyrus, the wax tablets, his favourite stylus, the dolphin seal. How typical of Gaius's attitude to life, she thought. Two dolphins in mid-leap. She felt a shudder run through her body. What a bloody, bloody shame it had to end like this.

Claudia broke the seal on the letter and opened it out. The page was shaking so violently, she was forced to spread it over the desk before she could read the words.

'I'm sorry, my sweet, but this is for the best. Love always, Gaius.'

Oh, shit. She sank down on to the bed. Oh shit, oh shit, oh shit!

Several long minutes had passed before Claudia Seferius stood up, blew her nose, brushed specks of dandruff from her husband's tunic, pinched her cheeks and strode to the door.

'LEONIDES!'

The lanky Macedonian, hollow-eyed from shock, was wringing his hands. Small wonder, she thought. It was bad enough when Melissa topped herself, the whole contingent of household slaves thought retribution would fall upon their uncombed heads. Who could imagine the terror in their veins now the master was dead as well? Tempting as it was to reassure them, Claudia realized that she'd get far more out of them by letting them stew for a while.

'Leonides, go straight to the temple of Venus up on the Esquiline. You'll need to register the death immediately.' She wasn't prepared to let Marcellus start meddling in affairs that didn't concern him. 'Cypassis?'

'Yes, madam.'

At least this one looked in control of herself.

'Go with him. Order the best mourners, musicians, dancers money can buy. Spare no expense, do you hear me?'

'Pardon me, madam.' The steward stepped forward. 'But I think the undertakers will want to organize that themselves.'

'I'm sure they will, Leonides, which is precisely why I'm sending you and Cypassis. I don't want any outside interference, we'll do this ourselves.'

The banquet might not have been the eye-popping extravaganza Gaius had hoped for, but, by Jupiter, his funeral procession would be. She owed him that at least.

'Report back to me as soon as you can. I'll be in my room.'

Julia, Flavia, Marcellus, Antonius, they'd all be huddled in the garden, pretending how sorry they were, the hypocritical sons of bitches, and she couldn't trust herself to speak to them. Not at the moment.

'Junius! I don't want Gaius's old bed on display in the atrium, see if you can lay your hands on something a little grander, can you?' Poor sod deserved a decent lying-in-state. 'Something fancy, with a bit of gold on it, perhaps. Or ivory. And, Junius, I know you're not his personal slave, but would you mind . . . laying him out?'

It was a filthy job, but the boy not only shook his head with considerable vigour, he actually seemed happy to do it. Which only goes to show, you can never really get inside these strange Gaulish minds, can you?

'It means . . . taking the sword out?'

'No problem, madam.'

'He's already stiffening . . .'

'Leave it to me.'

'Yes – well – ' Claudia cleared her throat. 'His parade uniform should still fit, so once you've got him, er, cleaned up, perhaps you could . . . ?'

He'd need help, of course, but she was sure the boy was more than capable of sorting that out by himself. What Claudia had needed more than anything else was peace and quiet and time to think. Think, think, think.

She caught the Macedonian at the door. 'Leonides, before you slink off I want you to tell me exactly what happened this morning.'

The steward was unable to meet her eye. He was very sorry, but there didn't seem to be much to tell. The master started drinking the moment he came downstairs, apparently oblivious to the argument raging around him, and when he retreated to his room to consolidate the job of getting drunk, it seemed the family wouldn't leave him in peace. How easily Claudia pictured the scene. Flavia, screaming that she wasn't going to marry Scaevola, never, ever, ever. Julia, nagging her brother to put his foot down. Antonius, demanding what the hell was going on. And finally Marcellus, shoving his two asses' worth in by suggesting that Gaius wasn't pulling his weight here. Some of them went up two or three times, the steward said, and he felt very sorry for the master in the end.

'Although I didn't think he'd kill himself because of it,' he added hastily. 'Had I realized—'

'What was his mood like?'

Again Leonides had been reluctant to answer, but eventually Claudia got him to admit that Gaius had been crying constantly, refusing to see clients who called, refusing even to wash. The only clear word he'd uttered all morning was 'Lucius'.

Well, he was with Lucius now . . .

A feather drifted down through the open roof of this fine patrician house to settle on Odysseus's big toe. Immediately a young slave girl pounced and carried it silently away.

Claudia thought of the green glass bowl containing Gaius's ashes. Tomorrow they'd be carried in a leaden basket to be interred, alongside the son he adored, in a handsome tiled chamber along the Appian Way. She leaned forward, supporting her head in her hands. Who could have predicted a month ago, when he was giving Lucius's funeral oration, that his own would have followed so quickly?

Without a male heir it had fallen upon the widow to deliver Gaius's tribute, which, because the occasion demanded something sensational in view of the rumours, she'd secretly hired Syphax the playwright to script for her. He may only have had twenty-four hours to knock it into shape, but if she said so herself it was exceptional, and she would have defied anyone listening to keep a dry eye when she read it aloud. And here lay the flaw in the entire arrangement.

No one had turned up to listen.

Oh yes, this was the funeral to set Rome talking about for generations, all right! The funeral of Gaius Seferius, that jolly old wine merchant. Remember him? How we liked the fellow – thought him the salt of the earth?

And then look what happens. Turns out he's the one who gouged out the eyes of his colleagues!

Rumours began to circulate almost before the body had cooled. Some you'd expect, considering that, contrary to custom and expectation, Gaius left his entire fortune to that young wife of his. Talk about scandal! And as much as Claudia denied knowledge of the will, it was clear Julia, Marcellus and especially Flavia believed otherwise. They could not, however, contest it. The signatures of five prominent Roman citizens testified to Gaius's wishes and that should have been that.

Except it wasn't.

On account of the letter Gaius had attached to his will, a letter for Claudia's eyes only.

A letter which she had subsequently burned.

But the new will contributed to the fact that Gaius Seferius had lain on his bier for two days – feet towards the door, coins over his eyes, cakes in his hands – in perfect preparation for the afterlife, yet with not one single person from his own lifetime coming to pay their respects. Including his family, who suddenly disowned him.

'Bastards!'

Her oath echoed round the stillness of the room.

Of course, it wasn't the rumours about the will that put off the rest of Rome. Scaevola brought the news late on Monday evening.

'Callisunus has closed the case,' he said, red in the face and puffing profusely. 'It's official.'

She hadn't believed him. 'Rumours,' she'd said. 'The city's full of them—'

'Claudia, I heard it from Callisunus himself. Seferius is the killer, he said; he was one hundred per cent positive. That's why I'm out of breath, I came straight round. There's something else, too. He's asked the Senate to issue an edict forbidding people to attend the funeral. Says it's the day of the Volcanalia, people should attend the rites at the Circus instead.'

Give me strength! 'And just what explanation does this adjectivally challenged dwarf offer for arriving at this idiotic conclusion?'

'He refuses to elaborate, except to stress the case is closed.'

Indeed? Well there was only one source from which such waters flowed, so Claudia had come straight to the spring ... to Marcus Cornelius Orbilio.

A door slammed in the distance and a long-legged girl came running through the atrium, tears streaming down her face. The tall Libyan came trotting after her, but it was too late, she'd seen herself out. She heard a second set of footsteps.

'Claudia?'

There was a distinct feeling of satisfaction, watching his handsome face redden. He shot a glance at the Libyan, who promptly dissolved into thin air, and combed his hair with his hands.

'Claudia . . .'

'So far, so good, Orbilio, you've got my name right. I'm afraid it's the only thing you *have* got right, but I'm sure you're not responsible. Tell me, did you inherit imbecility from your mother's side, or your father's?'

'I'm sorry about Gaius.'

'Not sorry enough to attend his funeral, though. Or did I miss you in the crush?'

'Blame Callisunus. I told him I didn't think it right for Gaius to be shunned, that I was intending to join the procession regardless, but' – he held out his wrists, which showed raw, red bands round them – 'he clapped me in irons for the day. Said it would be, and I quote, an embarrassment to him, the Emperor and the citizens of Rome for anyone to turn up. Especially me.'

Claudia rose to her feet and shook the crinkles out of her stola. 'Especially you, yes, seeing as how you were the person who convinced Callisunus to close the case in the first place.'

He scratched at a freckle on his thumb, his eyes riveted on the operation. 'Claudia, I'm sorry Gaius was the killer, because I liked him, I—'

'And he liked you, you treacherous bastard.'

Funny. The room had gone misty.

'You worm your way into his house, prying and snooping, hoping to find some poor bugger to hang these murders on, and you pick on Gaius Seferius. What had he ever done to you, eh?'

'Claudia, sit down. Dammit, woman, I said sit down and listen to me. Just listen, all right?'

Orbilio pulled up a chair and sat opposite her. Her eyes were flashing, her lips were pursed white, but, thank goodness, she was at least prepared to hear him out.

'What Gaius did, falling on his sword and all that, it was for the best, you must believe me.'

'Bullshit!'

'You don't accept Gaius killed six men?'

'Never.'

Orbilio ran his hand over his chin. There was stubble there, because he hadn't had time to shave this morning. Callisunus, the little toe-rag, had kept him locked up all night, and, when he returned home, Petronella was waiting. She'd left the locksmith, she told him. Oh, she didn't expect a man like Marcus to marry her, but she'd send for her things straight away and be everything he'd want of a wife. Orbilio felt a proper heel telling her it was over and the last person he expected to find under his roof after that pitiful encounter was Claudia Seferius, defending a husband who, no matter how affable on the surface, transpired to be a single-minded lunatic on the inside.

'Suppose I gave you cast-iron proof?'

To his astonishment, she twisted her head on one side and smiled. 'Suppose I asked you how many murder cases you've solved?'

Orbilio scratched his head and blew out his cheeks. 'Ooh, let me think. Including this case?'

'Including this case.'

'Um . . .' He stared at the flame flickering beside him. 'One,' he said quietly, feeling the colour flood his face.

Claudia nodded serenely. 'That's rather what I suspected. Orbilio, I want you to re-open the case.'

She was mad!

'Even if I could – and I can't – Callisunus wouldn't wear it. However much it hurts, Claudia, the evidence is solid, believe me, and he's tied me up so tight on this Verianus fraud case that I haven't got a minute to call my own.'

'Then we'll have to clear up this wretched Verianus business, won't we?'

'What do you mean, we?'

'Don't interrupt. Now is it Verianus who's accused of fraud?'

'The Senator? Good heavens, no! But someone in his

employment, probably his own brother, has been syphoning off large sums of money over the last couple of years. It's a question of proof.'

'Decimus?'

'No, the younger brother. Tullius. Hell, why am I telling you all this?'

Claudia ignored him. 'Suppose I provide you with a confession? Will you re-open the murder case?'

'No, I will not. I can't condone forged confessions simply because you want—'

'This'll be perfectly above board, Orbilio. Friday morning, you have my word on it, Tullius will be spilling his heart out to Callisunus. On the strict understanding, of course, that the affair will be covered up quietly! He'll return the money, Verianus will drop the case, you'll be a hero. How does that sound?'

Orbilio wrinkled his nose. 'Highly suspicious.'

Claudia waved a hand dismissively. 'Trust me,' she said simply.

She'd head straight to Tullius from Orbilio's and deliver her ultimatum. Own up, cough up, shut up. Or else what? he might bluster, though if the man had any sense between his ears he'd understand that the prospect of his wife and family, including Verianus, hearing how he liked to be tied up and peed on wouldn't necessarily be in his best interests. Far better to settle quietly, old fruit. They're on to you anyway.

'So now the Verianus business is sorted out, will you or will you not re-open the murder case?'

Waves of scepticism were emanating from the man sitting opposite, but he remained silent, tugging on his earlobe. Outside, a column of soldiers clanked past, their hobnail boots marching to perfect time. The smell of fried chicken came wafting across the atrium, yet still the investigator's eyes bored into hers.

Finally he said, 'Give me one good reason.'

Claudia leaned forward, aware of the rapid beating of her heart, the brightness in her eyes. Her tongue darted over her lips.

'Because, my clever investigator friend, Gaius was murdered.'

XXIV

He didn't scoff, he didn't blink, he didn't roll his eyes. He didn't even ask her why, he simply stared up at the vaulted ceiling for several minutes, then said, 'Why don't we go into the garden? It's cooler.'

It was spoken so casually that Claudia began to wonder whether he'd heard her correctly. Still, he was a dark horse, this one, it wouldn't hurt to humour him.

Considering how small this place is, she thought, following her host through the house, it's little short of perfect. Splendid statuary, elegant friezes, expensive aromatics in the braziers, and the garden was probably as close to heaven as you can get here in Rome. Cool colonnades, shaded bowers, flowers planted like an artist's palate, toning blues and whites, lilacs and pinks to give an impression of space in a minuscule plot. At one end, a very large cage contained a lot of very small birds, yellow, red, brown, green, all singing their tiny hearts out, while in front fish nibbled serenely in a pond fringed by lilies.

Claudia thought that, in time, if she put her mind to it, she could eventually learn to hate this place.

Orbilio indicated a seat by the pool. 'Now suppose you level with me,' he said at last.

'Why, Cousin Markie, I just have!'

A truer word was never spoken, for hadn't she spent

two whole days and nights agonizing over this decision? By rights, Claudia Seferius ought to keep her pretty head down and her mouth tight shut, because surely Gaius's suicide solved all her problems? Only she and the real murderer knew Gaius hadn't been responsible for those gruesome killings and, faced with a closed case (not to mention a culprit who couldn't contradict), it was pretty much a foregone conclusion that the murderer would be content to rest on his laurels. So! No more murders, barrels of money, what was the point in re-opening a case that was not only closed, it was locked, barred and bolted to boot? There was nothing to stop her from continuing her search, if she felt so inclined. A knife in the ribs, a poisonous mushroom, the method wasn't important, only the outcome.

'Well, that's a good start, the Cousin Markie stuff. Explain that.'

Claudia twisted a curl round her little finger. 'You started it, remember, pretending to Gaius we were related?'

'Claudia, I was investigating a murder, for gods' sakes. I had you placed at the scene of the crime and to continue those enquiries *discreetly* I needed to get as close as I could. That way at least I made contact with Gaius. Why didn't you bite my head off and deny the relationship straight off?'

The curl unravelled. 'Because that's precisely what you were expecting,' she said sweetly. 'Now is this level enough for you?'

His mouth twitched at one side. 'Tell me about yourself, Claudia. Before you married Gaius.'

'Old, old history. What's the point?'

'Indulge me.'

'Oh, don't hold your breath for that, Orbilio, but as for my life story – I was born in Liternum twenty-four years ago. At fourteen I married Titus Posidonius; he was thirty at the time and a judge, posted up in Cremona. We had three bouncing babies before the plague swept through and killed my family and half the town.' Claudia reached up and plucked a peach. 'I do not, as everyone knows, care to be reminded of such painful memories.'

'I'm not surprised.' Orbilio draped one arm across the back of the bench. 'Especially since you also died in that dreadful epidemic.'

The peach fell to the ground and splattered.

'Then I'm the healthiest ghost you're ever likely to meet.' Although she had a feeling she was fast resembling one . . . 'What are you driving at?'

Orbilio picked another peach, examined it carefully then tossed it across to her. 'Nothing in particular. I'm simply making a point.'

Claudia's finger traced a pattern on the fuzz. 'I hate to be the one to break the news, Orbilio,' she tossed the peach back, 'but point-making is not one of your strengths.'

'I asked you to level with me,' he said slowly. 'If you want me to take your claim seriously—'

'Then you agree Gaius might have been murdered?'

'I didn't say that, I'm merely saying it's about time you started telling the truth. Irrespective that this is my first murder case, I've solved every crime I've investigated so far, be it theft, rape, arson or corruption. I do know what I'm doing, Claudia.'

She drew her knees up along the length of seat, tucking the small of her back against the arm. The carved horns of the satyr's head dug in something wicked, but she twisted another curl languorously round her finger.

'So I was born in Bucentum? Hell, I'm not the only woman who's forged her past.' The curl sprang free. 'Gaius knew all about it.'

'Fibber!'

Her eyes said prove it. His eyes said if needs be. Her eyes won.

'What about the will?'

Ah yes, the will. 'Finance isn't really the issue at the moment.'

'It's a motive.'

'Orbilio, I have not hiked all the way up here this morning simply for you to dredge up my past and come to the conclusion I murdered my husband.'

'Oh, sit down, I'm only teasing. Of course you couldn't have done him in, you were at the Circus Maximus.'

He'd been checking. Dammit, the bastard had actually checked up on her! She wondered whether steam was physically coming out of her ears.

'Incidentally, I know why Gaius brooked convention, and left everything to you.'

He did? How? The letter was sealed, no one else could have seen its contents except the scribe who wrote it. Had Orbilio bribed or bullied his way into reading it? That meant this oily little ferret had suspected Gaius for some time . . .

'Tell me why you think he was murdered.'

What? The change of subject, swift and clean, took her by surprise. Claudia dabbed her hand in the pool. 'Several reasons. For one, his character.'

'Oh, come on, when Lucius died he went right downhill, and once he realized he was on the brink of arrest it swung the balance.'

'I'll ignore, for the moment, the fact that this accusation happened to stem from you, but don't think I've forgotten – because if Gaius *had* killed himself, you'd have had an innocent man's blood on your conscience. I'm presuming here that you know what a conscience is?'

'According to your rules, it's the fear of being found out, rather than any noble principles. Am I wrong?'

The look she shot him would have made a lesser man wince. 'Two,' she said pointedly, 'his eyes were closed, his face was at peace.'

A wasp began buzzing round the splattered peach, and an expensive black leather shoe came down hard to squash it.

'Most people who top themselves are looking for the ultimate peace,' he said. 'Maybe he found it.'

'Orbilio, you think yourself smart, why don't you tell me what corpses look like when they've been run through with a sword? Do they look happy? Well do they?'

Thank goodness he had the grace to look abashed. 'No,' he admitted. 'Their faces remain contorted. However,' he brightened visibly, 'if it wasn't a clean wound and he bled to death – and I heard there was a lot of blood – that would make a difference.'

'I'll concede that, but, point three, there was a large bruise on his head, consistent with his being knocked out cold. Probably by the small marble bust of Apollo he kept on his table.'

'Don't tell me, it had blood and hairs stuck all over it?'

'Laugh if you want to, Orbilio, and I might be wrong about Apollo, but it seems a likely object to me.' It's what I'd have swung, had I wanted to clobber someone. 'Gaius always kept it at the back of his table as a paperweight. When I went to his room it was on the side.'

The investigator's eyes widened. 'Anything else?'

'As a matter of fact, yes. Had Gaius decided to commit suicide, he'd have chosen any number of methods over that sword. It was his pride and joy, you see, and he might have died clutching it, but he would never, ever have killed himself with it and dishonoured the name of Seferius.'

Orbilio ran his hand over his stubble. 'And that's it?'

'No. The most conclusive piece of evidence is this.'

There was a flurry of jade linen as Claudia fished around inside her stola.

'Gaius's suicide note?' Orbilio snatched it out of her hand and read it aloud. '*I'm sorry, my sweet, but this is for the best. Love always, Gaius.*'

His face puckered into a frown as he read and re-read it. 'I'm sorry, I can't see anything wrong,' he said. 'In fact, it rather ties in with my case against him.'

'Only superficially. Assuming Gaius would ever write anything so terribly trite, he never called me his sweet when we were alone; I was always his dove. And even you have to admit this was a particularly private moment.'

'His mind was unbalanced.'

'Balls!'

'Claudia, he'd killed six men, don't you get it? Stuck a dagger through their hearts, then chiselled their eyes out. The last one was still alive and screaming when he did it, for gods' sakes.'

'He didn't do it, Marcus. He couldn't have. I knew

this man, he was as straight as the proverbial die, and if he had any tendencies to kill, it was through a business deal, not through the sword.'

Orbilio covered his face with his hands. 'Claudia, you are seriously suggesting the murderer heard the scandal mooted about Gaius and killed him so that he could take the rap instead?'

No.

'Yes.'

'Dammit, Claudia.' He slammed his fist into the trunk of the peach tree. 'When will you ever learn to trust me? I know everything. Do you understand what I'm saying? Everything.'

He leaned across, filled cupped hands with water and sluiced it over his face. The heady scent of roses drifted in the air as the birds trilled and the fountains splashed. He dried his face and the blood from his knuckles on his handkerchief.

'What's the real reason you want me to open the case? Is it because someone's been picking off his family and you want them caught?'

She stared him out. 'I don't know what you're talking about.'

What he was talking about, he said angrily, was Calpurnia, then Secundus, then Lucius and now Valeria's baby. Four untimely deaths, if she hadn't noticed, and she wasn't to give him any bullshit about how high infant mortality is; three of them weren't infants.

'Coincidence,' she said, carefully, pleating the hem of her tunic.

'Coincidence be damned, Claudia.' He shook his head. 'By Jupiter, you picked a right bloody family to marry into, didn't you? Now tell me, honestly, why you want this case re-opened.'

With Gaius dead, she was positively rolling in it. More than she imagined. More than she had ever dreamed of. More, even, than the old linen merchant had left that common little Marcia cat, would you believe? So who cared that the authorities had mistakenly labelled him a murderer? Did it really matter? And that was the crunch. Because, to her astonishment, Claudia found that, when it came right down to it, yes it did matter. She knew Gaius hadn't killed anyone as surely as she knew who had killed Gaius. But the point was, unless the case was publicly re-opened, a man who had worked hard all his life to get to the top through honesty, fairness and respectability stood to have his good name in tatters for ever. For all his faults, and they were considerable, Gaius Seferius did not deserve such an epitaph.

The revelation that she might actually have a conscience had come as something of a shock to say the least, and she certainly wasn't prepared to share this experience with this . . . this womanizing monster.

'First you tell me how you came to the conclusion that Gaius killed six of Rome's finest and most upstanding citizens.'

'We're going round in circles here. Callisunus will make his announcement in the morning. Why don't you wait for that?'

'Patience isn't one of my virtues, I'm afraid, although I excel at screaming rape. Remember, Cousin Markie? Clam up and you can expect a repeat performance of what happened last month at my house, except this time I'll make it look more realistic.'

His shoulders slumped. 'You win. The statement reads "Gaius Seferius murdered these men in the insane and mistaken belief that they were his wife's lovers." I know you don't like it, but murder is murder and I couldn't give a stuff about covering up Gaius's reputation—'

She stood up and stretched her spine. I'm going to regret this, I can feel it in every single bone of my body.

'Marcus, believe me, someone else killed those men. Now suppose I do level with you and say I was intending to kill this scumbag myself. I don't know who he is – not yet, anyway – but I'm this close I can smell him.'

'And are you levelling enough to explain why you should want to play judge, jury and executioner all at once?'

Her eyes flashed. 'That's none of your business,' she snapped, 'but the point is, Gaius deserves to have his name cleared. Now an hour ago you were practically threatening to push cast-iron proof down my gullet. You can't have it both ways.'

Orbilio stood up and walked over to where she was standing. He could smell her musky perfume, saw the sun sparkle on the tints in her hair, watched the pulse in her throat.

'Let it drop, Claudia. No good can come of this.' Was that husky voice his?

'Would you prefer me to go straight to that foul-mouthed boss of yours?'

'Claudia, you've got so much rope you're hanging yourself, can't you see that? Must I spell it out? Very well, but don't blame me if you don't like the story. Shortly before he was killed, I overheard Paternus gossiping in the baths saying you weren't what you seemed, and it got me thinking that maybe I should check up on you. I have to say it didn't take long to root out that Claudia Posidonius may not have died in Cremona, but she was a damned sick woman when she left. Her tomb is about twenty miles south, isn't that correct?'

Claudia shrugged noncommittally.

He brushed a strand of hair out of her eyes. 'Besides,' he added quietly, 'you can't honestly expect a red-blooded man to believe you've kept a figure like that after three children, can you?'

She turned away to study a butterfly feeding on a poppy. If that was supposed to be a compliment, he could bloody well stick it in his ear. She'd had it up to here with compliments. Gaius wasn't even buried and letters had come flooding in. Some were condolences, admittedly, but half of Rome's bachelors had wasted little time in winging off proposals of marriage. Some were clients of Gaius's, one even was a client of hers. As if she'd marry a pervert like Flamininus the censor, for heaven's sake! Who was married already, the twisted little tick. He wasn't the only one, of course. There was Ligarius, who had got it into his thick skull that now she was free they could carry on where they'd left off. Left off from what? They'd never been more than friends, certainly never lovers. Was the man completely mad? There were seventeen proposals in all, ranging from senators to centurions, the latest from that clot Balbus, who could only be after her money because in three months he'd have bored her to death. Juno, it would be funny if it wasn't so bloody pathetic!

'What else did your grubby investigations turn up?'

'Precisely what you'd expect them to, I'm afraid. Once I knew you were an imposter, I was . . . curious. Since you were there the day Quintus Crassus was killed.'

The butterfly was long gone, but Claudia continued to stare at the poppy. 'So you make up some feeble story about your house burning down and move in with us?'

'I was on to something, and if that's what it took to save lives I frankly couldn't give a toss.'

'I'd think before I boasted if I were you, Orbilio. Two men were butchered within five days of that clever little scheme!'

'They were scheduled to die anyway; don't you understand? Claudia, when I said I know about your past, I meant all of it.'

'All of what? A mother who worked in a dyer's, a father who was an orderly in the army? Big deal.'

'I'm talking about Genua, for pity's sake. The poverty, the dancing, the—'

'—the men.' She might as well finish it for him. Claudia felt her knees turn to water. The colour must have drained down to them from her face. There was a long silence before she could bring herself to ask, 'How did you find out?'

'There was an anonymous letter on Gaius's desk—'

'You two-faced son of a bitch, you said you hadn't searched the house!'

'That was as far as I'd got. Going through Gaius's papers like that, it made me feel . . . dirty.'

Funny, there are some things in life you just can't legislate for. 'There's a certain irony in this situation, Orbilio. You see, my mother-in-law wrote that, and she's a venomous old bitch who makes mischief for the sheer hell of it.'

'I think you're wrong. That letter was penned by an

educated hand and I've checked this family out. Larentia is illiterate and even if she dictated it . . . The words, the grammar, the careful phrasing? No, she didn't send that.'

Come to think of it, Larentia sounded puzzled at the time. Why didn't I pick up on that? If Orbilio could work it out, I bloody well should have.

Serves you right, a little voice answered. You shouldn't have assumed Gaius threw it away, even though he promised. You knew he was preoccupied over Lucius, you stupid cow, you should have checked.

'And then there was Ligarius. Your steward mentioned he was hanging around in the street every night. It was only a question of following him to his tavern, throwing in your name, and that was it. The floodgates opened.'

Bastard. Her swore he'd never let her down. Men!

'So the night he burst in, you clonked him over the head to spare my blushes. How frightfully gallant.'

'Chivalry's always been my downfall.' Slowly Orbilio crossed to the aviary, keeping his back turned towards her. 'Same as I didn't want to believe it was you in the tenement last month.'

'I thought we'd established it was Melissa.'

'Melissa, yes, Melissa. I was searching her room for money, remember? It occurred to me Crassus might not have been tied up by the man who killed him, suppose something kinky was going on? Could Melissa have been offering such a service? Why not? And suppose Gaius was her pimp, the man who tipped her the wink about which punters were willing and how much to charge? When I heard about her selling the brooch and found the green tunic, it all fell into place.'

He paused. A rock seemed to have lodged in his throat

as he remembered seeing Callisunus with his twin.

'But I was wrong. A man will see only what he wants to see, and I wanted to believe it was Melissa with those men, not you, but the evidence was piled against it. Rufus was so cocksure the woman he'd seen wore a stola, I couldn't shake him on it. Now a slave might pull on a fine linen tunic and pass as freeborn, but she'd never dare don that distinguishing symbol of Roman motherhood the stola. Whichever way I tried, you see, there was only one solution. It was you. You were in the tenement, Claudia. You found Crassus's body. Because you were working again.'

'Rubbish. Why would I do a thing like that?'

'To pay off Lucan. That debt stood at well over two thousand sesterces the night young Otho called to pay his respects. Correct me if I'm wrong, Claudia, those six men were tricks.'

Vulgar word. Claudia tossed her head in disdain. What the hell. No one can prove Gaius didn't know my background, the will's still valid. Nothing can take that away. It means moving on, of course, but I've done it before and no doubt I'll do it again.

'So now you know the risks I'm running by re-opening the case.' She hoped from that distance he couldn't hear the quiver in her voice.

Orbilio turned round. There was little trace of the boyish charm on his pinched features. 'Tell me one thing, Claudia, and answer me honestly. Do you have a lover?'

'A lover? With that list of punters? Do me a favour!'

His face relaxed, as though a weight had been lifted from his mind. The dancing light in his eyes was back as he squared his shoulders. 'Then I categorically refuse to re-open the case. You see, if you don't have a lover, who else would kill for you?'

'No one's killing *for* me, they're just picking off my clients. I've told you, I don't know who it is yet, but it has to be one of them. I've . . . eliminated all bar six.'

'How many were there? All right, all right, you don't have to answer that. All the same, I can't buy it. Sorry, Claudia, I don't believe Gaius was set up by one of your punters.'

Neither do I.

'I want his name cleared, that's all. If you re-open the case, that will happen automatically.'

'Good grief, how many times do I have to tell you before it sinks in? *Gaius* killed them!'

'Orbilio, are you being dense deliberately? Why should he do a thing like that?'

'I've just proved it, for gods' sakes. He loved you, isn't that enough? You were sleeping with these men—'

'I was not! They want to be spanked, beaten, whipped, you name it, but believe me, these guys don't want sex.'

'Really? You mean you didn't . . .' Orbilio cleared his throat. 'Stop splitting hairs. The point is, Gaius and you had separate rooms, he thought they were getting what he wasn't so – wallop! Exit the competition.'

Claudia put her hands on her hips, cocked her head on one side and smiled. 'You know, Marcus, we seem to have come by a convoluted route, but I think we're finally getting there. Haven't I been telling you all along Gaius didn't have a motive for killing these men?'

'For crying out loud, woman, I've just given you one!'

'Uh-uh. You've merely talked yourself out of one. Gaius didn't love me, I was another of his trophies, that's all. He married me for my looks and my character, another symbol of his success. Now why do you suppose I was so keen to get rid of the oik? Did you really think I couldn't handle whatever he might let slip? No, Marcus, I wanted that boy out of the house before Gaius could lay his pudgy white paws on him.'

She paused and looked up at him. 'Now are you beginning to understand?'

XXV

The light was fading by the time Claudia returned to the house. Orbilio had insisted she stay to eat, but instead of thrashing out the business in hand the conversation drifted on to all manner of subjects, weighty and light, and to her astonishment the afternoon just vanished. For several minutes she simply sat in the litter, composing herself. It left you raw, a day like this. You felt as though you'd been peeled and turned inside out. Claudia leaned back on the cushions. They were grubby and the drapes far inferior to her own, but for once she didn't grumble about using public conveyances. To be honest, she was glad Orbilio had sent for one of these, rather than her own litter; much longer and Claudia might have started to enjoy herself.

The dining room had been as gracious as the rest of the house, the cushions the most comfortable she'd reclined on for many a year, and the food exquisite. Scallops from Chios, fried chicken, baked bread with garlic, and sweet, unblemished fruit. She'd been waiting for him to lean over, to try to kiss and fondle her, to suggest they retreat to his bedroom and spend the night there, yet he hadn't so much as touched her. The hours drifted by, with him propped up on one elbow as they laughed and argued and ate and drank. Finally, when she stood up to leave, she asked him again whether he'd re-open the case and he answered with a simple yes. He would call in the morning, before the burial; they could thrash out a list of suspects.

He was adamant Gaius hadn't been killed by the man who murdered the others, although he was prepared to go along with it for the moment, since it would be sufficient to swing Callisunus against making his announcement, at least for a day or two. He made a great point of stressing his hope that there weren't too many skeletons in the Seferius closet, because once he started his investigations, nothing – but nothing – would stop him from seeking out the truth. Did she still want him to probe? She nodded vehemently. By the time he'd dug down that deep, there'd be nothing to find – she promised *herself* that!

Claudia puffed out her cheeks. She'd got what she came for; Gaius's name would be cleared, yet instead of a sense of satisfaction her brain was in turmoil. Orbilio had sown so many kinds of doubts in her head that if only half of them germinated she felt she'd explode. In his book, he said, everyone was a suspect; she would do well to bear that in mind. She ought to think carefully, he said. Recap events before Tigellinus was killed back in January, because you couldn't afford to overlook the slightest detail. Same as you couldn't rule out without checking and double-checking. Why was she so certain it was a punter? It made no kind of sense, he said; there was no motive. She might be the link between, but without identifying a motive she was whistling in the dark. She should take his word for it, he said. Love was the motive for these crimes, he would bet his boots on that. Finding herself uncomfortable under the intensity of his stare,

Claudia quickly pooh-poohed the idea, but Orbilio pressed on.

Had she, for instance, considered Junius as a candidate for Gaius's murder? No, she replied, she had not, finding that for some reason she was unable to look the investigator in the eye for once. Then she should, he said, and as for the man knocking off her tricks, had she considered Ligarius? This time she could say honestly that no, she hadn't reckoned on Liggy's involvement in this. Since Antonia died he'd gone to pieces, certainly, and lately he'd become somewhat unstable, but that didn't make him a violent man. Not in the cold-blooded way Marcus was talking about. Ah, but suppose Ligarius thinks he's protecting you in some way, he'd said. After all, the first murder took place shortly after Antonia's death, didn't it? Claudia scoffed. Good life in Illyria, whatever was he thinking of? She knew Liggy of old; what he lacked in brains he might make up for in brawn, but a killer? Never. All the same, the spectre – once raised – seemed extremely reluctant to depart . . .

Cypassis was standing outside in the street as Claudia tipped the litter bearers and dismissed them.

'The family's inside,' she whispered, wrinkling her nose. 'Been cooling their heels since noon.'

Claudia resisted the urge to hug this big-boned peasant girl. She catches on quick, she thought. She's only been here a week and she's sussed out the situation already. It hadn't taken them long, she thought, before they realized the will was inviolate. She'd expected them to come creeping back soon enough, but obviously they wanted to ingratiate themselves before the burial tomorrow. One big happy family, et cetera, et cetera. United in grief and, goodness me, no – the money doesn't mean a thing. Claudia shook her skirts, adjusted her curls and prepared for action.

'Claudia!'

'Marcellus.'

She wondered how long he'd been waiting by the front door. Hours and hours, with any luck.

'I'm sorry we were forced to stay away from the funeral. It was agony knowing there was no one but you to mourn Gaius at the pyre, but we'll be with you tomorrow, love. Right behind you all the way.'

'Splendid.'

There would be ample time afterwards to tell him that, however much Gaius might have put up with his incessant sponging, she was not prepared to tolerate it one moment longer.

'Claudia, don't walk away, there's something I want to say to you.'

'I'm still waiting, Marcellus. Four minutes have ticked past already, and you haven't opened your mouth yet.'

When he grinned, you could see every gap in his teeth. 'Do I sense a smidgen of frustration here, Claudia?'

'Well if anyone can, you can, because I'm sure it's something you have a lot of experience with. Now unless you want us both to die of old age, kindly spit it out.'

'Phew! How can I say this?'

'Try quickly.'

The pitted face moved closer to hers. 'Very well, then, I'll be blunt. I know Gaius had been depressed for some time and I know he wasn't doing right by you, but I will, Claudia. I'll do right by you.'

'Marcellus, what on earth are you talking about?'

'You know.'

'Call me thick, but sorry, I'm not quite up there with you. Could you give me a tinksy-winksy clue, just to get me started?'

'Claudia, I know what's missing from your life and I can provide it.'

Give me strength!

'Exactly what can you provide, Marcellus?'

'Sex, of course.'

'Sex? *Sex*? Am I hearing you right? My husband's ashes are sitting in his room waiting to be buried, yet you're offering to fuck me as a favour?'

'Well, I wouldn't put it quite so crudely, but – yes. I'm thirty-four, in my prime, I'll have you know. Oh, I've felt the shivers that run down your body every time I stroke you, the way you twitched when my hand caressed your breast. Remus, Claudia, we can make sweet, sweet music, so . . . What do you say?'

'Just this, Marcellus.' Claudia stepped back, balled her fist and punched him squarely on the nose.

Oil lamps had been burning for an hour before Claudia returned to the atrium. When she saw Antonius coming out of the latrines, she made a silent beckoning signal then turned back up the stairs to her room. A good ten minutes passed before he slipped in. Drusilla, woken from her sleep on the bed, raised her hackles and began to growl.

'Sssh, it's only Antonius.'

The cat didn't seem mollified, neither did Scaevola. Having heard what had happened to Otho, he backed against the wall.

'I hate to do this, Drusilla, but it's the only way. We need to talk and you? You'll bring the whole house running. That, I'm afraid, will never do.'

Claudia scooped up the cat, stiff with rage and indignation, and tipped her gently through the open window amid howls of protest. There was a ledge below; she'd probably sit on that and sulk. Claudia closed the shutters behind her.

Antonius grinned. 'Holding up all right?'

'Not too bad. You?'

'Suppose so. May I?' He nodded towards the jug of wine that lived on her table.

'Help yourself, Tony, you always have.'

'Yes, but it's different now. I mean, I've never been inside your bedroom before.'

Claudia smiled. 'Well, the same can't be said of you, my friend. I know every cube of mosaic like the back of my hand. Floor *and* ceiling!'

Antonius laughed with her. 'Good times, Claudia. Bloody good times, in fact.' He poured two glasses of wine. 'To good times to come!'

She slipped out of her sandals and positioned herself on the bed, tucking her feet underneath her. 'You're a very handsome man, Tony Scaevola.' Lean, grey, muscular. 'Can't imagine why Flavia didn't snap you up right from the start.'

Who else would have her? If Claudia had told her once, she'd told her a thousand times. Don't bite your nails, don't suck your hair and don't hunch over like that or you'll be round-shouldered by the time you're twenty. On the other hand, taking a bath occasionally might be to your advantage.

Antonius sat beside her and leaned over. 'You won't believe this, the little bitch actually wants to marry me now.'

'Well, she would, wouldn't she? Gaius cut her out of his will, Marcellus is broke and you, my old cobber, are not exactly destitute. Julia will have convinced her it's a smart move, considering your elevated position in the Treasury. It's goodbye tears, hello flattery.'

'She tried that with our patrician friend.'

'Orbilio? She never stood a chance with him. He was flirting with her to wind me up and, again, I think you'll find Auntie Julia told Flavia the facts of life about patricians and equestrians. Particularly penniless equestrians. You're the best bet that child's got.'

'Tough. An heiress I'd marry, but to take Old Grizzle-guts for free? No way.' He refilled both glasses. 'I haven't told her yet. I thought I'd wait until after the burial tomorrow, because Gaius deserves a decent showing, and it's better I attend as a son-in-law than merely an old friend.' He gulped his wine. 'That edict was a bloody disgrace.'

'I didn't see you at the funeral.'

'Gaius is dead, life has to go on. What good would it do me at the Treasury once word gets round I defied the Princeps to attend the funeral of a mass murderer?

'You believe Gaius killed those men?'

' 'Course not. But Callisunus thinks he did, so why stick my neck out? There's no reason now why we can't carry on as planned.'

Grieving widow comforted by stepdaughter's jilted

fiancé. They fall in love and marry, and in next to no time there'll be children on the scene. Sons for whom the Senate is not out of the question. Sons for whom the admission price of one million sesterces is no obstacle. Claudia sipped silently for several minutes. With both door and windows shut, the heat was intolerable. She knew Scaevola well enough, of course, to take off her tunic – to sit in the nude if she so desired – but this was not the moment. Indeed, it never would be again.

'I have something for you,' she said finally, running her hand under her pillow and drawing out a small opaque flagon.

'For me?'

When Antonius smiled, deep crevices appeared in his cheeks. Claudia had not flattered him, he was a very attractive man. She wouldn't have slept with him other-wise, even at twenty sesterces a shot. Certainly wouldn't have chosen him to be the father of her children.

'What is it?'

Claudia held the tiny flagon up to the light. It was half full. 'Poison,' she said quietly.

Beside her she felt Scaevola stiffen. 'I . . . I don't understand.'

She could barely breathe, and it wasn't only because of the heat. 'There's no other way, Tony.'

'Hey, come on.' He tried to inject amusement into his ragged voice. 'What sort of stunt is this?'

In the depths of the house, Claudia heard a pot smash into smithereens. A heated argument broke out among the slaves.

'You shouldn't have killed him, Tony. Everything was

going so well, it was practically within our grasp. There was no need to kill him.'

Sweat trickled down Scaevola's forehead and into his eyes. 'Claudia, you're crazy. Kill who? Who am I supposed to have killed?'

'You got him drunk, you sat him down, you picked up that little bronze statue of Apollo and you smashed it over his head. You positioned his sword – and then you pushed. Hard. Tell me, Tony, did it squelch? Did it—'

'Shut up, shut up!' He buried his head in his hands. 'Oh, shit, Claudia, you really know how to make a point.'

Several long lonely minutes rolled past before he spoke again. 'He didn't suffer; he was out cold, I swear.'

'I know that, Tony, but he didn't deserve to die like a dog and he didn't deserve to have his name sullied.'

'For pity's sake, how could I know he'd be labelled a murderer? He was depressed, for gods' sakes, he'd lost two sons, a daughter and a grandchild. Any man could top himself under that burden.'

'He was your friend.'

'He was your husband, so don't start moralizing! This whole thing was your idea, remember. I'll never make it through the ranks, you said, but by heaven I'll bear sons who will. This was shortly after you realized Gaius's interests lay elsewhere and you approached me, Claudia, so don't you forget that.'

Claudia leaned back against the wall and closed her eyes. How could she forget? The betrayal had tormented her from the moment she first looked down on Gaius's corpse.

'Look, you're tired. It's hot, you're bound to overreact.' He waggled the phial. 'There's no need for any of this, you know. We'll give it a few weeks then get married quietly and everything will go as smooth as a kid glove. Trust me, Claudia.'

'You still don't get it, do you? A scam to put sons through the doors of the Senate house by deception is one thing; murder is an altogether different kettle of fish.'

Antonius slipped his arm round her shoulder and drew her towards him. 'Kiss me.'

'No.'

'You think that because Gaius left you a million I'm trying to claw into that?' The look on her face told him he guessed right. 'Don't be silly. The plan was we'd cobble together the requisite million by me marrying that whinging cow downstairs then divorcing her on trumped-up charges of adultery. I would then denounce the child I was so eager for as another man's – hell, Claudia, we'd already earmarked the patsy – because that way I'd hang on to Flavia's dowry *and* put in a hefty claim for compensation. By this time you'd have a not inconsiderable settlement of your own, since Gaius Seferius – overweight and unhealthy – would have shuffled off his mortal coil.'

At least he'd have died from natural causes.

'Now since I was prepared to do all the dirty work, it doesn't stand to reason I'd change the rules simply because Gaius left you all his dough.'

'Gaius changed his will in the firm conviction that Flavia killed her siblings out of bitter rivalry. He made the new will, he said, in case she tried to kill him, too. He left me a letter explaining it all.'

'Flavia?' Scaevola blew out his breath in a whistle. 'Well, I'll be damned.'

'I daresay we both shall, but that's not the point. The point, Tony, is that Flavia didn't kill them, you did.'

His arm fell away. 'You're not serious . . .'

'Never more so.' She opened her eyes and looked at him. He looked terrible. 'You were engaged to Calpurnia when she died of a fever and it gave you an idea. Gaius's fortune was divided three ways instead of four, so you asked to marry Flavia. I thought it was my idea, but it wasn't, you already had your plans in motion. You were with Secundus the night he died. *You* took him on a tour of the taverns. *You* got him pissed. Then *you* pushed him under a wagon.'

'He fell. When I realized he was dead I panicked.'

'You pushed him, Tony. You waited for a wagon piled with grain and you pushed him. You poisoned Lucius and you paid the midwife to lie about Valeria's perfectly healthy baby.'

And no doubt grizzly little Flavia would come to a sticky end along the way, poor cow. Claudia could feel, rather than see, that he was shaking. Perhaps he was crying, she didn't particularly care. He'd murdered four people, she hoped he fried in hell. And for what? Greed, pure and simple.

'It's over, Tony. Go home and take that bottle with you.'

'You don't mean you've told the authorities?'

'There's a letter, yes, and should anything happen to me it'll be handed over.' She was bluffing, of course, but he wouldn't know that. 'This way they'll be none the wiser.'

'Claudia, please—'

She turned her head and covered her ears. She didn't

want to see him, she didn't want to hear him. She just wanted him gone.

A century must have passed before she found the courage to turn round. The room was empty, apart from herself.

Feeling like an old woman, she crawled off the bed and opened the shutters to let in the fresh night air. Drusilla, miffed at being thrown out, was nowhere in sight and it was quite possible that, knowing her, she'd stay out until dawn to teach Claudia a lesson. She yawned. The night was still young, but her bones ached, her head was pounding, there was a filthy taste in her mouth.

'Good evening, m'dear. Received your message.'

She spun round. There was a figure in the room, the figure of a man. He wore a toga, which didn't disguise the fact that he was small in all directions.

'Jupiter!'

She turned up the light to find herself staring into the blank features of Ventidius Balbus, a flagon of wine under one arm.

'I think there's been a mistake in communications, Ventidius, I didn't send any message.'

'Oh.' His face fell. 'Um. Sent you a letter . . .'

'Yes, I know.'

She was too damned weary to bawl him out and he looked so pathetic standing there. Besides she could use that drink.

'Plus proposal of marriage. Wondered, er, whether this has been considered?'

'Ventidius, could we discuss this another time? I'm very tired.'

'Ah! One didn't mean to, um . . . Although this matter is of some urgency to one's self.'

One's self? Or was that, one's elf? Really, it was quite impossible to take this twit seriously! However, since he was the one who might still make that Genua connection it wouldn't hurt to be tolerant. He had, after all, recently divorced a wife who, he told her endlessly at the banquet, had been bonking every man in sight. His ego was probably fragile.

'The thing is, Ventidius, I've decided against remarriage.'

'Somewhat hasty, don't you think? Early days, and all that.'

'Possibly, but you know Roman law. I'd be putting myself under the rule of another man, and somehow the concept of subordination doesn't appeal.'

His eyes, those ghastly boiled gooseberries, widened in shock. 'Oh, but you must. What would people think?'

'Convention, Ventidius, is not something that interests me.'

Neither was the prospect of bonking this insipid little worm.

'So if you'd excuse me . . .'

'Quite. Quite.'

He looked so crestfallen, she had to shield the smile on her face.

'One is, um, not without funds, y'know.'

'Ventidius, I didn't think for one moment you wanted to marry me for my money.' This one would want to get inside a different sort of treasure chest. 'But,' she feigned a yawn, 'it's late, and this girl does need her beauty sleep.'

'Apologies. One didn't mean to . . . Um, perhaps one could persuade you to accept this small token of my esteem. A delicacy of mine, sweet violet wine.'

Oh. She handed him the glass Scaevola had been using.

'Well, here's to sweet violets.' Claudia dredged up her best professional smile. 'And to you, Ventidius.'

Good grief, it was ghastly. Rich, sweet, sickly. Claudia began to blink rapidly. Was the room swaying or was she? She put a hand to her forehead.

'I think – I'm feeling – a little dizzy,' she began.

But before she could finish the sentence, the floor had risen up to meet her.

XXVI

The ship was rolling and wallowing, pitching and tossing. Hammers pounded incessantly. Slow, heavy hammers which shook your bones. Rapid, tinny hammers which shook your nerves. Not to mention every hammer known to man in between.

Claudia groaned. She lifted one eyelid, closed it immediately. No ship. Wherever she was, this was no ship. Too dark to make out the ceiling, but the walls move, there's no floor. I'm drifting on a pink sea. A bare-breasted woman with the head of a goat wades up to her thighs, her arms outstretched and beckoning . . .

I'm dead. The bastard's killed me!

What else explains the heat. The heat and humidity and that thick, cloying scent. Heavy. Choking. Nauseous. And limbs weighted with iron. When she tried to swallow, it was to discover a small, furry rodent had been wedged inside her mouth. After three attempts to spit it out, she realized something. It was her own tongue.

Not dead, then. Hallucinating.

Her eyes swivelled round. Slowly – very, very slowly – quaking walls solidified in the simple flicker of a candle and, as her vision adjusted, the naked woman became a humble statue, the goat's horns nothing more sinister than its skin drawn up to form a helmet. The pink sea, however, refused to go away and as Claudia struggled to sit up, another fact became plain. Her wrists and ankles had indeed been bound. She was strapped naked save for her breast band and thong to a couch in the middle of this wretched hell-hole. Even the pins from her hair had been taken.

Dear Diana, save me from sweet violet wine and worms that turn!

She slumped against the soft wool. What on earth could that idiot be thinking of, kidnapping her? And where was she, for heaven's sake? Not his own house, it was too dark, too damp, too neglected for habitation. The plaster had crumbled, the frescoes all but disappeared. A tomb? She wriggled her wrists until the bindings chafed. Give him credit, Ventidius Balbus could tie a mean knot, she'd say that for him.

'Balbus, you raving lunatic, let me loose!' Her voice echoed round the empty stone chamber. 'Balbus, can you hear me?'

Futile, but it made her feel better, shouting and screaming. You can almost forget how helpless you really are . . .

It was the intermittency of the hammering which made her realize the pounding came from outside her head, yet no matter how hard she yelled she wasn't making herself heard. At least there was consolation in that she was still in Rome, because these reverberations and rumbles meant it was another temple in the process of restoration. Temple! Of course. What if this was once the home of a long-forgotten cult which, like Consus, was also revered underground. She could feel her pulse racing. Where, though, where? Juno, it could be anywhere! No. No, it couldn't. The clues are here. Goddess. Wears goatskin. Arms out, left one bent at the elbow. Got it! The old shrine of Sospita. That left hand would have clutched a shield, the right a spear. I'll bet if I could see her feet she'd be wearing shoes with turny-up toes! Claudia winked at the statue. The old vegetable market, am I right, Sospita?

Her hands, being over her head, were beginning to tingle and she wriggled her fingers to chivvy the circulation back. Balbus had chosen his spot with care. Apparently he wanted to play sex games, but – a rash of goosepimples broke out on her skin – suppose he's the type who likes to torture his victims? It would be naïve to imagine she was the first woman pinned to this altar. Her eyes squinted in their search for bloodstains, but with only that one small flame burning in the corner it was impossible to differentiate shadow from stain. Bugger! Frantically she clawed at the bonds. Bugger, bugger, bugger! Panting from the exertion, her wrists and ankles raw, Claudia slumped back and forced herself to stay calm. Emotion could only be her undoing. Men like him feed on fear. Fear and power. Balbus was a worm who had acquired himself a victim, relying on his power and her fear to get his kicks. Or so the poor, misguided bastard thought! So if you plan to escape from this rathole, you'll need a cool head and a clear brain. Deep breaths, Claudia. One, two, three, four—

Her ears picked up measured footsteps, yet even as she braced herself to scream, instinct held her back. The footsteps grew louder. Clomp, clomp, clomp down the stairs. Eight of them. No, nine. He'd hesitated at the last. There was a grinding of a key in a lock, a draught, the grating of a badly fitting door over stone. Once inside the chamber the footsteps were instantly muffled but she could hear him wade through the pink froth and suddenly the room was filled with light.

'The effects have worn off faster than one calculated.'

The clinical assessment sent a shiver down Claudia's spine. She composed her features into a show of non-chalance as though this were normal behaviour, something she did every Wednesday and occasionally on a Friday if the moon was full.

'I'm a quick healer. Why's the floor two cubits deep with rose petals?'

Once he'd got all five candles burning, Balbus wove his way towards the couch. Difficult to believe this creep was still in his early thirties. Or that he won't be as weak as he looks.

'Cleopatra would seduce her men knee deep in them.'

Vulgar little trollop.

'Thus I decided to honour you in the same tradition and then tomorrow, when one's work is fully complete, we can repair to Asculum. I have purchased the most delightful villa not far from the town which I believe you will find perfectly amenable. Privacy is naturally guaranteed and—'

'Are you off your chump? I'm not going with you to any poxy villa, Balbus, not now, not ever.'

He looked like a puppy who'd been kicked for chewing a shoe. 'A wife is duty-bound to obey her husband, Claudia. I protect you and in return you obey me. It is the law,' he added without the slightest hint of deprecation in his voice.

'Bugger the law. Let me go.'

The bland features looked affronted. 'Your place is

with me now. We shall consummate our marriage in the privacy of this shrine, although, alas,' the boiled gooseberries lit up as they skimmed over her body, 'one's commitments prevent one from doing justice at present. We shall need to savour the moment, Claudia, but I do not think you shall find me wanting in that respect.'

'Balbus, I find you wanting in every respect and I'd sooner chain myself to a rotting corpse than marry you.'

It was a mistake. She realized the instant she'd spat the words out. The colour drained from his face, there was a tautness around the mouth, a fanatical glint in his eye which was mesmerizing.

'You will marry me, Claudia.' He leaned closer. 'Say it.'

She felt a surge of defiance. 'Don't be absurd.'

The blow to her cheekbone came out of nowhere, slamming her head round as far as it would go and sending pain soaring through her left eye.

'I proposed to you in your room and you turned me down. Are you refusing me again?'

There was a roaring in her skull, a throbbing down the left side of her face and Claudia could taste blood in her mouth. Probably from where she'd bitten her lip. It should be so easy to say yes to this maniac, she thought.

'Never.'

She braced herself for a second backhander. Instead, Balbus grabbed a handful of her hair and jerked her off the couch so violently she saw double.

'One more chance, Claudia.' There were two high spots of colour in his cheeks. 'Will you do me the honour of taking my hand in marriage?'

'Go to hell.'

The second blow knocked her breath away and she felt his ring slice her cheek. As her head fell backwards, blood, warm and runny, dribbled down her jawline. Drip, drip, drip down her neck, slithering over her shoulderblade to form a damp patch on the wool. The wool was red, the same colour as her blood, and the blood didn't show. It just spread and spread. How many others' blood had spilled on to this couch? And what happened to them? She fought back the panic and in doing so made one small triumphant discovery. Ventidius Balbus hadn't taken every pin out of her hair. Right now, that jab of pain behind her right ear was as welcome as a cold bath on a hot day.

She thought of Otho. A brute of a man, yet even Otho could be reasoned with. It was difficult to see what logic you could use with a man like Balbus, other than to keep on agreeing with him. With one cheek throbbing and the other puffing up like a dead fish, Claudia wondered how many 'wives' he'd brought down here.

'Very well, Balbus. I accept your proposal of marriage.'

Nothing. No reaction. Nothing at all.

Maybe he couldn't understand her through the split lip? She swallowed, ready to try again, then saw he was staring into space with a strange smile on his face. When she realized the source of his pleasure – the blood he was licking off his knuckles – the hairs on the back of her neck began to rise. As assiduously as any cat he followed the trails with his tongue. Down the back of his hand, in between his fingers. Slowly, sensuously, careful not to miss any. She dared not break the spell by speaking. When he was sure he'd licked away every drop of blood, he drew a small knife from his waistband. Claudia sucked in her breath. Expertly he slit through the thin cotton of her breast band and pulled it away. She heard his breath come out in a hiss.

'You have publicly given your body to me, Claudia.'

'I . . . have?' Bats squeak louder than that.

'At the races on Monday, after the Festival of Consus, I sent you a letter. Unsigned, yet you knew it was from me, didn't you, Claudia? And in front of thousands, you surrendered your body to me in a supreme gesture of sensuality.'

Never mind I tore the letter up. In front of thousands. 'Yes.'

'Because you love me.' Balbus leaned over and ran one clammy hand over the flat of her stomach.

'Yes.' She could barely form the word.

The hand moved upwards to circle her breast. Dead meat on her flesh.

In the wavering candlelight, Claudia found herself staring at the menace of the blade in his other hand. Balbus seemed to have forgotten about it, but the knife lay only inches from Claudia's throat. She tried to remind herself of what she'd said earlier, that it was only her fear which fed his power, yet she couldn't break the barrier. He had tied her hand and foot, she was as helpless – and powerless – as a kitten. Resistance had resulted in violence. Further resistance would only result in more violence, and who could imagine the boundaries of this man's brutality? He stopped kneading her breast and the knife disappeared from view. Wide-eyed, she watched him, with one swift flick of the wrist, slice through her thong and press it to his lips. Claudia couldn't quell the shudder of revulsion that shook her body. Half of her wanted him to take her and get it over with. The other half, the logical half, told her that would only be the start . . .

Suddenly the knife came flying through the air towards her. Her eyes snapped shut. Every muscle tensed. The blade cracked into the couch's frame. When she dared to open her eyes, Balbus's face was a finger's width from hers. Contorted with hatred.

'You won't take lovers when we're married.'

She was shaking from head to foot, she couldn't help it, and her teeth were chattering. The blade was wrested from the wood.

His lip curled. 'I said, you won't take lovers when we're married, do you understand?'

'Yes. No.' She was confused by the ambiguity of the statement. 'I . . . I won't take lovers.' Sweat poured off her body and, heaven help her, she was this close to the ultimate humiliation of wetting herself.

He laid the flat of the blade against her cheek, the one which absorbed the first blow, and Claudia couldn't prevent herself flinching. Slowly it traced the arch of her neck, the cold metal skimming unhurriedly over the ridge of her collarbone and down her breast. When it hesitated over her nipple, Claudia stopped breathing. Jaws clamped tight, she felt the blade glide over her stomach to follow the gentle contours until finally it came to rest between her legs. He didn't intend to kill her. At least not yet. But—

'Please, Balbus . . .' It was barely audible. 'Please don't hurt me.'

She didn't mean to say it. In a moment of weakness, it slipped out, the worst possible thing she could have done. To plead. To fuel his power by showing her naked fear. Already her body was quaking like an aspen in a high wind while her teeth chattered uncontrollably. This pathetic whimper should just about seal it. To her astonishment, his eyes widened.

'Hurt you? Claudia, how could you think such a thing? I *love* you.'

Her mind was reeling. What was going on? What did he mean? Why this sudden change of attitude? One minute he was making Otho look like a playful cub, the next the knife had vanished and he's stroking her forehead, pouring out words of endearment. How he'd loved her since Genua, when she danced those sinuous dances, how he'd divorced his wife just so he could be with her . . . For the first time since Balbus arrived in this stinking cellar, Claudia found a faint glimmer of encouragement. She resisted the urge to struggle free of her bonds. He wasn't the headcase she thought, because it was clear from his ramblings – the glowing tributes and gushing compliments – that he didn't make a practice of bringing women down here. He was genuinely (if somewhat misguidedly) in love with her.

Damn funny way of showing it. The old Claudia began to claw her way to the surface. Sadistic bullies she could handle (more or less), but the revelation that Balbus wasn't the twisted psychopath she'd imagined brought both strength and reason. Not to mention a whole bucketload of relief. Tension drained away. Calm was restored. Thank heaven, she'd be able to reason with him after all. The reaction that set in threatened to become almost as physical as the terror. Projecting her senses above pain and blood and terror, Claudia forced herself to listen to him droning on about how she would learn to love him in time, of the things he had planned for them and the sublime joys the future would hold. Yes, and I expect you'll want to repeat this performance every bloody night and all! Fat chance, Balbus. You really are the most unpleasant specimen of mankind I've ever had the misfortune to meet, so—

What's that? Her ears pricked up. What did he say? A pity she'd never be able to attend the games and races, but he'd report back as faithfully as he could?

'Just what do you mean, Ventidius?' She tried to quell the resurgence of panic in her voice. 'I . . . won't be able to visit my friends or the theatre again?'

'Well, you do see how it is, don't you, my dear?' Glints from the candlelight bounced off the metal which was back in his hand. 'Claudia Seferius is already dead, we can't allow any stirring of the waters.'

Claudia's skin began to crawl. From the elbows and knees, upwards and outwards, until her whole body prickled with fear of his reply. She closed her eyes. She didn't want to hear. She didn't want to know.

'Why do you think I took your clothes? Do you think me some barbarous beast who cannot control his sexual impulses?'

Numbly she shook her head.

'I needed them for the whore. Same height, same build, same colour hair.' A high-pitched giggle slipped out. 'Any time now her body should be discovered wearing your clothes, your jewellery, your pins in her hair and Claudia Seferius will be found dead, her face beaten to a pulp in a frenzied attack by an unknown assailant.'

She tasted bile in her mouth and fought the uprush of

hysteria. Her heart was beating faster and faster, her breath quick and shallow. She was wrong. Unbelievably wrong. Balbus wasn't a clown turned sadist. He was as twisted as a gnarled vine. Twisted – and therefore utterly unpredictable. One tiny flame of consolation sprang up and Claudia began to fan it. You're wrong, Balbus. There's one man who'll know the body doesn't belong to Claudia Seferius. A man with the tenacity of a terrier who will come looking for me.

'I have to leave now.' He might have been excusing himself from a banquet. 'When I return you will sign the marriage contract?'

Twice the word lodged in her throat. 'Yes.'

He stared hard at her for several moments then suddenly his face took on a malevolent appearance, accentuated by the flaring of his nostrils.

'Tell me again you won't take lovers when we're married.'

'I . . . won't.' It was little more than a whisper. 'I promise.' At that moment she'd have promised him the world.

His lip curled. 'I can understand you taking them when you were stuck with that rich old faggot Seferius, but you must understand I can't go round mopping up after you for ever. I demand fidelity.'

Claudia's body began to convulse. Oh no. Please. Oh, please. Anything but this. Mighty Juno, tell me I'm dead, tell me I'm dreaming. Tell me anything – but this! In the far distance she heard a tremulous voice ask:

'*You* killed those men?' Faces thrust themselves in front of her. Tigellinus, Fabianus, Horatius and the others, vying for position at the forefront of her memory. Tears stung her eyes. 'For gods' sakes, why?'

The boiled gooseberries were staring past her, trance-like. 'They'd seen you. Seen your nakedness. Couldn't allow that. Had to teach them a lesson. But then Paternus – oh, that Paternus. One dare not repeat his vile insinuations about you, suffice to say he paid a very special price.'

Claudia felt the blood freeze in her arteries. You gouged his eyes out while he was still alive, she wanted to scream, simply because he called me a whore? Is that what you're saying, Balbus? But the words wouldn't come. And amid the horror and the terror and the revulsion, suddenly all she could think was that her nose was running and she was ashamed . . .

The faraway look was replaced by a maniacal glint. 'There's still one more.' It was like the hiss of a snake.

He began to wade towards the candles, snuffing them one by one and sending wavering shadows of smoke round the shrine. Despite the heat, Claudia shivered.

'Once I've disposed of the man you left so recently, we can start our lives afresh.'

Somewhere in a distant recess of her mind, Claudia was conscious of the absurdity of the situation. Scaevola, poor bugger, would be found poisoned, stabbed, the whole bloody lot.

'They'll find the body.' Was that croak hers? 'The authorities will twig that Gaius wasn't responsible for the murders.' Idiot! What made you blurt that out? Scaevola is dead by now, you might have had a chance to escape when Balbus goes off.

'So?' His tone was contemptuous. 'Callisunus is a fool, he'll never work it out, and, since the killings will have stopped, this will remain one of the great unsolved myster-ies of our time.'

'You're wrong, Balbus. One man will work it out, even if it kills him. He's as stubborn as a mule.'

'Oh, really? And just who might this superior character be?'

'Marcus Cornelius Orbilio. He'll—'

Contempt became impatience. 'He's the very least of my worries.' Claudia heard the door grind open. 'That's my mission now, to dispose of that idle braggart.'

XXVII

How long she lay there, numb with horror, was anybody's guess. A minute? An hour? At one stage, what might have been a cockroach scuttled over her thigh, yet she remained motionless – too shocked to react. The feeling in her hands and feet had long gone, and now her whole body was rigid. The heat, the humidity, the overwhelming stench of rose petals all served to embody Balbus's insanity. Oh, she would stop him. Sooner or later he would have to untie her, sooner or later she would kill him. But not before Marcus Cornelius Orbilio had been tortured to death.

She stared at the peeling plaster on the ceiling as the one remaining candle smoked and gutted. How long before he begged for mercy? He would be brave. He would be tough. At first. How long, though, before he prayed for death? Balbus's stability was spiralling further and further out of control. Paternus had put up a fight, an error which would quickly be corrected. This time the victim would, like her, be strapped tight, the screams (and however hard you try, Marcus, there *will* be screams) exciting Balbus to who-knows-what sadistic heights?

Rubbish, she told herself. He'll be out wenching; Balbus will be thwarted. Yes, a small voice replied, same as that little quail you ate for supper is going to sprout feathers and lay eggs! Stretched out on the couch, Claudia felt she was suffocating. Suffocating in heat and darkness and fear and hopelessness. A man was going to die and there was absolutely nothing she could do. She ran a dry tongue over dry lips. The blood had crusted. She could well carry a scar on her face from his ring and her cheekbone might yet prove to be broken. It was swollen and throbbing and the pain was swamping her spirit. Spirit? You flatter yourself, my girl. Terror has crept into every corner of your mind and you've done nothing – *nothing* – to fight back. You should be ashamed of yourself, letting him win like this. A small spark of anger flared within her. How dare he! Just how dare this psychotic worm with his arrogant disregard for life be allowed to get away with it? Boast about beating the authorities, would you? I'll give you boasts, you miserable little weed. Oh yes, you can be strong and masterful when your victim is helpless, let's see what you're made of when it comes to a fair fight. Claudia jerked to free her hands. Man to man, let's see your real potential, you abject little turd.

Resonant hammers continued to mark time in her struggles. Time! Impossible to judge how much of it had passed since Balbus drugged her. Impossible to predict how much of it Orbilio had left. Was it still night? Assuming her calculations were on course and she was under the old vegetable market, men could easily be working nightshift on the city's massive restoration programme, especially if progress had been lagging behind of late. Claudia stopped squirming. Think for a minute. Don't you remember when Balbus lit the candles and you first saw your bonds? Ever the romantic, he'd tied her up with strips of pink linen. Tugging merely tightened the knots, but linen, Claudia . . . linen stretches. Except— Dammit, she'd need assistance from that little hairpin. Cautiously twisting her head from side to side, she wriggled it free, taking great care lest it slip into the sea of rose petals, then eased it slowly upwards using her forehead until her hands could take over. It wasn't easy. They felt five times their normal size, clumsy hams which couldn't grip a loft beam much less a delicate three-inch pin, but eventually she wedged it under one of the linen strips and using the heel of her hand for leverage, began the interminable process of stretching. At least two lifetimes drifted past before the fabric finally surrendered and her left wrist worked its way free. Silent prayers wafted up to the gods and Claudia's eyes closed in relief. Now let's get the hell out of this rathole.

Jumping off the couch, she pitched straight into the statue of Sospita. Serves you right, you silly cow, she thought, massaging the tender lump forming on her temple. More haste, less speed, and for heaven's sake, wait till your limbs function before you start into the heroics. Spitting out rose petals and struggling to stand, one hand encountered a hard, metallic object. Sospita's shield! Decorative use only, but she'd be able to crown Balbus with it, that's for sure. She scrabbled around in the half-light, feeling her way over the uneven floor, until she found what she was hoping for. Bless you, Sospita. That's a mighty fine spear. Pity it's broken. Still – she tested the tip – it was sharp enough for the job. Now for pity's sake, shift your arse, and I mean now, do you hear me? *Now!*

Gritting her teeth, Claudia inserted the bone pin in the vertical slot of the lock until she made contact with the peg. Lift, damn you, lift. After several ineffective attempts she withdrew the pin, clamped it between her teeth for safekeeping, then wiped the sweat from her palms on the wool couch. Deep breaths. One, two, three. Thatta girl. Now – in. Make contact. Lift and . . . click! Quickly she pulled the leather strap and heard the bolt scrape back. Cool night air blasted into her face and Claudia punched the air.

'Yes!'

No. She'd not get halfway up the Capitol clad only in shield and spear. She pulled the pin from the open lock and stabbed it into the couch, cutting the soft wool away from the wadding until there was sufficient to wrap round her body. It covered her breasts, it covered her hips, but if she bent over . . .

By the time Claudia Seferius walked up the steps from the ruined shrine of Sospita, she hardly recognized herself. Apart from the wrap, held together only by willpower and her faithful friend the hairpin, she wore red woollen bootees stuffed with rose petals and the goddess's goatskin flung over as a cloak. Dear Diana, the sickly smell of the rose petals was nothing compared to the stench of this hide. Talk about badly cured! I ought to head straight home. Call the police, have a bath, go to bed and leave it to the experts. Orbilio can look after himself. This sentimental claptrap is merely reaction to the horrors in that stinking little chamber. Unreal. Go home. Forget tonight. She raced across the Forum towards the Esquiline, cursing under her breath. I don't know why I'm bothering. He's smart enough to sniff out trouble. He won't be fooled by that lunatic Balbus. No way. And it's not as if he'll appreciate the trouble I'm going to, either.

'Allo, darlin'.' A centurion with his swagger stick blocked her path. 'Goin' my way, is yer?'

'I'm in a hurry.'

The centurion made a chuckling sound in the back of his throat. 'So am I, darlin',' he said, rubbing his crotch. 'So am I.'

Claudia smiled and brought her knee up hard in his groin. The centurion retched and pitched forward. She frowned. Only when she was satisfied the soldier was spewing his guts up did she stride out again.

Thought for a minute I'd lost my touch.

Would Orbilio appreciate all this? Would he hell. I'll bet he gets into scrapes like this every other week without blinking. Besides, what's he to me? Nothing. Nothing at all. A good looking bastard with a mop of curly hair and a boyish smile. They're ten a quadran in Rome. And as for that dreadful habit of covering his mouth with the back of his hand when he thinks something's funny – huh! As if his eyes don't give the game away! And did he think I actually enjoyed those verbal duels? He was a pain in the backside was that Marcus Cornelius Orbilio, turning up wherever you looked. Oh, he had a fine body, she'd give him that. Good muscles, firm thighs. She'd seen his thighs when they tussled in the garden. (Childhood wrestling games, indeed!) By the time Leonides came running his tunic was barely covering his dignity and you'd think it was Marcus accusing her of rape, not the other way round . . .

Dawn was beginning to break. A faint phosphorescence in the sky over the Temple of Vesta. There's something particularly special about the break of day. No matter how many times you see it, your arms break out in goosepimples, your breath catches in your throat. It has a unique smell, a sharpness, a whiff of infinity about it that makes you stop for a moment, whatever you're doing, and thank the gods for this magical new beginning. Claudia's pace faltered. And Marcus? Does he have a new beginning? Does he? To her amazement, fat tears were rolling down her cheeks. Can't imagine why. Defiantly she scrubbed them away. Never liked him. Right from the start I said this man was trouble. Don't like the way he looks at me – straight through to the soul – and his jokes aren't remotely funny. So what's he to me when it all boils down? Nothing. Some stupid investigator who comes to all the wrong conclusions, that's all.

The mournful Libyan opened the door and blinked. 'Mistress . . . Seferius?' His jaw dropped at the bedraggled spectacle in front of him.

'Who did you think it was, the Emperor's wife?' Hadn't he been in a fight before? Seen bumps and bruises and cuts and blood? 'Fetch Orbilio.'

'The master? I'm afraid he's out, milady.'

'What! Dammit, where?'

'I've no idea. I'm sorry. The Emperor's envoy called him away on a secret mission about an hour ago.'

XXVIII

So that was it? You escape from hell, race halfway across the city to save a man's life – only to find you're too late? That it's all been for nothing? She was cold. So very, very cold. Her whole body was in spasm. Around her the crush of carts, street-sweepers, drunks and vagrants went about their business unaware and untouched by the tragedy.

Hold on. Why not a genuine ambassador?

'Did you examine the seal yourself?'

Yes, he said, it was definitely the sphinx of the Emperor, and when asked to describe the envoy the man-servant's description was so vague there was only one man in the whole of Rome whose features were so forgettable. This was surely a contributing factor when it came to witnesses, for Ventidius Balbus might as well be invisible for all the impression he left behind. It explained, too, how he'd entered the tenement to kill Crassus. Few people would think of their landlord as a visitor. And only an arrogant egotist like Balbus would consider forging Augustus's seal!

Claudia slithered down the door jamb to slump on the threshold, not bothered whether the gods which inhabited it were offended or delighted by the sight of her bare bottom on top of them. First she had threatened the man-servant. Then she bribed, wheedled, cajoled and cursed

him in case he harboured the mistaken belief he was protecting his master until finally, convinced the poor wretch
spoke the truth, her knees could support her no longer.

Defeat wasn't a word generally attributed to Claudia
Seferius, but even she had to admit the chances of guessing
where Balbus might have taken Orbilio were remote in
the extreme. Conscious suddenly of her throbbing face, the
tightness of the swellings, the tenderness of the bruises
and the raw wheals round her wrists, she stared at the red
woollen bootees. They'd served her well, up and down the
hills. The rose petals had made a perfect cushion for her
feet. And when she caught up with Balbus, she'd force
them down his puny throat, he'd choke to death on bloody
rose petals, so help her. You might have won this round,
you perverted little scumbag, but by heaven you'll regret
it. However long it took poor Marcus to die, I'll double it
for you. Treble it. I'll slice the skin off your feet and burn
them with coals. I'll pour oil down your gullet and set it
alight. I'll rub nettles on your skin and stick pins in your
balls. I'll seal ants in your ears and—

'I clocked 'em.'

Damn you, Ventidius Balbus. Damn you to eternal
hell. Claudia looked up. The sky was turning pink now,
and already the temperature of sultry air was rising. The
last of the delivery wagons were weaving their way
towards the gates. Bakers were baking, millers were mill-
ing, street lighters were extinguishing their torches and
heading for their beds.

A small finger prodded her on the collarbone. 'Didja
hear? I said, I know where they went.'

She didn't see where he'd sprung from, only that he
was annoying her. Then his words filtered through. Rufus?

Rufus knew where they'd gone? Claudia was on her feet in an instant. 'Where?'

'Don't snap me head off, I'm only—'

'I'll snap you limb from scrawny limb if you don't squawk, you horrible little oik.'

He pulled a face. 'Well, seeing as how you've got the hump, like, suppose I'd best not ask what it's worth, eh? Ooh, ouch! All right, climb off yer high horse, they went to an old warehouse on the far side of the Aemilius bridge.'

Bugger! Balbus had me incarcerated by the Capitol, I was practically there. She glanced up at the brightening sky. What a waste of bloody time. Had I but known, I could have been there an hour ago!

Despatching Rufus for the soldiers and the Libyan for Callisunus, Claudia hared back down the hill. That manservant, the fool, was more concerned with cleaning her up, tending her wounds and finding decent clothes. She supposed he meant well, but he couldn't seem to understand it was a matter of life and death. Vaguely she wondered whether he thought she was drunk.

The streets were clearer now, less traffic, fewer pedestrians, and the early morning light meant she could see her way more clearly. Which brought different hazards to dodge. Bruised fruit, donkey droppings, spilled oil. One careless footstep could mean a trip and a sprain – hammering home the message that a man's life might yet hang in the balance. Any incapacity on her part might well sever the slender thread from which it dangled.

Apart from a few eager pigeons grubbing around in the cracks of the flagstones, the Forum was largely deserted and as she raced past the Rostra she was grateful it wasn't thronging with the usual bankers and advocates, soothsayers and whores. By the time she reached the bridge, she was wheezing pitifully and the cushioning effect of the rose petals had worn off, but Claudia was barely aware of the pain in her lungs or the rawness of her feet. She was cursing herself for tearing headlong down here without thought to how she could stop Balbus single-handed. If only she'd thought to grab a knife from Orbilio's house!

Below the stone arches the winding Tiber swirled and eddied, and she forced herself not to think about Marcus's broken and bloodied body which might, at this very moment, be sucked into its murky depths. Across the bridge she hesitated. A grey stone building, Rufus said, but in this light they all look grey! Wait. The boy said it was next to a grain silo . . . and there's only one grain silo. Claudia weighed Sospita's spear. It mightn't be much, but so intent was she on catching Balbus that she hadn't been aware of it clutched in her hand. Until now. She pursed her lips and nodded with satisfaction. Gotcha, you little pervert. I've gotcha! She was no longer afraid of him. And the instant you cease to fear the oppressor, he's rendered powerless. Dust to blow through your fingers.

Nevertheless, sweat was pouring down her back and her heart pounded louder than a blacksmith's hammer as she circled the building. She had to believe Marcus was still alive.

Slowly does it, Claudia, slowly does it. She could not afford to risk failure at this stage. Easing the door open a fraction, she wriggled inside. It was pitch black, though from the dry, dusty air, quarried marble had probably been stored here at one time. Right now it looked – and sounded – as though it was empty. Then her ears picked up a sound. A scuffle. It came from overhead. A series of grunts. Ach, it could be anything. Rats, vagabonds, you name it. Then she heard a groan. Not a groan of discomfort, not a groan of pity, this was a groan of abject misery.

In the gloom her eyes picked out an upper storey, rather like a hayloft in a stables, at the far end of the storehouse. There was a ladder leaning against it. Keeping close to the wall, Claudia inched her way forward, her padded bootees silent on the boarded floor. She was clutching the shield and spear so tightly that her knuckles shone white in the darkness. Her ears caught a second, more urgent scuffle, a gurgle and another groan followed by a high-pitched giggle, and suddenly Claudia realized she'd not only found her man, but that his victim was at least strong enough to fight for his life. She tested the ladder and crept up, rung by rung.

No wonder you couldn't see anything from below. A huge black curtain partitioned off this upper storey. Claudia lifted the hem and peeped underneath. A circle of oil lamps, each no further than a cubit apart, surrounded Orbilio. He had been stripped naked and tied to a chair, his arms to its arms, his legs to its legs. Beside him, a small table displayed a precise arrangement of surgical implements. Now Claudia wasn't too hot on surgical instruments, but she could identify saws, scissors, forceps and knives as well as several she'd never seen before, many of them with a sinister screw mechanism. She felt her blood turn to ice. Balbus, too, was stark naked, his legs blue-white from lack of sunshine, ribs poking through the skin on his chest. He was leaning over his victim, holding a jug in his hand.

'More vinegar, my friend?'

He tipped Orbilio's head back, pinched his nose while Orbilio squirmed and pursed his lips until the need for air overtook him, then Balbus tipped the liquid down his throat. At the same time he twisted Orbilio's nipple with his free hand, making him jerk and swallow. Carefully he set down the jug, balled his fist and rammed it into Orbilio's stomach to produce another groan.

Claudia dropped the hem of the curtain. It was obvious what was happening. The bloodlust had overtaken Balbus to such a degree that he intended to prolong it as long as he could. To that end he'd selected a site where he could torture his victim slowly and in complete privacy. Screams would go unheard, he could take all the time in the world, cutting Orbilio into a thousand pieces if he so desired. Well, maybe this wasn't the way Marcus would have chosen to start a Thursday, but at least he was alive and with all his organs intact. Trouble was, although she'd sent for help, chances were that Balbus would kill him the moment he heard legionaries clanking towards the building and there was precious little she could do to prevent it. If she burst in, brandishing her spear, he could easily kill Orbilio before she reached him and there was no way she could spit him with the bloody thing, she'd never thrown one in her life. Think, girl, think. Create a diversion! That's it, you could . . . what? Saunter in and say, Hello, Ventidius, having fun? and trust he's so overcome with surprise he drops his weapons? Start a fire? Rush in, kick the lamps over – then by the time Balbus and you have finished wrestling, Marcus'll be burned to a frazzle. For pity's sake, use your noodle, Claudia.

She lifted up the curtain again. What the hell was that two-pronged fork doing in his hand? Oh no! Sweet Jupiter, no! The implement he was flourishing seemed purpose-made for Ventidius Balbus, and perhaps it was – two arched prongs three inches apart. She stared, mesmerized. Balbus was lunging first at Orbilio's eyes, then at his testicles. Orbilio's face was bleached as he flinched and ducked. With each lunge, the prongs came that little bit closer . . .

'I have something of a problem, my friend.' He might have been talking politics or ordering a chicken. 'One is torn between plucking your eyeballs out in the knowledge that afterwards you'll never know where the next strike's coming from. Or, and this is the difficulty, whether to let you watch so you can anticipate my next move.'

He bridged his fingers and frowned. Head back, Orbilio stared at the pronged instrument wavering in front of him.

'Something of a conundrum, but one thinks, on balance, the latter takes precedence and I'm sure you will agree – it would be very remiss of me not to allow you to watch the proceedings. Now, where should one begin? I still think the emasculation, don't you? Yes, of course you do. You want me to teach you a lesson for fucking my wife.'

The adam's apple in Orbilio's throat moved up and down. 'I don't know your wife,' he said hoarsely.

'Liar!'

The fork in Balbus's hand slashed down Orbilio's chest, leaving two parallel red streaks in its wake.

Soldiers, where are you? Callisunus, you foul-mouthed, feckless son of a bitch, get your carcase down here before it's too late!

It was already too late. Balbus slowly laid down the

bloody fork and selected a vicious-looking saw. His other hand picked out a pair of tweezers.

Oh shit.

There was only one strategy Claudia could think of. Wild, feckless, maybe even hopeless. But she had to try. A frontal attack would be suicide. Balbus had orchestrated his sadistic operation like a theatrical performance, with him and his victim centre-stage. For Claudia to make a dash towards him was impossible, there was a distance of at least forty paces. Assuming Marcus wasn't killed, she would be. However, if she could pass herself off as the personification of the goddess Sospita . . . ? Most Romans feared offending their gods, believing they would receive personal retribution. Mighty Juno, let Balbus be one of them! As Sospita she would denounce him, he would prostrate himself before her, she would bring this bloody great shield down on his head—

Trembling fingers untied the goatskin and slipped out the bone pin. The woollen wrap drifted silently down to the floor thirty cubits below. She pulled the rank-smelling skin over her head like a helmet and slipped under the curtain. Silently in her bootees she crossed to the back of the platform, advancing with shield and spear outstretched from the blackness. Balbus's jaw dropped.

'Hear me, for I am Sospita, you defiler of my temple.'

The words boomed out in the silent warehouse, her voice disguised by dropping several octaves. The colour had drained from his face, the boiled gooseberries stood out on stalks.

'Only virgins may seek blessings at my feet for fecundity, yet you bring a harlot, experienced in the ways of men, to mock me.'

She brought the spear down hard on the boards, sending reverberations over the upper storey. The shaft, already broken, threatened to break completely. She couldn't use that dodge again.

'On your belly, you transgressor, and make obeisance to Sospita.'

'You!' It sounded like a strong wind in a long tunnel.

Oh shit! He wasn't staring because he saw Sospita. He was staring because he saw Claudia. Anger suffused his pallid cheeks. Anger not so much at her as at himself. For allowing her to escape. Claudia saw in his face that he would kill her for this omission.

'Bitch!' He flung the tweezers across the room and grabbed a knife. 'Faithless, whoring bitch!'

The glint on the blade was nothing compared to the insane glint in his eye. With a manic cry he lunged towards her, the amputation saw flashing in his other hand. Claudia parried the knife with the shield, twisting to the left. He spun round, hacking downwards. Again she raised the shield, but Balbus was too fast. It spun out of her hand, wrenching her fingers, and she felt herself falling. The bootees had no grip, her feet were sliding, kicking air. Balbus lunged, but his foot caught in the goatskin. There was a crack as he landed on his knees and Claudia felt the rasp of the saw as it grazed her naked shoulder. She heard it clatter out of his hands and skid across the boards. Using the spear for leverage, she sprang to her feet just as the knife whizzed past. A bony hand fastened itself round her wrist and twisted. The spear fell out of her grasp as Claudia gasped with the pain from her raw, bleeding wrist. She was losing, she knew that. Her strength had been sapped from her ordeal in Sospita's shrine, from the two fast runs across the city. His, meanwhile, was growing stronger, fed by insanity and bloodlust. Her foot caught Balbus in the groin, but there was no weight behind it. The knife flashed in the semi-darkness. She could hear a string of bitter obscenities under his breath.

Wildly Claudia's eyes searched for the table of instruments. Circling and fighting for her life, she'd lost track of direction. Dear Diana, where was the bloody thing? Then she saw it. Faking a dive, she took advantage in the split second Balbus was diverted to dart towards the ring of oil lamps. From nowhere a hand clamped round her ankle and she pitched forward, the breath knocked out of her. Behind her she could hear Ventidius Balbus in the blackness.

'Now you will die, you treacherous whore.'

The hand fell away from her ankle. Gasping for air, Claudia scrabbled to her feet, but found herself stumbling over the shaft of the spear. Her hands clamped over it, but before she could regain her balance, Balbus was upon her, his blade raised.

She heard a man's voice shout 'The spear!' and instinctively brought it up to protect herself, but it was too late. Claudia closed her eyes and waited for death. Her whole body jolted, she heard a sickening squelch, but surprisingly felt no pain. Confused, she opened her eyes to see Balbus floundering on the spear he'd run into. Suddenly the shaft snapped in her hand and she jumped backwards as though it were burning. She waited for him to fall, but instead he calmly pulled out the spear-tip, grinning horribly. Blood spurted everywhere. Vast red pools began to form.

'Die, bitch!'

Balbus lurched forward, clutching his knife, but she

was transfixed now. Like a rabbit in torchlight, she was his for the taking. She could see every pulse in his throat, every blink of his eye. Then, on the second pace, he slipped in the sticky puddle. Suddenly he was slithering and sliding, his palms thrashing on the boards. A hoarse rattle sounded in his throat, his eyes rolled, and he pitched forward. Four times he twitched then lay still. For an eternity Claudia waited, then – slowly and carefully – she approached his motionless form. With trembling hands she lifted his head by the hair. Ventidius Balbus was as dead as they come.

She glanced over at Marcus, who was white as birch bark, his face drawn with horror. Daresay mine's no better. She drew a deep breath, counted to three, then let it out, wiping the greasy blood on the wooden floor.

'Orbilio—' She cleared her throat and started again. 'Orbilio, are you going to sit there all night gawping just because I'm buck naked?'

He shook his head slowly from side to side in wonderment. 'Claudia Seferius, you are incredible. You are absolutely incredible.' His voice was as shaky as she felt.

'Oh, come on, Orbilio. I'm better than that and you know it.'

Unexpectedly self-conscious under his scrutiny, Claudia snatched at Orbilio's tunic. It was far too long, but it was a damned sight better than that skimpy woollen wrap and it smelled sweet. Besides, it was cold. She was shivering, so it must be cold, mustn't it?

'One clean stroke. Have you been practising?'

She grinned back at him. 'All the way down here, Orbilio. I needed to find a better way to keep fit than running up and down these bloody hills all night long.'

She pulled the tunic over her head and ruffled her hair. It stank from being stuffed inside that rancid carcase.

'Hey, where are you going?'

She paused at the top of the ladder to belt the tunic. 'Home,' she replied. 'For a bath.'

'You can't leave me stranded! Claudia, for heaven's sake, I'm tied up and stark naked. This is embarrassing.'

She put her foot on the top rung of the ladder. 'I assure you, Orbilio, you have nothing to be ashamed of on that score. Believe me.'

She began her descent. Callisunus and the soldiers would be along soon. They could sort it out between them. It was what they were paid for, for gods' sakes.

'Untie me, Claudia. CLAUDIA!'

She took two steps upwards and popped her head over the top of the boards. 'Orbilio, do you mind? This is Thursday already and I really do have a lot on my plate at the moment. A business empire to run, two households to manage, a husband to bury, a cat to feed and a farm that needs urgent attention.'

'Mother of Tarquin, woman—'

'The farm's a priority. We're still waiting for the augur to pronounce the vintage, but there's straw to cut, land to plough and didn't Rollo mention something tedious about irrigation? Now if I'm to catch the games in two weeks' time, I've really got to get cracking.'

I still don't know who paid off Lucan, but while I'm on a roll it'd be a shame to miss the fun. Claudia planted a kiss on her fingertips and blew it across to him.

'So you see, Orbilio, I really can't afford to waste time running around after you.'

With a toss of her curls, she flounced down the ladder

and across the dusty boards of the warehouse. What sort of alleycat had Drusilla been consorting with? she wondered. As long as there aren't more than four kittens, it would be all right, because she'd have to keep them, of course. Maybe two here and two up at the villa?

Marcus's plaintive cries for freedom floated down to her and she smiled. You're all right, Orbilio, do you know that? You're all right.

Pausing on the bridge, watching a fisherman come home with his catch, Claudia breathed in the early morning air and looked at the city waking above her. Yes indeed, there was something exceedingly satisfying about Thursdays.

Hadn't she always said so?

MARILYN TODD

Virgin Territory

It just wasn't fair. When you marry a man for his money, you expect him to leave you a shining pile of gold pieces. *Not* a crummy old wine business. So newly widowed Claudia Seferius jumps at the chance to escape Rome and chaperone Sabina Collantinus back to Sicily after thirty years as a Vestal Virgin. Unfortunately Sabina is an imposter . . .

Back in Rome, investigator Marcus Orbilio fears Claudia is in very great danger. He must go to Sicily to save that delicious neck of hers.

But before he gets there a woman's brutalized body is discovered . . .

What follows is the first chapter of *Virgin Territory*, the latest Claudia mystery, which is available in hardback from Macmillan (£15.99).

I

It wasn't his fault. Captain Herrenius hardly knew her. How could he possibly predict that, despite keening winds and raging seas, no amount of persuasion would winkle this beautiful young creature from her niche in the prow?

'It's for your own safety,' he urged, and the lack of response threw him. He was sure his voice had carried above the clamour of his crew, the crash of the waves. 'You'll be more comfortable in your cabin.'

He couldn't mean that dingy mop-hole where she slept? Bilge rats had better bunks. 'Don't be ridiculous.'

When there were problems to be faced, there was only one way Claudia Seferius tackled them. Head on. Besides, storm or no storm, she had no intention of being bundled out of the way like a redundant artifact.

But her words had been carried into the churning Ionian, and all Herrenius could make out was the shake of a mass of dark curls as she drew her cloak even tighter. Scared, was she?

'Don't worry, m'dear, I'll look after you,' he said – only this time he found himself on the receiving end of a glare capable of cracking walnuts at fifty paces. Checking that the water cask was secure, he wondered whether, given time, he would ever understand women.

As the ship rolled to starboard, Claudia's cloak went

skimming down her back to form a black heap on the boards. For one ghastly heart-stopping moment, she could see nothing but the liquid marble of the water, then the ship righted itself. She snatched up her wayward garment. Made of goat's hair, it was favoured for its resistance to salt water and as she shook the dirt off this old workhorse, she had a feeling it was about to be put through its paces. Spume was being whipped up like egg white.

Noting the set of her chin and never one to admit defeat, the *Furrina*'s captain inched closer. Young girl alone on the seas, needed looking after, what? He cleared his throat. Charming filly and no mistake. Needed a man, though. A strong, capable man to help her weather the storm. A man with – what was the word? – *experience*, that was it.

Inching closer, he caught the heavy scent of her perfume and felt a stirring in his loins as he remembered her at the stern rail yesterday, the breeze ruffling her hair and flattening her tunic against the outline of her body. Fully aroused at the memory of those taut, high breasts, the points of her nipples, the curve of her belly, the sweep of her thighs, Herrenius nevertheless waited until the ship gave another violent lurch before making his move.

'Take your paws off me, you odious little greaseball!'

To his credit, the captain's expression didn't alter as his fingers unlaced themselves from her waist. Stuck-up bitch, he thought, but it was with immense care that his hands remained firmly clasped behind his back as he made his way aft as nonchalantly as he was able.

'Come by the boat!' he snapped, and the bosun looked up sharply. The jolly had been hoisted aboard this half-hour past. But he knew that mood, and to avoid being put on a charge, tossed another anchor over the side. That still left three, didn't it?

Claudia snapped her fingers and the limp form of Junius, the head of her personal bodyguard, made a manful effort to straighten up from where it was hanging over the rail. Interesting colour formation, she thought. White for the main part, tinged with a spot of green here and a spot of grey there, and a tinksy bit of purple round the eyes.

'Junius, if you ever let that scumbag Herrenius within one pace of me again, I'll have you dangled from the masthead by your toes. Understood?'

The look he gave her was that of a whipped and starving puppy who'd just learned he was about to become the ball in a game of 'countrymen', but it was wasted on Claudia. The storm had all her attention.

They blamed Claudia for this easterly. Not in so many words (they wouldn't dare), but in September these straits are blessed with westerlies, they are calm and pleasant and a veritable joy to sail. This, she had been assured time and again, was fact. So why, then, had the Tempestates been unleashed by the gods to wreak mayhem and havoc?

Drusilla, it transpired, was the key.

Suddenly the keel was thrown high out of the water, sending Claudia crashing against the side of the ship. She clung desperately to a ratline as the freighter wavered, as though skewered on Neptune's trident, before pitching forward with a spine-jarring shudder. Another check at the cliffs. This is not a good place for a shipwreck, she thought. Definitely not.

She licked the ropeburns on her palms and thought of Drusilla. It was a rough ride, she hoped she was coping.

Poor Drusilla! She didn't deserve the crew's hostility, but for some obscure reason, the presence on board of one small Egyptian cat with blue eyes and a wedge-shaped face had turned the entire contingent into gibbering, super-stitious shadows of themselves. It had now reached the stage where two of her bodyguard – big, black Nubians, the toughest she could find – were permanently stationed outside the cabin door.

A mischievous gleam twinkled in Claudia's eyes as she wondered how the crew would react to the announcement that, as of this morning, there was still one small Egyptian cat with blue eyes and a wedge-shaped face ... but with the addition of four tiny replicas.

The impending storm and the prejudice of the men had not, it seemed, deterred Drusilla from the practicalities of motherhood.

The long-threatened rain began to lash Claudia's cheek and, gripping the rail with one hand, she tucked flyaway curls under her collar with the other. That letter, she thought, was a godsend. An absolute godsend.

It *had* seemed the answer to her prayers when, five weeks ago to the day, she inherited from fat old Gaius his entire fortune. Now Roman law might not insist a man divide his estate among his natural children in preference to his third wife, but it was pretty well accepted practice. Fortunately her husband, may he rest in peace, had swal-lowed every baited hook – and the whole lot had come straight to his twenty-four-year-old widow rather than to his daughter, Flavia. Every single copper quadran. Except...

How on earth was Claudia supposed to know Gaius's fortune was tied up in property? Did he discuss his business? Did he confide in her? Did he ever so much as mention money to her? Did he hell! Instead of inheriting a shining pile of gold pieces there for the spending, Claudia was lumbered with a bloody great house in Rome, a vineyard and villa in the middle of nowhere and a wine merchant's business that she knew bog-all about and cared even less for. It simply wasn't fair. You marry a man for his money and he leaves you with this to sort out!

What Claudia Seferius knew about viniculture could be written on the back of . . . well, a vine leaf. I mean what is there to know? Vines have thick, twisty stems, they throw out dark green leaves and lots of twiddly bits and at some stage they produce bunches of grapes to be picked by slaves who then trample them around in some buckety thing. Frankly, what happened between that and the filling of her glass was of no interest whatsoever. Yet within days of her husband's funeral, Claudia had been swamped. Buyers to meet, contracts to honour, shipping to arrange – there was no end to it. Pricing, irrigation, pruning, manuring, it was enough to make a girl's head spin and there was only one solution, really there was. The races.

In fact the very first thing she'd determined was that Gaius had left in his moneybox a float of 23 gold pieces, 1 silver denarius, 835 sesterces, 6 asses and 12 quadrans. Hardly a fortune, but ample funds to finance the odd flutter. Her mouth twisted down at the corners. She ought to stop. Hadn't she been taught a lesson once already? Except the old excitement had taken hold, more and more with each wager – which in turn became heavier and heavier, wilder and wilder. The addiction was back. With a vengeance.

'Boredom,' she told herself.

And so rather than face up to the fact that the weight of her inheritance was too great and she simply couldn't cope, Claudia immersed herself in the thrill of the chariot race, the combat of the gladiators. Here it was easy to ignore pressing commercial problems and decisions up at the farm. Here you can escape in-laws clamouring for a decent settlement. With breathtaking alacrity that liquid float turned itself into a paper deficit of over 700 sesterces, the equivalent of a labourer's annual wage. Claudia sighed. It was true, the old saying. The best way to make a small fortune is to start with a large one . . .

Therefore that letter from Sicily, coming out of the blue, had been nothing short of a godsend. One Eugenius Collatinus, an old friend of her husband, sends condolences to the grieving widow and invites her to stay with him and his family for as long as she needs. If, however, she does decide to visit, would she mind chaperoning his granddaughter, Sabina, returning home after thirty years' service as a Vestal Virgin?

He lived just outside Sullium, he said, not far from Agrigentum. Claudia, who barely knew where Sicily was, much less Sullium, rooted out an ageing map etched on ox hide, blew the dust off and unrolled it. Triangular in shape and large enough to be a continent in itself, Sicily was plonked right in the middle of the Mediterranean and it wasn't so much a bridge between warring nations as a breakwater. It was easy, now, to see how the province had become Rome's first conquest. Where are we? Ah yes, there's Agrigentum, on the south coast. So where's, what's it called, Sullium? Claudia's finger trailed along the cracked surface of the hide until she found it. West of Agrigentum. Oh good. Right by the sea.

After that, the hard work had begun in earnest, but a thorough – and she meant thorough – search of Gaius's business papers for transactions involving this Collatinus chappie came up empty-handed. There was nothing in his personal correspondence, either.

But she did find something else.

Something very, very important . . .

Something which put her whole future in jeopardy . . .

STEPHEN BOGART

Play It Again

£4.99

FILM LEGEND BELLE FONTAINE FOUND MURDERED
IN LOVE NEST. UNKNOWN KILLER STILL AT LARGE.

There was nothing else Manhattan private detective R. J.
Brooks needed to know. His movie star mother was dead.
And if your mother is murdered you have to do something
about it.

He doesn't have a lot to go on, though. Until he sees a face
at the funeral that is hauntingly familiar . . .

What R. J. cannot know is that he's just looked into the eyes
of a ruthless psychopath who has already selected his next
victim – R. J. Brooks.

'The characters feel real, the dialogue is killer bee, and the
book smells like New York. *Play It Again* offers the reader
what every good mystery novel should.'
Kinky Friedman

'An enjoyable thriller in the tradition of Raymond Chandler
and Dashiell Hammett, made more enjoyable as one tries
to spot the biographical parallels.'
Sunday Times

'Recalls the glory days of *Black Mask* magazine . . . Smart
hijacking of the Bogart screen persona.'
Literary Review

ANABEL DONALD

The Glass Ceiling

£4.99

Alex Tanner, TV researcher and private investigator, is more than a little curious when she receives a parcel from someone calling herself 'Ms X'. Inside the package are £200, a list of four famous feminists and a grisly surprise. All this plus the impassioned plea:

'I MUST SMASH THE GLASS CEILING. STOP ME IF YOU CAN ... PLEASE STOP ME.'

But what sends the biggest chill down Alex's spine is the cross against one of the names on the list. For this woman is now dead . . .

'Brings the London of the nineties vividly to life in this fast, absorbing read.' Val McDermid

'More please! And more!'
Observer

'Prose as sparkly as a string of diamonds.'
Oxford Times

'Thrillerish, prodigiously lively crime novel. . . . Most engaging.'
Literary Review

JOHN GANO

Death at the Opera

£4.99

A wonderfully entertaining murder mystery set in the passionate world of opera.

When the Floria Tosca Grand Opera Company visit stately Bolitho Court to raise money for the local hospice, few in the audience can imagine the seething cauldron of suppressed violence that lies beneath the greasepaint smiles.

After a month on the road together, fraught with sexual and musical rivalries, the pressure has become unbearable for more than one among the company of nine.

When death comes, it is with more drama than the final act of *Tosca*.

And then a second body is found . . .

'Compulsive reading'
Birmingham Post

All Pan Books are available at your local bookshop or newsagent, or can be ordered direct from the publisher. Indicate the number of copies required and fill in the form below.

Send to: Macmillan General Books C.S.
              Book Service By Post
              PO Box 29, Douglas I-O-M
              IM99 1BQ

or phone: 01624 675137, quoting title, author and credit card number.

or fax: 01624 670923, quoting title, author, and credit card number.

or Internet: http://www.bookpost.co.uk

Please enclose a remittance* to the value of the cover price plus 75 pence per book for post and packing. Overseas customers please allow £1.00 per copy for post and packing.

*Payment may be made in sterling by UK personal cheque, Eurocheque, postal order, sterling draft or international money order, made payable to Book Service By Post.

Alternatively by Access/Visa/MasterCard

Card No.

Expiry Date

Signature

Applicable only in the UK and BFPO addresses.

While every effort is made to keep prices low, it is sometimes necessary to increase prices at short notice. Pan Books reserve the right to show on covers and charge new retail prices which may differ from those advertised in the text or elsewhere.

NAME AND ADDRESS IN BLOCK CAPITAL LETTERS PLEASE

Name

Address

8/95

Please allow 28 days for delivery.
Please tick box if you do not wish to receive any additional information. ☐